THE SEEKERS' GARDEN

ISA PEARL RITCHIE

TE RĀ
AROHA
PRESS

ISBN: 978-0-473-58332-3

Tell me, what is it you plan to do with your one wild and precious life?
— Mary Oliver

Often we are led to a wall, it is too high, we cannot get over it and we stand there and stare at it. Rationalism says there is no getting over it, just go away… There is another way in nature, the way of a tree. The tree stands still and grows and makes roots and eventually overcomes the obstacle.
— Carl Gustave Jung

Look to the seasons when choosing your cures.
— Hippocrates

We delight in the beauty of the butterfly, but rarely admit the changes it has gone through to achieve that beauty.
— Maya Angelou

MARCIA

I f you stand still for long enough, the past catches up with you. The phrase came back to Marcia Reed-Wilton as inevitable as the sun rising. She took one final look around her home. Her eyes came to rest on the wall clock, its antiqued second hand obscuring the view of the first as it struck VII. She listened to its grandfather in the hall chime seven times as she assessed the things that were left in the room, relics from the past twenty years of her life: her mahogany furniture and beautiful hand-sculpted pottery in bright turquoise, olive, tamarillo, butternut, all of these familiar, comforting things.

William's possessions were still scattered deceptively here and there: car magazines on the coffee table, overcoat hung next to the door. She was afraid to touch them. Anyone looking at the scene would assume it was a home in which a man and a woman lived. How wrong they'd be; he hadn't lived here for months, and she hadn't felt alive since his death.

She said goodbye to the Impressionist paintings she loved and that he had gently mocked although he had surreptitiously relegated his grandmother's flowery watercolours to the guest room and hung her bolder tastes on the proudest walls in the main living spaces. She focused her attention down at the suitcase at her feet, packed with bare essentials, tools and trinkets small enough to carry halfway around the world. Something stirred in the back of her mind.

Marcia had dyed her long, dark hair with bright red henna, leaving the grey streaks a striking garnet. She brushed it away from her tear-stained face, walked towards the cherry-wood hallway table, pulled open the lowest drawer, and extracted a small wooden box. She opened the lid, revealing beautifully painted cards. She cut the deck and stared for a moment at the picture: a young, vibrant being playing a pipe and walking merrily off a cliff over a ravine, a dog following happily behind. The card was numbered 0, the Fool.

An obviousness dawned on her, painted lavishly over the calm façade she had been wearing these past months. *At some point, fear becomes irrelevant. You have no choice but to trust the universe and take the leap: surrender.* It was something she had been telling herself for years, but at that moment, it was real. She looked back down at the printed card in her hand. *This is the first step in a journey.* She spilt the cards out on the floor and selected the twenty-two major arcana. Then she quickly put them in order, back in the box, and into her bag as she heard the horn of her taxi sound outside. She hurried out into the thick London summer night, all sentimentality forgotten.

Marcia clutched her boarding pass tightly as she walked through the terminal. She distracted herself by gazing at the horizon out of the wall-to-wall airport windows where she was confronted by a ghost. Every time she recognised his jacket, his cologne, his hair cut, she was faced with the impossible reality of William's presence. For the first few months, she had seen him everywhere, as if her mind was reaching out for the familiar, trying to fill the space that he used to occupy, which was now a bottomless pit, a black hole that destroyed and consumed everything around it until she felt it was all she was. The figure stood at the airport window, silhouetted in a posture that was as familiar to her as breathing. Something irrational stirred in the back of her consciousness, hope that was buttery and light, but as he moved, the glitch in her mind vanished, and she was empty again. *How long will it take…?* She wondered, *before all the pieces of me realise he's gone forever?*

She felt her nervousness building as she boarded the plane, flanked by blank-faced flight attendants. As she took her seat, the anxiety was unbearable. What about her herbs? What about the mail? She comforted herself in the knowledge that she had good friends who she could call upon, understanding friends who knew the importance of her leaving even if they could not understand her motive. They thought she was running away from her grief, and indeed, this did feel a bit like running away, but where she was going, she had no friends or comfort, nothing. She was not escaping the past but following her intuition, and, holding tightly to the last shred of sanity she had left, she was going to face her past head-on.

Gossamer asparagus fern shrouded the driveway. Marcia's neglected childhood lay, ominous, in the Waikato fog. The high concrete fence stood silently in memorial: a tombstone. The driveway, in ruins of rubble, gave way to her footsteps, welcoming the familiar as she breathed in the atmosphere: intimate, sweet jasmine, *coming home.*

Marcia shivered in the damp cold. She had flown more than thirty restless hours, left behind the summer heat and her familiar, comforting world for this.

This Victorian villa was the house her parents had bought before the Age of Aquarius dawned, and liberation became the Western anthem, as the world struggled between conservatism and brave new human rights. *When we still had hope.*

She didn't remember first moving here. The turmoil might have been buried deep in her six-year-old mind. She remembered playing on the lawn in the sun, the roses all around, the garden clear and bright before dad's gardening style, neglectful, like his parenting, let it overgrow into this rampant, delightful jungle.

The house felt dormant, expectant as if it was waiting for her. As she got closer, she noticed the peeling paint and cracked windows. The signs of abandonment were so obvious. It crossed Marcia's mind that it was easy to tell if a house was run down.

Houses could not hide their reality the way that people could, the way that she had for so long, masking her true feelings to shelter herself from the well-wishes and pity of other people.

Approaching the front door, she felt like a shell, a hollow porcelain doll. Her painted smile did not reveal any of the five and a half decades of life she had experienced, of wisdom and pain and joy. It did not express the agony of having her whole universe ripped away from her in one night, leaving a half-life where things appeared to exist in the same way, but she saw right through them. The thing that scared her most in the world was that when she dropped the act of holding everything together, the hollowness was the only thing she felt, the only part left of her.

As she reached up, key in hand, poised to unbolt the deadlock, she felt very small, like a child in a world that was too big. She had an urge to call for her mother. She needed someone to hold her hand and distract her from the terror she suddenly felt. Then the door was unlocked and closed firmly behind her. She rested against it, catching her breath as she took in the surroundings that were so familiar yet tarnished with decay.

Standing in the doorway of her old bedroom, Marcia saw the empty room as it had been in her youth, cluttered with the remnants of her various unfinished creative projects: scarves and toys strewn about; every crevice and corner stuffed, like the fissures of her mind, with food stolen from the kitchen in the dead of night; the remnants of unwanted school lunches rotting silently, odious. These were her desperate attempts to fill the void she'd felt inside, to compensate for her neglect, to neglect, in turn, all that she did not care to deal with, mirroring the behaviour of her parents.

She burst into tears as she usually did when a childhood memory struck her. This so often happened at night while she lay, hour after hour, trying to sleep. It was when her defences weakened. The tears poured forward like healing rivers, and not so long ago, she'd had William to comfort her, who would turn automatically to embrace her, whether conscious or not, and who would never ask questions. Not until this point did she realise how lucky she had been.

She crumpled to a heap on the floor, feeling as desolate as her childhood had been.

As the tears abated, Marcia felt they had soothed away most of the pain. *If we chose our parents...* she thought. *If we chose them for the important task of raising us, of teaching us, what was the lesson here?*

She'd had to teach herself to deal with her wayward tendencies. She had taken responsibility, but not in the way her mother had always told her. The tears flooded back again. Responsibility was not something that can be requested from one person to another, not something to be ordered. *We are always taking responsibility. Each one of our choices is just that.*

It was part of her counselling training. She had learnt to let the pain flow through her, releasing her blame, releasing guilt, never bothering to rationalise. All these were just ways parents controlled their children and themselves, trapped in a cycle of misery, having learnt from their own parents that a solemn look could do more than a slap, that blaming another relieves one's own guilt. *Choosing for yourself is allowing freedom.*

Marcia chose to pick herself up from the floor just as she had chosen to leave home all those years ago, just as she had chosen to come back. She wrapped her courage around herself and continued to walk through the deserted house, noting the peeling wallpaper and mildewed ceiling. She opened the back door and walked out onto the sunny deck, a 1970s add-on. Squinting as her eyes adjusted to the light, letting the sun warm her, she allowed the past to slip away, to be in the moment, in the joyful experience of being.

As she looked around at the overgrown garden, the lemon balm and mint, native flax and cabbage trees, her attention happened upon an understanding. She could almost feel the buzzing influence of the planet Mercury. This was a time for shaping, creating, and she knew why she had come back to this place so haunted by the memories of her childhood. She had work to do.

On the first day, Marcia walked to the supermarket, where she purchased cleaning supplies and a large box of rubbish sacks. She sifted through each room, filling the sacks with old newspapers and empty bottles, trying to ignore the stale stench left behind by the tenants who had rented the house after her parents had moved into a retirement village.

She scrubbed down the benches and the windowsills with baking soda. She swept then mopped the hardwood floors with diluted vinegar. She pushed and heaved a couple of old couches and a mouldy mattress outside, ready for their disposal. She called the power and phone companies and waited patiently, listening to tedious New Zealand pop music, to get reconnected.

Halfway through the day, she realised she hadn't eaten. There was, of course, nothing edible in the house at all. So, dizzy and a little bewildered, she wandered down the road to investigate the café she had spotted from a distance earlier that day. She was pleasantly surprised at its quality. When she had left New Zealand decades before, she had never heard of espresso or parmesan or prosciutto, but evidently, these Italian delicacies had pierced through the traditional Kiwi cuisine of 'meat and three veg'.

She returned home with a pleasantly full belly. Her progress was noticeable, but there was still so much more to do. She began scouring the oven with a liberal amount of baking soda, then turned her attention on the bathroom. Her cleaning products were ordinary but effective; it had always been her philosophy to keep things simple and practical. She used some old newspaper and vodka to clean years of mildew, dust and cobwebs from the many windows and then collapsed on the only decent couch in the house. It was a little tattered but clean and structurally sound. Marcia appreciated it now far more than she had ever valued her expensive suede sofas draped in mohair throws.

On the second day, she hired a carpenter, a plumber, and an electrician to assess the house and repair its many flaws. Fortunately, most problems were small, and as things were set in motion, she caught the bus into town to shop for furniture and upholstery. Although her art deco London flat was decorated in bright, extravagant colours, she wanted something slightly more subtle for a Victorian house. She chose crème and pea-green, which she accented with mild cherry blossom pink and, because she couldn't help herself, splashes of Chinese red.

On the third day, she arranged the furniture, which was delivered that morning, before realising that the walls desperately needed painting. So she moved everything into the garage with the help of the neighbour's teenage son Greg and paid a visit to the local hardware store to buy paint in various neutral shades.

She spent the fourth and fifth days covered in paint splotches as she endured the somewhat daunting task of painting the main rooms in the house with Greg's help: the kitchen and dining area, the living room, the sunny room she had chosen as her bedroom. They had to navigate between the carpenter and electrician, who were busy patching up holes and replacing old wiring. After an hour of scrubbing mould from the walls and ceilings, the bathroom was finally painted and ready for use.

On the sixth day, she arranged the furniture and hung the curtains, and on the seventh day, she went to the farmers' market and bought food fit to cook with. Her unpacked bounty covered the entire kitchen bench, and she wondered whether she had gone a little overboard and bought more fresh food than she could eat in a week. The winter market had more stalls than she had expected, proudly displaying root vegetables, apples, and citrus. There were the cucumbers and lettuces grown in greenhouses, safe from the frosts and a wide array of preserves. She bought ciabatta and raw honey, hummus and smoked salmon. She even found homemade brie and feta, as well as several varieties of free-range sausage. She greedily gathered almost every fruit and vegetable she could find, inhaling the scent of fresh basil, delighted that so much abundance could be found in even the deadest of seasons. Her bounty was such that she'd had to purchase two large reusable bags so she could carry it all home on the bus. As she enjoyed her purchases, it occurred to her that this whole escapade might not have been as horrible as she had dreaded.

2

IRIS

I ris Cooper stopped, the wretched iron clasped in her hand, her blond hair a frizzy nightmare. She'd had enough. Just then, the microwave beeped, Alex stomped down the stairs, yelling something about homework, and the doorbell chimed. She took a deep breath and let it out to thoughts of calm, tropical waters and palm trees swaying in the breeze, *escape*. Iris put the iron gently down, wondering, for the first time, what irony had to do with flattening clothes so that they could be worn in a socially accept-able way.

At the front door, two young men stood in suit and tie, shivering in the frosty, June morning air. Iris looked at them, bewildered.

"Excuse me, ma'am," the taller one said in a hoarse, cracking voice. "Have you ever thought about the meaning of life?"

Iris took the brochures with colourful drawings of people smiling and living in harmony. She mentally tossed a coin. Heads: be rude, tails: polite. Tails. She thanked them, pleading, "this is not a very good time," and closed the door, frazzled. Irony visited her for the second time that morning: *I'm too busy worrying about important things like my hair and being late for work to think about something as insignifi-cant as the meaning of life.*

She returned to the kitchen to find Alex, shoulders slumped like any other sixteen-year-old boy, already halfway through her bowl of porridge.

"Aren't you old enough to make your own breakfast?" Iris called into the kitchen as she returned to the ironing board. *Although maybe, I should be rejoicing that he is eating something other than cocoa pops.*

"It was in the microwave," came the sullen adolescent reply.

She glanced at her watch. She was late. No time to finish ironing. She would have to wear a wrinkled skirt and blouse to the meeting.

"In the car!" she ordered.

All the traffic lights were plotting against her. As Iris gave up her last semblance of control and swore loudly into the steering wheel, the words of the door knocker swept through her mind like a breath of fresh air, "...the meaning of life?" She was jolted back to reality by the sound of a car horn. The green light was glaring at her.

After dropping Alex off at school in Wellington peak traffic, Iris was embarrassingly late. Heads turned as she scurried in through the main entrance. She quickly nipped into the bathroom to try to defy the nature of her hair and straighten her skirt. Her heart beat loudly in her chest as she made her way into the boardroom to the reproachful stares of all those who had put in the effort to make it on time.

As she sat down, her smarmy boss Neville smiled toothily.

"Is there something you'd like to say, Iris?"

She was taken aback, having not been asked that very question since she was ten. She opened her mouth to apologise, and instead, some very different words burst out and hung in the air.

"I quit."

Iris slumped forward in her chair. The room was deafeningly silent. She tried to form some kind of miraculous sentence in her mind, the kind that she was well known for in her PR work, that would put everything back in balance, but she surprised herself again. A different internal voice emerged, a voice that said it was time for a change, echoed by feelings of exhaustion. She was tired of rushing around between appointments and meetings, mealtimes and soccer practice. She found herself resolved to her initial words. She plastered on a slightly shocked smile, picked up her handbag and left the room, leaving behind a trail of stunned faces. She dashed outside into the cool breeze and into freedom.

A few hours later, Iris sank gloriously into her rose-scented bubble bath. She let her body relax and her mind float away from the reality of the day she'd just had. In her mind, she danced over pink candy floss clouds to the sounds of an angelic choir, which was rudely interrupted by the phone ringing.

"It's for you!" Alex sidled in with shielded eyes and the cordless phone. The voice on the other end was familiar and warm.

"Hello there, Miss-Full-of-Surprises. Neville told me what happened at morning tea." It was Ariki, Iris's closest friend, who worked on the floor above hers in the policy department.

"Well...?" She said when Iris remained quiet.

"I don't know what to say... but this bath is divine," Iris said, smiling, drunk on her own nerve.

"What are you going to do now?" Ariki's voice formed a conspiratorial whisper. Iris felt a sudden rush of dizziness; she'd thrown away her perfectly reasonable and well-paid job in a fit of insanity, yet an inexplicable joy bubbled inside her.

"I think I'll write a book."

"Good on you, darling. You're a star! And speaking of stars, I best be off to the Matariki celebrations at the Waterfront. We're going to bring in the Maori New Year in style. *Ka kite.*"

Iris put the phone down in a daze; her mind was calmer than usual. *Matariki*, the word floated around in her head until it settled on an explanation. It was one she remembered reading in a pamphlet at the museum. *Once a year, twinkling in the winter sky just before dawn, Matariki, the constellation of Pleiades, signals the Maori New Year. Traditionally, it was a time for remembering the dead and celebrating new life.*

Ariki and her extended family would be out celebrating the

newly rejuvenated festival. Meanwhile, Iris found herself on the verge of a new life. She pulled the plug and stood up quickly, ready to wrap herself in her pink, fluffy dressing gown. She looked across at the bathroom mirror into her powder blue eyes and the face that always made her uncomfortable because she could never anticipate its expression. Her face, with its pale, patchy, pink-white skin, smiled back at her. Suddenly she was caught in a white fog that engulfed her. She was falling, falling…

The horizon spread infinite, flat, the wind howled, eerie in the indigo half-light.
The ground: dry tiles of ice, silent as she crossed towards the cave.
On a ledge, she saw her, recognising her higher self: muslin kimono, painted face,
Vietnamese hat, cherry blossoms, sitting peacefully.
These are the symbols that seemed so foreign before and emerged from nowhere as
luxurious fascinations: teacups, rosaries, precious.
She spoke, a ribbon of consciousness.
Do you trust me?
Yes.
But was this superficial? Warm despite the ice, awareness flooded through her.
Trust me.
Yes.

She was lying against the cold enamel of the empty bath, feeling, well... nothing. Except for perhaps freedom.

It was dark when they arrived. *So much for serenity,* Iris thought. After their eight-hour drive, the driveway, described as "a bit rough" on the rental website, turned out to be a terrifying safari into the darkness with fern claws scratching at the car from all directions. When they finally stopped, Alex wanted to stay in the car.

"In horror movies, you're safer in the car," he mumbled into his collar.

It was more of an adventure than Iris had bargained for, but they had come this far, and the promise of hot chocolate was enough to get her teenager moving. They stumbled up the stony steps using their cell phones as torches.

"Can't you imagine a scary taniwha hiding in the trees?" Iris chided.

"Shh, Mum," Alex whispered. "Turn off the light."

In the stillness, Iris's eyes adjusted to hundreds of tiny lights. She sighed in awe of the galaxies of luminous glow worms.

"Now that's a spectacular welcome to our new home," she whispered.

The website had paraded pictures of spectacular sea views framed by native bush, but on their arrival, all Iris wanted was a cup of tea and comfort. Her spirits were revived when she finally found the light switch (about a foot lower than any rational person would have put it), and light poured through the open-plan pole house. The wooden walls glowed warm and welcoming, and Iris let out a sigh of relief; she had made a good choice after all.

She put down her bags, leaning her hand against the rough surface of one of the four wooden poles that supported the structure and took it all in. The house had been advertised as furnished, although almost all the pictures showed off the view rather than the interior. She took stock of the small round dining table, wooden of course, with three matching chairs, the orange corduroy window seat tucked away in the corner and the worn purple sofa, which faced the sliding doors that seemed to lead to pitch-black infinity.

To her consolation, the kitchen was well stocked with standard appliances and mismatched crockery. She put the jug on and joined Alex out on the deck. They silently looked up at the stars together, so much brighter than in the city. The milky way expanded overhead, making Iris feel small and insignificant. Strangely, this gave her a deep, peaceful sense, as though nothing she did could be *that* bad, no decision she could possibly make could have even the slightest ramifications on this grand a scale. It turned out a bit of perspective was all she needed, and this place was everything she had hoped for: the perfect scene to write from.

The sound of gentle rain eased her into consciousness. Iris opened her eyes to the peaceful green of the trees swaying outside, dancing between the raindrops on her window panes. She let her eyelids close, allowing herself to drift deeper. She was aware of herself, aware of the vibration of matter she identified herself with, her body.

Her mind expanded until she was only in a state of being, a drop in the ocean of awareness. She could hear the rhythmic sound of her breath, the distant ocean, and intermittent chords of bird-song. Underneath this, she could also hear a vibration, the hum of the planet revolving beneath her. She felt infinitesimally small and yet connected with everything, part of something so much bigger than she had ever conceived before, followed by an overwhelming sense of awe.

This was something she needed to capture in words and share with the world because through knowing this, through experiencing this oneness, this broader perspective, all other problems were rendered insignificant. It wasn't until the feeling had faded that Iris remembered she had a teenager to get to school, laundry to do, and a kitchen to clean, and the moment was all but forgotten. Even in this paradise, she was still captive to necessity. But later, when all the chores were done, she would return to her natural shrine, the beautiful view that awaited her, and her writing would flow. The thought was enough for her to rise without internal protest and prepare herself for the increasingly impossible task of waking Alex up.

Iris hummed to herself as she took out her laptop and sifted through the history of her thoughts, feelings, and working life. She dragged all the files that seemed useful into a new folder, the only folder on her desktop, labelled "Book". She sang along to the songs that played inside her head as she washed the breakfast dishes and sipped herbal tea on the deck. She hummed through a mouthful of toast, something she had not done since her teacher at kindergarten had told her off for it. She sang a slow sixties ballad as she scoured her wardrobe for any clothes that needed ironing, including several expensive yet dreadfully boring suits and bagged them up ready to donate.

She flicked through her CDs when she got into her car and selected her favourite Kay Templar album for the trip to pick Alex up from the school bus.

I used to dwell in the Danger Zones, the trouble zones, the drama zones
I used to be absorbed, but then I got a little bored
I grew up making miseries, solving problems compulsively
I used to think this insanity was the real world

Iris sang along to the gentle acoustic guitar as she guided her car up the driveway, guarded closely on either side by native forest.

Then I realised it was mad when I saw I was creating
All the problems in my habit just to get a fix
So I sought out some perspective, saw the forest for the trees
And I learned to flow like a river, not a drop out of place
I learnt how to slide... slide... slide
Slide, slide, slide, slide

She drummed her fingers on the steering wheel as she turned the rocky cliff face corners and admired the view; the sea stretched majestically out toward the horizon. She felt lighter than she had in months, as if she had shed a thick layer of skin along with her work clothes and old life. She had granted herself a pass at freedom.

Iris sat on the deck for breakfast, her damp hair wrapped in a rose-coloured towel, consuming the magnificent view. The ocean was so close she could hear its waves rushing to the shore. The subtle, earthy scent of the native trees mingled with the tart, sweet smell rising from her breakfast: half a grapefruit marinated in brown sugar. A chorus of hidden birds and cicadas chimed around her over the sound of the fridge, which had a strange hum about it, a resonance, purring like a satisfied cat. Memories of past experiences crossed her mind: the people whose recollection still speared her in the chest, emotionally, every time she thought of them. She was distracted momentarily by a loud wave crashing below, interrupting the rhythm of her thoughts, carrying her, like driftwood, to a new state of mind.

She had escaped the stresses and tedium of the city and, in her fit of insanity, she had made rash decisions: to spend all her savings on a year's rental of a wooden pole house by the sea near Raglan, uprooting herself and her child and leaving her friends behind. All this to write a book that she had no idea about. *All this on pure faith.* But the idyllic view did more than soothe her worries. The morning breeze brought with it a sense of new hope.

Iris had always felt compelled to help people. There was a nagging desire within her to let the world know the truth – to tell people what they needed to hear to make their lives better. Whenever she found herself in a crowd, her heart went out to all the lost souls, scowls on their faces, so caught up in their own worries that they weren't living their lives. It was a tragedy that people turned to fundamentalism or addiction rather than face the aspects of themselves and their lives that they didn't like. She knew the book she was writing was coming from her desire to help. She wanted to show people how they could think in a way that shaped their lives into the way they wanted to, to teach them how to love themselves, to help them face their inner demons. She wanted her work to be a gift that could do some good in the world.

All those years of helping people, of re-framing their perspectives to suit their needs, of manipulating the thin membrane of reality so that it resembled somewhere worth being, was finally amounting to something bigger. In her job, she had been, now that she looked at it, nothing more than a walking self-help book. All her philosophies fitted this drive for personal fulfilment, productivity, and general wellbeing. She had always been the person people came to. When Danielle, the junior receptionist, had arrived in Iris' office in a frightful state, pregnant three months into her job, Iris had talked her through a number of options that she had never thought of, and Iris herself had seemed to pull them out of thin air. The poor girl was reassured by Iris's confidence and by her stories about

Alex. She had left with a bright smile on her face, reminding Iris of the emotional roller coaster of pregnancy hormones. She still kept in touch, sending Iris Christmas cards of a chubby baby that had since grown into a gorgeous little girl.

Gladys, the most efficient tea lady Iris had ever met, had lost her husband to cancer, and she had turned to Iris for support, although Iris had admitted she was out of her depth with this level of grief. As far as she knew, everyone she loved was still alive and well. Iris had found her a support group for grief and had started an office initiative of putting positive quotes of the day on the whiteboard in the tea room.

Even the office manager had pulled her aside to ask for help when dealing with the differences with his in-laws. For some reason, people just seemed to turn to her for advice, and when they did, from nowhere, in particular, Iris seemed to be able to summon the words that they needed to hear.

She had given talks on power dynamics in employment relations and the importance of empathy in making ethical decisions, but there was something else. There had always been something more important.

A memory of ridicule swam to the surface of her mind. As a child, she had felt her true calling early and announced to her family that she was going to be a nun when she grew up. Her siblings had howled with laughter, and she'd been so wounded that she put away the habit she had made out of a pillowcase. The drive remained with her, drawing her like a magnet towards unseen ends. She longed to show the world that spirituality was more than a fad, more than after-life insurance, more than ritual, that it had practical applications.

Iris didn't know where to start, but she needed to start somewhere. She opened her laptop and began to write.

Babies are not born with guilt or shame. It is not a natural emotion. It has been taught to us by our parents and other people in our lives. Guilt and shame make people feel bad, which often creates a situation that is worse. Guilt is even embedded in our everyday language.

As many wise people have pointed out, the word "should" implies that it would be wrong if its instruction is not followed. Most of the time, there is no external punishment for not following a "should" directive, yet people punish themselves internally with guilt.

Let's say, hypothetically, you want to lose weight because you feel fat. You decide, as many people do, to go on a diet because you should lose weight. You tell yourself you will follow it with strict discipline. Three days later, you are tempted by a piece of chocolate cake, which results in you breaking the diet, even though you know you shouldn't. You feel terrible guilt, and because you're so low, you decide to pick yourself up with a little treat of some other contraband food.

Can you see how guilt, in this situation, only makes things worse? This is fairly typical. When people feel good about themselves, they don't need guilt. Guilt is not necessary for you to do the right thing; in fact, it may result in the opposite. We learn self-punishment in our childhood. Reflect on the following questions:

Are you trapped in a guilt cycle?

How were you punished as a child?

What kinds of things did your parents do to you?

What kinds of things did they say?

How do you punish yourself now?

Iris wanted to build on the teachings that had helped her. She wanted to help people understand that they had much more power over their lives than they realised, that their thoughts could change their realities. She knew that healing the emotional injuries that lurked in the past was a vital part of living a healthy life. All of a sudden, there were too many things to write about.

3

ZANE

Zane Strachan's onyx black hair fell over his face. The pulse of the music throbbed intensely through the recording studio, cementing his every word, stamping it into the minds of all future listeners.

The father and his son
Jesus and all his merry men
All coming down to watch it burn

His voice broke into a whisper, like waves crashing over the rocky drum rolls.

His mind flashed back to the dream he had the night before. The woman with the light hair calling to him from across the sea. He'd woken, feeling unnerved and vulnerable, as if his past had caught up to him.

He recognised her, but bitterness stopped him from naming her directly. She had no power over him.

He'd missed his cue for the lyrics, and his bandmates and producer were giving him curious looks from behind the studio's control room. The music cut off, and the section started up again. Zane shook off the lingering haunted feeling from his dreams.

He focussed back on his lyrics.

Watch the sun expand
Ready to swallow us all

His voice rose again, loud enough to drown out the discomfort of the dream.

The great floods are coming
To purge all our sins
Wash away churches and prisons alike
Drown out the impotent corporate dictators
Heal the world of this two-legged virus

He paused, waiting for the pulse to return and then finished the song. Beginning softly and cascading to a roar, triumphant.

Let go
Let it wash over
Carry us awaaaay.

He looked up and through the glass divider at his bandmates. Jimmy, the band's oafish Buddhist drummer, stroked his beard thoughtfully. Their staunch English guitarist, Mitch, gave a curt nod of approval and Baz, the bassist, every inch of him tattooed, offered an eye-gleaming smile. This, collectively, was their latest master-piece, their offering to the masses.

Zane walked out of the studio with Jimmy, leaving the other band members to chat to the sound engineer about effects.

"This recording is blowing me away," Jimmy mumbled in a misty voice that seemed oddly fitted to his unruly beard. Zane nodded through his thoughts.

They rounded a corner and headed for their LA home. On their last world tour, they had thought up the idea of renting apartments in the same building and had found the perfect block: four self-contained, minimalist apartments with a large lobby area, which they'd furnished with sofas and bean bags while covering the windows and doors with coloured cellophane.

Zane thought of all the good churchgoers in their Sunday best who would be making their way home from services right now, jubilant from their religious experience, safe in the belief of being guided and protected.

The image of the dream flashed in his mind again, but he pushed it down. It used to be a different dream he had – a recurring dream with an older woman with dark hair. Sometimes she was a witch or a goddess. Once or twice he'd wondered if she was some kind of guardian angel or spirit guide, but the dreams never made any sense.

The dream carried with it that feeling of emptiness that Zane had known all his life – not knowing where he came from, not knowing where he belonged. The kind people who raised him were never the problem… it was just that there was a gaping void where his history should be. His music sustained him day-to-day, but he was forever searching, forever seeking a substitute for what he'd been denied.

The June summer sun burnt through the remnants of the morning air. They were among the few people dotting the dry concrete pavement while hundreds of cars sped past on the street. It was this thought that led him to change the subject abruptly.

"It must be good to have some faith – to have something to hold onto."

"Faith?" Jimmy responded, smiling as if it was his favourite topic of conversation. "True faith is not about holding on; it's about letting go; it's about trusting enough to take a leap when you don't know where you'll end up." He paused, looking up at the hazy sky.

"It's about opening up, allowing yourself to be vulnerable, like a blossom." Jimmy held up his clasped hands and allowed his thick fingers to unfold like delicate petals.

The next morning, Zane found the kitchen in a state of disrepair.

"Tightly-wound girls are the hardest to unravel." Mitch always dealt out his pearls of wisdom like party favours, gilded by his Yorkshire accent. His eyes were fixed steadily on his morning paper as his latest girlfriend slammed the door on her way out. He had a thing for Californian Barbie types who always wore bikinis but didn't swim because it would spoil their makeup. Zane found it ironic that Mitch would spout anti-capitalist philosophy while the women he liked were suckered into the consumerist dream.

Baz came into the room, eyeing Mitch with mock condemnation. "Heck man, what did you do to Malibu Stacey? She looks as if she's about to go on a killing spree."

"Nothin'," Mitch said, discarding the commerce section. "I think that's the problem." He was the only one of them who bothered with the news. He said it gave him the inspiration to try to stop humanity from destroying itself.

Zane chuckled quietly as he looked out at the perpetually grey Los Angeles sky. He wouldn't bother with that kind of girl. Trying to get a decent conversation was like getting blood from a stone, a saying he vaguely recalled his mother using when he stubbornly refused to sleep in pyjamas. He preferred the strange, shy women who lurked in the corners, unnoticed by everyone else. He liked to draw them out and listen to their stories, but he never gave much back himself. He was in it for the conversation, not the romance, and one by one, they gave up on him. He took it in his stride; he was his own person, and he wanted to stay that way.

Jimmy was going through one of his celibate phases, and Baz was the only one of the four who had anything resembling a long-term relationship. His was unconventional. Yolanda was a postmodern sculptor who shared Baz's taste in tattoos and did most of the parenting of their four-year-old son, Marco. She lived in Pasadena, in a house Baz had bought her for their sixth anniversary. When Baz was in town, they spent weekends together as a family but lived apart for the rest of the week. This, Baz professed, was the reason they had managed to stay together for so long. They gave each other space. They lived their own lives.

This summer was turning into a memorable one for Zane and

his band. Their fans were eagerly awaiting the arrival of this new album, and he knew they would not be disappointed. They had spent the last few years perusing the world for new ways of expressing profoundly human experiences. Exposing the raw underside of Western civilisation for what it really was: exploitative, greedy, and malevolent. Now it was all coming together, a divine celebration of the infinite beauty and horror in the world, the ironic, the wonderful, and the tragic.

Zane resented that the radio versions of their songs had to be toned down, made less explicit, but it was part of the recording contract. He would be the first to admit that it was selling out, allowing the record company to milk their art for all it was worth: sound porn, reverberating through iPods, plastered all over the media. He knew his perspective was cynical, but he preferred that infinitely to being thought naive or, worse, ignorant. In this day and age, ignorance was the new evil, and evil was the new label of cologne.

After this album release, they would be free of their record deal anyway. The band had vowed to release all their future music for free on the internet, where they could be as explicit as they wanted.

The messages in Zane's lyrics ranged from thuggishly blunt to those so subtle they would be missed by all but the most perceptive fans or those who already understood. His band were committed to manipulating sound and meaning to create music with depth, to rip away the pretty facades created by politicians and capitalism and to unite people in an understanding of their true humanity.

Zane awoke to a strange, unfamiliar feeling of electrical excitement. He felt as if he was in control, shaping the mattress beneath him with resistance between the atoms of his body and the bed. His stomach dropped. He was falling through time and space. He awoke again to the sound of something moving intimately closer. He was running through a forest, his heart pounding, and he knew he was dreaming. Then she was there, ghostly white, looking down on him with love, a hand on his sleeping forehead, a soothing voice.

His eyes opened, and a more concrete reality dawned, anchored by the stagnant taste in his mouth. He was alone, but at least he was not powerless. He was in a world in which he knew the rules. He knew that if he dropped something, it would hit the ground, if he was caught committing a crime, he would, most likely, be punished, and if he was unkind, he could expect unkindness back. Maybe there was an essence of truth in the idea that thinking affected reality. Perhaps all the subtle thoughts he was sending out were making a difference in his future. Who knew? He had built up his current life from nothing; he had wanted things this way.

He agreed with the existentialists that one chooses one's own reality, but he refused to believe in the existence of a god, of a pre-ordained paternalistic holy one who would let such tragedies befall his children. In fact, Zane had made a fortune expressing his resentment of such a mythical being and of a society that blindly trusts. But what did these dreams mean? Every night, they seemed to become more vivid. There was always the same woman from his past, the same engulfing fear, the same abrupt ending. Something big was catching up with him, and he wasn't sure he was ready to face it.

Zane arrived at the studio early to find Jimmy already there, standing at a window, looking down at a trail of marching ants.

"If you could choose to be a small insect for the duration of its lifetime, would you?" He spoke as if still deep in thought, not looking up.

"Why?" Zane asked, taken aback by the question.

"See the world completely differently," Jimmy responded.

Zane pondered this for a moment. He supposed if this was possible in virtual reality, he would sign up straight away, but not if it meant losing everything he had.

"If I could come back and be me afterwards, I guess I would."

Jimmy smiled a slow smile. "You are attached. The things we are surrounded in are not as absolute from a broader perspective."

"What do you mean 'broader'?" Zane asked. "Ants have a much more limited perspective, don't they?"

"We are the ants," Jimmy replied, in a voice childlike and innocent.

He was always coming up with mind-blowing concepts that left Zane reeling. It was part of the reason Jimmy was one of his favourite people in the world. Thinking about things in entirely new ways challenged him; it kept him from becoming old and bigoted like his church-going father. Even though Zane was in his thirties, he didn't feel like an adult. He didn't think he would ever grow up. In a business like music, there were always younger and younger faces, but he wasn't threatened by them. No one made music quite like Wrench, and any bands that were even close to their complexity of sound were just as old and world-wizened as they were.

4

LEA

Lea Breage flung herself onto her bed. Too many emotions were coursing through her; she needed to get it out. She brushed aside the purple and black strands of her fringe and, reaching for her school bag, fumbled for her diary. *How did my life become such a teenage cliché?* she wondered, opening it to a blank page and letting the smooth white paper slide beneath her thumb for a moment. She released everything she could put into words, marvelling at how such a small notebook could hold so much suffering.

I need something to believe to rescue my tattered soul, to diminish my unexplained paranoia. I need something to hold forever.

Self-doubt lodged itself more firmly in her mind. Surely this was too much pain for a body so small to contain. How had her life come to this? She was all alone, powerless in an unfair world. She was locked out of the happiness that she knew other people shared.

Vulnerability struggles
Exposed by the bleak light of day
Under the cover of darkness, she creeps and chokes out all that is left to hope

Her life had gotten steadily worse in the last eight years ever since her mother married Mr Dalton, as she referred to him in the privacy of her own mind. Her mother's beloved Chad, with his coiffed blond hair and plastic smile, was obviously some kind of cosmic punishment for something Lea had done wrong. No matter what she did, he always criticised her. "I think you can do better" was his favourite line. His words were always edged with disappointment. She had complained to her mother about him countless times, but her mother always dismissed it.

"He just thinks you have a lot of potential, honey. It's his way of showing he cares."

Of course, his twin sons, her half-brothers, could do no wrong, and she hated them for it despite their innocence. It was better without them, even after her dad had left them to find a new wife in Thailand, even when her mother spent most of her days lying down in her darkened room with headaches. At least, the house had been quiet, and she had been able to do almost anything she wanted. Now she could barely get five minutes to herself without being ordered to do chores or interrupted by brats. It was all too much.

Nothing lasts. Colour fades in sunlight, black and white to grey, drifting through my head like a storm cloud, but it circles. It circles me. I am alone and afraid, empty as the endless pit in which I fall forever. Or until I see myself differently.

Her changeability was the one thing she liked about herself. At least, depression could be replaced by something else in an instant, even if it was self-hatred or anger. At least she didn't get bored of herself. Fickle sounded like a negative word, but it seemed to be one of her most redeeming qualities. Of course, it had its price: she could never settle, never be content.

Nothing physical, spiritual, or mental can sustain me, capture me long enough to contain me. My mind heartlessly devours my innocence as it does my beliefs, fading, sinking, drowning...

"Leanna, get in here!" Her mother's shrill voice rang from the kitchen, interrupting Lea's thoughts.

"What?" She was sullen. She hated being called *that*.

"You said you'd do the dishes last night!" The accusation. "The kitchen is a pigsty! How am I supposed to get the boy's lunches made?"

It didn't seem like that big a deal. "Chill, Mum, I'll do them if you want."

"What were you doing last night?" She thought her mother might be having a hernia. "That damn computer again, wasn't it? You're banned from using it for a week."

"What? That's not fair. I went to bed early because I had a headache. I wasn't even on the computer."

"Well, you use too much of it anyway. You need some fresh air, and I'm sure your homework needs more attention than you've been giving it." So now it was for her own good, was it?

"Thanks a lot, Mum. That's a great excuse to punish me; because it's good for me!" She stomped off to her room and slammed the door.

Lea burst into her room, closed the door firmly, and sank down behind it. She wanted them all to go away, Chad, the twins, even her mother. She never wanted to go to school again and endure the glares of the peroxide blonds who thought they were better than everyone else, or the good Christians in her history class who judged her dyed black hair to be some kind symbol of devil worship.

She took the box out of her bag. It rattled invitingly. She split the foil and removed one of the smooth, rounded, blue pills. Tears welled up in her eyes, and she fought off the feeling of something being wrong with her. She needed to write away the pain.

All I have is artificial happiness that comes in a bottle or from hormone imbalances, infatuation, or is just plain fake, shown on the surface, blocking the frozen tears that are permanently set on my face, my true face, that I won't let anyone see.

She hated the thought that there was something wrong with her, but she had nothing left to indulge in but self-pity.

The calmness, numbness settles. It descends upon me like a thick fog, cutting me off from the world, cutting me off from myself. At least, anger and pain have emotions, feelings in them. This just blurs everything. Nothing's real, ever.

She wanted to stop taking them. She wanted to feel, but there was always the look of worry in her mother's eyes, her insistence that trying the pills, anything, was better than taking the risk. And she knew what risk that was. Her mother was afraid the depression would get the better of Lea, that it would win, and she would do something stupid.

I want to go to her, to spill out my heart and disclose my soul, but she always looks for a solution, and all I want is for her to understand, to empathise with me, but I don't really deserve empathy, not even from my mother. She will never truly understand. No one ever will.

She supposed her mother and the counsellor and the psychiatrist all wanted her to feel better so that they didn't have to worry, so that *their* consciences could rest. She supposed this was what she wanted. She was creating this, her fake peace of mind, numbing the pain with prescribed drugs.

My memories fade, like pages in sunlight, as if I had only read about them. Experiences blur into the past, and all I have is the bleak withering reality that my mind has created to ease the pain. The pain my mind has also created.

From deep inside her came a silent wish for a deeper peace, for an end.

Lea sat on the school bus, her heart pounding, mind racing. She didn't know why. Pressure built in her chest. *This is too much.* That was when she realised she hadn't been breathing and started to inhale quick heavy breaths. She was light and heavy at the same time. Reality stopped and then was jump-started again, like the time she had touched her cousin's electric fence on a dare. Only, this was much less severe, as if a minute shock had been issued from her head. It was a strange feeling. She turned her head from side to side, testing to see if it would happen again. She felt almost normal, and then her mind clicked in and out again, twice.

There was only one explanation for this odd experience: she had neglected her anti-depressants. The last time she could remember taking them was the night before last. It seemed strange that a little pill, or its absence, could have this effect. Her concern dispersed as she felt two more little shocks. *Tick-tick* through her mind. They weren't unpleasant; they were somehow almost satisfying in the same way that clicking her spine could be.

The bus pulled into a stop. Just then, she was distracted, her attention caught by a guy with a khaki jacket, his brown hair almost touching his shoulders. He walked past her, appearing to be deep in thought. The concept flicked through her mind, the one ideal she most coveted: the Soulmate, someone to take away her loneliness.

It was a silly thought – absurd. She didn't know that stranger, and he probably wasn't her type. He was probably loud and optimistic and stupid, or bearing some other trait she despised. He had probably gone out with girls from her school; in a town the size of Hamilton, it was bound to be the case. The kind of town where your mother bumps into your teacher in the supermarket and knows her from school, or they took a pottery class together, or their parents were friends. The lady at the post office was married to her doctor; a girl in her group of friends, Sienna, was also the daughter of her dentist's receptionist. Lea's mother was often delighted by such coincidences. She would call her friends and update them on the new connections she had discovered.

It was the kind of place where some subtle form of incest was inevitable. Her friends had swapped boyfriends numerous times and gone out with each other's brothers. It made her slightly ill. The longer she lived in this hell hole, the smaller it seemed to become.

Thoughts slipped through Lea's mind like a running film, each slide a complete emotion, with setting, scene, theme, or picture behind it, running so fast they were almost falling. She could not quite tell where one ended and the other began.

Lea didn't know which of her thoughts, if any, were rational and which were just a consequence of the sticky joint she had held, inhaling its thick, pungent smoke moments before. She slumped on the couch next to Erika, who was ripping a piece of her school book to shreds.

The pictures slowed down, and she could feel icy fear behind each one. She could see herself and Erika as if from a third person's perspective. She watched herself intently, wondering if she felt weird. Of course, she was acting strangely. She was staring at the cactus that sat on top of the dusty television in Erika's garage. She must have been staring for hours, or was it only minutes? Time had slowed. She looked over at the tiny white flecks of paper Erika was arranging into patterns. Erika looked up at her. *Oh god,* Lea thought. *Am I staring? Am I being a total freak?*

"Are you ok?" Erika crooned in a voice that was slower and deeper than usual. Lea marvelled at the way the sound waves must be bouncing off her eardrums, somehow conveying meaning.

"I'm fine." Her response seemed to have come an age after the question was asked. She felt embarrassment prickle her cheeks as her voice seemed to echo in her head, sounding entirely detached from her body, sounding less like words and more like a comical re-enactment of them. She focused her intention internally again. The sliding had stopped, and the pictures flicked through her head mechanically, but something was behind them: comforting whispers that flowed liquidous, issuing clear meaning in a sound like the ocean.

Writing was her therapy, Lea had decided. Much better than her stupid psychiatrist or the patronising counsellor her mother took her to, who referred to her depression in the third person as if it had a body of its own. *What does depression want?* She could never tell them what was really going on, how she was broken into a million pieces. Hopeless.

I need something to loathe, to crush with the confusion in my mind, to balance the unjustified unfairness I witness, to blame for my misery. And since all other sources are safeguarded by my upbringing, and since I see my misery has no sign of any other source, I blame myself. I loathe myself. Accepting and nour-

ishing my misery, dragging down my pain, burying any sign of hope, any rays of light with contempt.

She knew it was dramatic. That was part of the reason she didn't want to talk about it. It was embarrassing. But she still needed to get the feelings out.

Sometimes she thought that writing about these things made them less real. They belonged to the page and not to her. Her darkest thoughts could be unleashed upon the paper, and she could purge herself of them, confess her sins, and be redeemed. The thought had occurred to her more than once that writing was keeping her alive.

Her thoughts were interrupted by a shrill scream. As she looked up to see who was being murdered, a naked tornado of a child stormed into her room.

"He's going to kill me!" Lincoln screamed. His blonde hair was matted to his head, and he was dripping with water.

Oh, to be six again, Lea thought as she watched Carter burst into the room and tackle his twin to the floor amid plumes of giggles. Lea still didn't know what her mother was thinking, naming her children after past American presidents. She had a suspicion that it was something to do with a certain young Hollywood starlet who had called her twin girls Rosa-Velt and Kennedy.

Lincoln had Carter in a headlock by the time she yelled at them to get out. It was bad enough her mother had had to have IVF babies at the tender age of forty. The twins now occupied all of her time and energy. It just made matters worse that Lea also had to suffer their existence. She pushed them carefully but convincingly out of her room and closed the door sharply. She leant her back against it and slid down to the floor. Even with the door closed, she could hear them romping up and down the hallway.

In her childhood, she'd had dancing lessons and hockey practice that her mother dutifully took her to. She would go to her games and recitals and beam at her from the sidelines. Lea had learnt to play the clarinet, badly, and she probably would have even improved if it weren't for the twins. *Now I might as well not even exist.* Lea burst into tears. To be fair, it wasn't *their* fault her mother had wanted other children, that Lea hadn't been enough.

31

5

MRS EVERGLADE

Mrs Alice Everglade loved daffodils and the way they crept up in the middle of winter, bringing in a cheery hope that spring was just around the corner. *Have they always blossomed in June?* she wondered, looking out the mildewed windows of her living room. Her memory was not what it used to be, but her mind was still sharp, and her eyes, though beginning to fail her, pierced through the morning light in a stare that even the young boys who served her at the supermarket were afraid of. They seemed to be getting younger and younger, perhaps because the youth wage was so low, but probably, she knew, because the gap of comparison got wider every year.

Even the matronly volunteers who delivered her meals on wheels had a delicate youthful glow these days. This did not bother Mrs Everglade, who had never found age to be much more than a curious and inevitable happening. Reality was a far cry from the rows of princess figurines adorning her shelves or the ever-young statuettes in her garden, the frolicking children and Roman goddesses, always poised in that perfect moment, only blemished by the moss that crept up their white, ceramic figures.

Her garden was becoming neglected now that she had stiff joints and diminishing strength. She still swept the path every week, removing the clumsy deposits made by the neighbour's monstrous redwood tree and fighting a losing battle with the weeds that crept up through the cobblestones. The lawnmower man helped her out, taking his weed-whacker to them, although it worried her that he didn't know a dandelion from a daffodil and many a precious bloom had come to an untimely end under his thunderous machinery.

This winter seemed colder than the last, although her meticulously-kept diaries had claimed that for the past ten years. Winter was a thoughtful time, when everything was quieter and crisper, and it struck her, as she looked out at the bare, spindly trees raking the grey morning sky, that she was well into the winter of her life, where she could easily observe but not so easily act. She was in the midst of her own demise, and she felt it creeping slowly up on her, an inevitable chore.

She watched the birds from her dark, book-cluttered cottage. The little blackbirds and wax eyes darted from branch to branch through the foggy mornings, occasionally accompanied by robins or fantails. She sighed, delighted by their spirited energy. *If only...*

Mrs Everglade had been in the same routine since she had decided to stop travelling in her late 60s. She awoke when it became light outside, made her first cup of tea, and watered the plants. Then she ate a slice of toast with butter and marmalade and read the paper. She made her requisite diary entry, noting the weather and the state of the garden. This took her through to her lunch of tinned soup, and the afternoon usually trailed away into television, which was increasingly difficult to hear, or one of the many non-fiction books that lined the walls of her little 1930s cottage, which her eyes struggled to read. Sometimes she would look at pictures of the castles in France, or she would enjoy the tidiness of Japanese styled gardens. Occasionally, she would pick up a book on Africa and reminisce about the short time she had spent there.

On Tuesdays, she bought milk, tea, bread, and butter from the grocery store around the corner, and there were infrequent visits to the doctor to see about her joints, which ached from rheumatism. Even more rare were visits from old friends. Most of the people she cared about had passed away or were confined to retirement institutions. Though she never spoke of it, the thought of *those places* terrified her. She could not bear to imagine a life confined to a bed in a building reeking with disinfectant and urine, surrounded by imbeciles and patronised by caregivers.

Her solitary life was one she was proud of. She had never remarried after her dear Albert lost his life in the war. Preferring her own company, she treasured her self-sufficiency with quiet pride.

So, on Tuesday morning, when she slipped on the frosty step outside her front door, she lay on the cold concrete, waging a silent battle in her mind. Did this mean something? *Of course not.* Was it a step towards her demise? *Certainly not.* Could she even walk? There was no denying her physical vulnerability, but she had not given up yet. She pulled herself into a sitting position, and, keenly aware of her throbbing thigh, she used the bannister to hoist herself up. She couldn't help but feel she had lost something, a shred of dignity, an ounce of strength. She had come face-to-face with the inevitability of her declining body, but at least for today, she had won.

Mrs Everglade had taken to feeding the neighbour's cat, Louise. She had never particularly liked cats, but she did enjoy the company, and as she sat in the pale winter sunlight, stroking the cat's dusky mane, she was reminded of something she had read years ago, perhaps in a magazine or a novel. She used to read novels in her youth before she retired from the world of make-believe and resigned herself to the factual. It certainly didn't sound factual – that the purring of cats had healing properties, but then again, there were many mysteries in nature that she had pondered over. How do termites in the desert know how to build such magnificent cathedral mounds when their brains are clearly insufficient? How did bees develop sign language? How do flocks of birds get so organised and how do they know when, and where to fly for the winter?

On a whim, Mrs Everglade nestled Louise next to her bruised thigh, petting her soft furry head and scratching her ears, allowing the slow vibration of the purr to echo over the wound. She felt quite childish in doing so and let out a giggle that did not suit her one bit.

Mrs Everglade felt her joints ache in the July morning air. She peered out of the window over the neighbour's fence into the disorganised jungle of a garden so unlike her own neat beds. She noted the last of the winter camellias and the first of the blossoms, preempting spring. At least, *her* garden used to be tidy when she was more able-bodied; now, it seemed to become more of a tangle every year, and her pension did not allow for much in the way of gardening help.

The Reed family next door had no such excuse. Mrs Everglade had watched in contempt each year for several decades as the garden appeared to decompose from the neat, long-stemmed roses that the previous owner, Mr Buick, had so lovingly and dotingly tended. As the years passed, the garden had degenerated, as more unusual plants were set in abnormal places. There were too many untidy natives and sprawling weeds, and the enormous redwood near her boundary shed its prickly leaves all over her path. Mrs Everglade remembered an abundance of children and dogs next door, but the house had now been empty for years and was slowly being engulfed by the garden.

Africa had been as wild, but it was meant to be. There was a harmony about it when she had visited in 1950 with her baby sister Maree. They had stayed in Nairobi, where their favourite cousin, Elsa, was settled with her husband Bill, an ardent missionary. There was sparseness to the landscape, and a presence of being she had not experienced anywhere else since. She had watched the magnificent scarlet sunsets and inhaled the warm, baked air deeply, wanting to capture it, to keep forever. The memories had lasted longer than Maree or Elsa, who had died in their sixties of cancer, or poor Bill, who was killed in 1958 in some kind of rebellion. She hadn't wanted to know the details, but she hadn't been surprised. There had been trouble brewing while they visited. She could feel it then, and she remembered thinking it inevitable. *There's no taming a country like that.* And she had told Bill as much, warning him, but he had launched into a speech about Jesus, which she had politely listened to without paying much attention, having no patience for religion since Albert's passing. A good god would have let him live longer than twenty years. At any rate, his boyish face would not want to see her in the afterlife, withered and sagging like this. What a pair they would make! No. This world was all she had time for, even if her time was running out.

The girl was back. Mrs Everglade had noticed her in the garden, although she was probably older than she looked. Thirty? Fifty? It was hard to tell these days. Therefore, she was still *the girl*. The oldest child with the dark hair – the one who'd left as a teenager.

It had caused quite a scandal, and Mrs Aberdeen, who used to live in the house behind them, had whispered over the fence; rumours of pregnancy. In those days, girls who found themselves in that sort of predicament would sometimes be sent away to "visit a cousin" or something like that. Apparently, they would actually go to a convent or to the house of kind strangers who took them in and cared for them, in exchange for their help in the household, until the child was born and adopted out.

She had always thought it was an awful lot of effort to go to over a baby – over a secret – but some people cared about such whimsical things as other people's opinions. Mrs Everglade had doubted that it had been the situation next door. There had been funny things going on in that house for months, years actually. The whole family seemed mad. The poor girl had probably just run away to escape them. In any case, she had not, to Mrs Everglade's knowledge, returned until just recently.

It had happened a long time ago, perhaps four decades earlier, but Mrs Everglade wasn't counting. She remembered her as a child, knocking on the front door of her little cottage asking whether she could pick lemonades from her tree. She wondered why the girl had returned after so many years. That crazy old Mr Reed, as she had called him in private, had gone, along with his wife – retired to some village constructed entirely for the care and entertainment of the senile and demented. Perhaps they had passed away and left the house to their missing daughter.

The procession of builders and such next door had not escaped Mrs Everglade's notice. She occasionally saw the girl pop up in one of the windows of the old house, wiping away grime and cobwebs. She watched her as she pottered around the garden.

Good luck, she thought. *With that garden – and that family – you're most definitely going to need it.*

6

MARCIA

Her father would have said, in a jestful boast, that it took fifty years of careful neglect to get the garden looking this way. Marcia could not compare it to the neatly manicured front sections in the surrounding neighbourhood. People were outside, bright and early on Sunday mornings, pruning the hedges and clipping the garden edging. Perhaps they enjoyed it as a hobby, but to her, there was an underlying obligation, a detectable *should*, some kind of guilt motivation.

The garden she stood in festered on guilt and shame, engulfing and hiding these emotions beneath the dense, chaotic foliage, rather than trying to hide from them, which Marcia suspected these elderly neighbours were doing. Perhaps they looked down on this garden; perhaps they liked to. Perhaps this was the wrong that made them right. Perhaps they were the kind of people who kept their issues tucked neatly beneath the rug, who clipped their nasal hair discretely, while her family had a tradition of pretending the lurking mass of problems in the corner was a coat stand and ignored the smell of rotting rats behind the refrigerator.

Neither approach satisfied her. *Not in my backyard.* It simply wasn't sustainable. Although after a while, a garden develops ecosystems of noxious weeds and stealthy insects all on its own, in the same way that people learn to live with the problems they are too scared to face – the same way that addictions reinforce themselves: vicious cycles. *If this is the result of so many years of neglect,* she wondered *how many years of loving nurture will it take to heal?*

She picked up a shovel, ready to unearth the past.

The ground was soft, easily giving way to the spade, and to Marcia's delight, she was making progress, absorbed in something bigger than herself. This garden was a metaphor for her family's unresolved history, and as she dug, she came across reminders of the past: old glass bottles, rusted metal wheels, rubber balls that her siblings most likely played with before losing them in the weeds. She noticed, too, that the different types of weeds all had a variety of strengths and weaknesses: wandering Jew, the anti-Semitic pest, was quick to grow and easy to rake away, the personal issues that keep coming back, needing to be cleared, like a cluttered mind. Ivy was tough, but one strand easily dragged others with it, like chains of bad memories. Jasmine, whose flowers were so sweet, and would bring death over her surroundings, could be cut at her strong, woody roots – cauterised at the source – which was what Marcia liked to think she could do with the thought patterns that unnecessarily drained her. Every problem could be solved – at least, in the garden.

The inner work was much tricker and needed other analogies. It was hard to tell which tensions needed stretching out, like sore muscles, which needed to be left alone to heal, like a bruise, or which needed deeper healing – cutting down beneath the layers, like a surgeon to remove the festering wound.

Marcia looked around at the wild garden. She was already exhausted, and yet, there was so much more to do. A wave of hopelessness and grief came over her, and it was all she could do to stop herself from collapsing. She coaxed herself back inside for a cup of tea and a reminder that the sense of being overwhelmed was all part of the process.

Yes… there's more work do to, but I don't need to do it all today.

Marcia awoke in the dark to a tapping sound. She sat up and looked toward the windows, visible in the faint orange glow of street lights reflected against the overcast night sky. Something was rapping against the glass. She got out of the bed she had dressed in mountains of feather duvets, shivering in her silk nightgown. A giant moth was knocking on her window, throwing itself desperately towards the reflection of the street lights, its wings a brilliant apple green. Marcia noted the peculiarity of a puriri moth so far from the trees it lived in, stranger still in winter. Marcia remembered reading in a native etymology book about the moths that burrowed into the Puriri tree, creating homes for themselves and living off the tree yet doing it no damage: a harmless parasite. She recalled that these moths lived as larvae for years and then after pupation, spent only one night as moths. This one was choosing to spend its only night in a mating dance with its own reflection.

Marcia found herself lost in memories of these beautiful creatures in the summers her family had spent in the nearby seaside town of Raglan. They had camped on a piece of land her uncle owned that was largely covered in native bush. She remembered her siblings fighting on the drive there, the carsickness from the twisting gravel road, the beach where they spent day-after-day, getting sunburnt and covered in black sand.

She had fallen in love with these moths, their delicious colour and implausible serpentine patterns. Her childhood recollections faded, and she felt the exhaustion again, giving way to the feeling of defeat, of utter hopelessness. She looked down at the moth, still adamantly careening into the window pane and wondered if moths fly towards the light because they were always tired, if their lives were so intolerably miserable that they wanted to sleep all their nocturnal waking hours.

Marcia had noticed the blossoms appearing over the fence, little white ones that seemed to be suspended in the air. They reminded her of dewdrops caught in a spider's web. On her way back from the greengrocer's, laden with vegetables and citrus fruit one overcast morning, she noted the arrival of small sunset-coloured blooms and wondered why these late winter flowers were so much more endearing, on their naked branches, than the classical spring blossoms soon to appear nestled amongst leaves. The cherry trees in the front garden would, in a matter of weeks, be in full bloom with their candy-floss tufts. But as ornamental varieties, they would bear no fruit, like the cats bred for show that would be utterly useless in the wild, the chickens and cows bred for meat that could hardly walk, let alone mate to save their species. *Another of humanity's great accomplishments,* she thought with a cynical smirk. *Tailor-made for our pleasure with complete disregard for the natural order of things.*

The frosts had come and gone, and Marcia was getting used to the solitary existence she had chosen. Her main conversational outlet was the neighbour's smoky cat, Nui. *Nui* was the Maori word for 'big', if her memory served her, although this little feline could not be described as such. She fed him scraps and sat with him on the deck, catching patches of winter sunlight. Apart from the cat, her only company had been the tradesmen from the yellow pages: fit and friendly builders, plumbers, and electricians, who were slowly restoring her neglected family home. She had the kitchen, last renovated in the 1930s, gutted and had installed something worth cooking on. Gas elements, marble benches and a sizeable pantry now lured her into the preparation of her meals, and she indulged in the creative outlet with relish. The dining area in the sunniest part of the house had its small windows replaced with large French doors leading out to the deck. This, along with the newly-painted light walls, gave the house a bright, airy feel, a striking contrast to the small dark rooms she had grown up in.

On the first Saturday of August, Marcia celebrated her solar return. The anniversary most people would call a birthday always seemed to bring strong emotions with it, as the sun crossed the point it had been when she was born. Alone in her family home, she turned out all the lights and watched the many shadows cast by fifty-five assorted candles she had placed all around the kitchen. All around her, the reflection was replicated on the glass of the windows and the French doors.

She brewed a herbal concoction, using her own intuition as guide. *Artemisia vulgaris, Verbena officinalis,* and *Lactuca virosa* – the wise ones, her old friends, combined in a seer's potion: a doorway to the subconscious.

Taking the draught, she felt the air thicken around her and let her mind clear. Her body relaxed into the softness of her futon couch, and she was pulled into a Plutonian trance.

The image of the High Priestess emerged then vanished, and she found herself surrounded by faces in a circle of people. She was their teacher, and they were eager to learn all she had to offer them. They smiled and laughed around her, and then the image swam away, replaced by the image of a woman, radiant, with rosy cheeks and golden hair. She felt a connection with this woman she had not met, a closeness, perhaps a friendship of souls. Her vision changed again, revealing the Lovers, two young ones together, making one, then the image was torn apart. It was replaced by a man standing before her in the prime of his life. Creativity swirled around him before he disappeared into the darkness, the peaceful void.

Marcia woke, her room flooded with September sunlight, her mind slightly dazed. She had spent the last two weeks in retreat, barely leaving the house, processing her solar return. The images of her vision washed over her mind, and she knew she had work to do. She had a class to teach, but she had to divine the exact nature of this class, and she had people to find. She felt a longing, stretching out from a pain buried deep in her womb.

For most of her life, she had focused all her energy on learning, and she still felt she had so much to learn, but there had been a shift; now, she had a new focus. *What do I have to offer? What can I teach?*

She had been a counsellor in London for the past fifteen years, helping people to wade through the troubled waters of their minds, but this was not what she had seen in her vision. She had studiously researched the properties of herbs, grown them, and gotten to know them as close friends; she had twenty-five years of yoga under her belt, but none of these things quite fitted the picture she had received. The group she had seen was clearly sitting, listening, laughing, and talking.

When she had first left New Zealand in search of new adventures and overseas experience, she had lived for six months with a Hindu family in Sydney and worked in their shop. The journey had helped her to reconnect with her mother's Indian heritage, the part of the family lineage that her father had never let anyone acknowledge, insisting Marcia's darker skin and hair was Spanish to anyone who asked.

Through later travels in India, Marcia had learnt about Ayurveda and chakras – the energy centres of different levels of awareness. She had hungered for spiritual mysteries and deeper truths and gratefully imbibed any mystical wisdom that came her way. Whenever she was inflicted with any sort of ailment, she sought out spiritual healers and naturopaths, trusting their subtle methods more than blunt chemical medication.

Over the years, she had taken courses in medicinal herbs, tarot and aromatherapy, and although all these things had a shared current running through them, they were all very different. She did not profess to be an expert in any of them but now she was called to share something of the wisdom she had accumulated over the years, in combination with her counselling training.

She felt mercurial as she sifted relevant words through her mind: wellbeing, awareness, health, healing, growth, spiritual, holistic. She arranged them until she came up with a combination she was happy with. Then, before she lost her nerve, she called the local community house to make a booking, and then the local papers, to advertise.

The garden was slowly undergoing a remarkable transformation. Grassy flowerbeds had been reclaimed one by one and layered with compost, mulch and fresh soil. Lavender, violets, and iris bulbs had been carefully planted. The lawns were slowly adjusting to their regular manicure. Marcia had spent the best part of a week pruning the plants that were healthy enough to keep, and an arborist had been consulted about the scores of dead and dying trees haunting the property.

The September weather was changing fast, and despite the frosty mornings, spring blossoms were popping up everywhere. Marcia was planning her vegetable plot, carefully estimating the amount of sunshine that would be available. She had dragged cinderblocks from their various resting places around the garden to use as edging and was now deciding which productive plants to grow. Her London flat only had room for a few potted necessities, and she was enjoying the luxury of so much space. Zucchinis were a must, as were tomatoes, but she decided to skip the carrots and onions, at least for now. She was in desperate need of some culinary herbs, so she added thyme, oregano, and parsley to her list. Lettuces she could plant out early and enjoy the benefits for months by picking the outer leaves for salads until the plants started to flower and became too bitter. She pondered briefly whether the plants chosen for the garden were as accurate a metaphor as the weeds to be taken out of it, whether choosing parsley to enjoy in tabbouleh was like choosing a political opinion to share with friends, whether lettuce was just as important to nurture as hope or kindness.

Her thoughts were cut short by the appearance of a head over her fence. Her elderly neighbour was peering scornfully at her.

"Hello, Mrs Everglade." Marcia felt as if she were fifteen again, which probably was the last time they had spoken.

"Good morning, dear." A pause followed in which Marcia was unable to find words to add to the conversation.

"That tree, dear," the neighbour said in her withered voice, pointing at the towering redwood, a gift Marcia's father had received from an American colleague some decades earlier.

"Yes?"

"It sheds terribly all over my path. I can't reach the leaves on the garage roof, and I'm afraid it's rusting. It's tearing up your… garden." She said 'garden' as if it was not the best word, but the most polite one she could think of. "The path's a right mess."

It was true. The concrete garden path had been cracked and lifted by enormous tree roots. The redwood was monstrous. It was also the largest tree in the neighbourhood, and Marcia didn't have the heart to tell Mrs Everglade that she had no intention of getting rid of it.

Marcia loved the sound of the rain as it cascaded down the corrugated iron roof and poured out of the old guttering, badly in need of replacement. She snuggled into her blankets as she listened to gusts of wind picking up raindrops and splattering them against the windows. The rain brought with it a tingling sensation akin to anticipation, and just before dawn was the most delightful time to weather a storm. She watched the grey light outside and felt grateful for this time alone. Fear had taken up residence in her chest, and it was growing.

She was frightened of the world outside and all the pain it held. Even greater was her fear of the things she wanted to do. She was afraid she would fail and, contrary to all reason, was even more afraid that she would succeed.

Self-sabotage presented itself in the back of Marcia's mind, offering an enticing way out. Excuses. There were always plenty of those, but she was tired of hiding from the world, and she was driven by a sense of impatience. There was a lot she still had to do in this life, and until she completed every task and learnt all she could, she was trapped here.

She wanted so badly to see William, to touch his face, to allow him to alleviate her misery and fear. She missed him so much her body ached, every cell screaming out to her to correct the imbalance: to bring him back and make her whole again. He had been taken from her in the night, and she had rolled over, looking for his comforting warmth and finding a clammy statue instead. Her horror turned into shock, and after a few days, maybe weeks of cold surreal hell, her world dissolved in rivers of tears. Grief mingled with a longing for freedom, for peace, that no amount of self-torment could possibly bring her.

She rose early. The birds were welcoming the dawn, and in the pale light, she put on her warmest dressing gown and bravely faced the new morning. The air was frightfully cold, turning her breath into clouds of steam. She could make out the sound of blackbirds and tui, robins and some kind of warbler.

Her bare feet froze on the damp wood of the deck. Anyone watching her as she scaled the wall of the garage would have considered her a raving loon – a fully-grown woman climbing onto the garage roof in her dressing gown at first light. But she did have a reason.

She was there to confront the little Saturnian voice inside that screamed, "I CAN'T!!!" A child having a tantrum, a self-fulfilling prophecy. Of course, it was about her workshops, the ones she had been planning these past weeks since her birthday. The closer the date got, the more excuses she had come up with to delay, postpone, or cancel. She was stubborn enough not to listen to her doubts, but they were growing increasingly dramatic.

She sat down on the cold, wet, corrugated iron, wrapping her arms around her knees, focusing all her attention on her feelings.

"NO!" the voice seemed to yell in a high pitch. "YOU CAN'T!" Now it wasn't coming from her. It was speaking to her as if it was outside her. This did not surprise Marcia. In her years as a counsellor, she had become familiar with these externalisations. She thought of them as little bits of the self that had broken off from the whole, creating dissonance. One little fragment such as this could be devastating to one's confidence. It could ruin a marriage, a career, a life, and this particular one was posing a threat to her, to something she wanted to do. She could listen to it; she could decide to throw in the towel and focus on all the hundreds of other things that needed to be done on the house. If she was really weak, she could run all the way back to London to escape a part of herself that would undeniably come with her. But, as she had already established, she was tired of running; she was ready to face herself.

She let the voice scream and scream until it quietened, the way

46

children become spent from their own exertions. She held it there, in her chest; this part of her that had become estranged. She welcomed it back, but it resisted. That was acceptable; it would heal in its own time. Its separate being would be consumed by the whole, and she would feel more complete. For the present, she was satisfied with the quiet calm her rather bizarre morning activity had provided.

7

IRIS

I ris pulled into the petrol station and immediately felt her body tighten. It was stress, worries about money. It was unhelpful. It may just have been a coincidence, but Iris had noticed, throughout her life, that the people she knew who worried about money the most were the people who always had financial problems, regardless of their income. She had worked with people earning six-figure salaries who were always broke and never happy.

Though many people all over the country were struggling, especially with the cost of housing, Iris also knew some people who drew on other sources of wellbeing – some of them on very low incomes always seemed to have enough to live their lives in a way that made them happy. Of course, there were structural factors to consider, and real poverty was nothing to make light of, but it was puzzling that even those earning similar amounts of money could be in such wildly different financial situations.

It was still a mystery to Iris, but she had spent a long time thinking about it. It seemed when she felt the most intense feelings of financial stress and scarcity, it had only made her more likely to spend the little money she did have on things she didn't need. From a survival perspective, that made sense. In the wild, human beings would have reacted to scarcity by going out to forage and hunt for food, but things had changed so drastically. Now, the equivalent to foraging was shopping which only resulted in more scarcity. It was hard for the brain to make good decisions while under stress, after all.

Iris had experimented on herself, encouraging her own positive thoughts about her money situation, which seemed to work for a time, until her worries crept back and she would find herself staring at the Eftpos machine, hoping for 'accepted' rather than 'declined'. It was a tightening feeling, the feeling of not having enough. It was almost as if she could feel her reality changing, and her bank balance obligingly responded. The less she worried about money, the less she needed to, but that didn't stop the feelings and thoughts of 'not having enough' which had been so ingrained in her as a child.

She unscrewed the petrol cap and lifted the nozzle from its post. As she clutched the lever, allowing the petrol to pour into her car, she was not bombarded by the usual middle-class guilt of using precious natural resources and polluting the environment. Instead, she thought of herself as a kind of hose, a channel through which the universe could flow or be blocked. She remembered something she had often come across in self-help books, *the universe is never lacking in energy; lack is just a human construction that helps our economy to function*. She felt herself opening up, allowing the abundant and generous energy of the universe to flow through her. It was a much more pleasant sensation than the tight feeling she had experienced moments before. *If only she could remember to do this all the time*, she thought. *Why is it that whenever human beings happen upon a universal truth, we are always so quick to forget it?*

Iris sat at her laptop, staring at the screen. She was inside today because of the rain. Perhaps that was the reason she was having trouble with her writing. She had been trying to express something that was almost too delicate for words, and no matter how many times she edited, it always came out sounding tacky.

When you were growing up, you learnt how to behave from your parents. When you were too emotional, they may have behaved towards you in a certain way. If you spilt your glass of milk by accident, your parents might have yelled at you, causing confusion and emotional pain, and from this type of experience, you will have learnt ways of treating yourself, internalising the behaviour of your parents. Now when you are emotional, or when you do something, which the parental part of you thinks is wrong, you probably continue this process internally.

Do you tell yourself off sometimes? This is the voice of your internal parent. We all want parents who nurture us and understand us. Take a moment to consider your inner child, that irrational, emotional, creative part of you. Think about what he or she wants. Now consider your inner parent and think about his or her needs. When you find yourself falling into a pattern of self-punishment, allow yourself to think about these two distinct parts of your personality. Encourage your inner parent to meet the needs of your inner child: for support and encouragement and love. Remind your inner child to respect your inner parent. When these two aspects of yourself are in harmony with each other, a major internal conflict is resolved, and you are able to live your life free from this internal struggle.

Maybe it's just me, she thought. She had read too many self-help books after all. The concept was important to her, the inner child and the inner parent, but the terminology reminded her of a 70s love-in. Her parents had always regarded such words with contempt. Her father had once remarked to her that men couldn't have inner children because they didn't have wombs.

Come to think of it, there was nothing wrong with what she had written at all. It was just the contamination of the ideas by her parents that was bothering her. That was something she didn't need. She accepted it and let it go. *After all,* she thought, *no one has a perfectly happy childhood if you dig deep enough.* It was probably because children were so sensitive in a world full of sharp edges, and people hardened to its cruelty.

Iris sighed happily as the fresh spring breeze picked up and whirled around the deck. The rain had gone, leaving bright sunshine. She looked down at her laptop where her first chapters, written in an excited blur, lay.

The thoughts we occupy our minds with are as important as the food we use to fuel our bodies. If we choose the thoughts that encourage the things we desire, we will attune ourselves to those things.

She had come upon the realisation that it took more than a can-do apple-a-day attitude to write in a way that would connect with the reality of people's lives. Iris sometimes had difficulty following the advice she preached when she argued with Alex over internet use, was stuck in a long queue, or felt she was being unjustly over-charged. *Yes, thinking happy thoughts will work, but life can be complicated. Change needs to occur consistently at every level to have a lasting, life-trans-forming effect.*

Iris had no idea of how to structure this work, but she did not let her thoughts dwell on concerns. She lifted her head to the horizon, to the peaceful grey clouds in the distance.

At times she longed for the stability of her old life, the certainty of knowing what she had to do next. This was not one of those times. Allowing her intuition to guide her, she began to write again, not consciously aware of her fingers as she typed.

Allow your mind to clear and visualise yourself as a newly-born child, in awe of the amazing new world around you, innocent and pure. Allow yourself to realise that all the guilt, resentment, and regret you have felt is not natural or necessary. It is merely something you have been taught. Free yourself of these burdens by acknowledging your own innocence.

Iris strolled carefree through the small, seaside town of Raglan, picking up groceries and looking into boutiques filled with local crafts. She passed a stony-faced, middle-aged couple, noticing that everything about them seemed to be grey. *In need of healing*, she thought and wondered why so few people sought a path out of their misery. She entered the herbal dispensary, filled with scented candles, peculiar bottles, and organic snacks, and watched a long-haired woman browsing through supplements. She remembered what Ariki had said about all the people she knew who studied alternative medicine being in need of healing themselves and wondered whether some people could be addicted to finding new panaceas or miracle workers, never satisfied with the present.

So many of the people she had seen milling through the town were instinctively holding close to their fears, and Iris couldn't help but think this unnecessary. Their serious expressions made it obvious. Survival was not something that needed a lot of attention for most people in this country, where the social welfare system was almost reasonable, violent crime was fairly low, and shootings were rare. These people focused on just getting by were missing their lives in an attempt to protect themselves. Iris knew a shift in perspective is all it took to transform a mundane life into a wonderful, joyful experience.

There had been times in her life when she had hardly smiled, days at high school when the pressure of exams had overwhelmed her, weeks at university when all her assignments were due at once, months when she was plagued by work deadlines and a sick baby. During these times, she had managed to politely turn the edges of her mouth up to form a semi-circle, but her eyes had not sparkled.

Iris had grown up focussed on survival, her family just scraping by, managing to pull together enough money to buy school shoes for her and her sisters and occasionally managing a rare treat, chocolates or a camping holiday. Iris had always longed for something more, not just financially, or even physically; there was a deeper hunger, for meaning, for understanding, for wisdom. As a child, she had desired the power to transform her world into somewhere enchanted, where she could fall through a trapdoor into a city of elves or find buried pirate treasure. She had been obsessed with superheroes like Wonder Woman and Superman and enthralled by science fiction movies. There was a trace of something magical that she longed to believe in. Looking back, she realised that more than anything, magic had been hope.

Iris called into the local café to pass the time before Alex finished school. A paper lay open on the table. An advert stood out as if in answer to her prayers: a seven-part workshop series on holistic awareness.

Iris set off on her usual walk, down the stone steps and gravelled driveway, passing over and through native saplings, as she made her way along the narrow path. As she walked, she took time to reflect.

Her writing was coming together better than she had hoped. New ideas streamed through her into the keyboard, and inspiration struck at all hours. Things were beginning to develop so quickly that she wondered whether this was really her own work or whether, as she sometimes got the strange feeling, she was just uncovering something that was already written, or perhaps she was just a marionette, dancing to the movement of someone higher up pulling the strings.

She felt like she was putting the pieces of a puzzle together and that the end result was already predetermined but impossible for her to see. The workshop she had signed up for was surely one of these pieces. Something inside her had clicked into place when she had seen the ad, and now she felt a strong wave of anticipation whenever she thought of it.

She was slowly adjusting to this strange new lifestyle that was governed by her whims and fancies rather than tightly scheduled meetings and other work obligations. She hoped Alex was settling in, but she had no clue what state his mind was in.

For the first few weeks, he had locked himself away, barely surfacing except for meals and school. Then the phone calls had started. Iris had smiled the first time she heard the girl's voice, small and nervous, asking to speak to her son. The same voice called almost every day now, and she wished she knew more about what was going on, but she allowed Alex his privacy.

He barely spoke two words to her in a day unless it was to argue over his excessive internet use, and each time, he would throw her choice to move in her face, as if he had no responsibility for his life at all.

Iris made peace offerings to fly him back to Wellington for weekend visits with his friends, which he just shrugged off as if he would prefer her to remain the villain and for himself to stay in his poor-me role.

Every now and then, her mind would automatically schedule in her morning bath and walk and begin to make plans for what to have for breakfast when she caught it and let go of the need for her time to be fully accounted for. Often her thoughts would stray to worrying about money or obsessing over the insanity of her current situation, but when she realised her thinking was of an unhelpful strain, she chose to replace it with positive affirmations. *I feel great. I have all I desire.* Every time she came across a phrase she particularly liked the resonance of, she jotted it onto a post-it note and stuck it to the side of her laptop screen to use in her writing. *I am happy with my life. I rejoice in the beauty of life.*

8

ZANE

The moonlight was mercilessly depriving Zane of sleep. He looked up at the iridescent lunar disc, merrily taunting him from the sky. He pulled the sheets over his head despite the disgusting Los Angeles summer heat and managed to drift into a light dream state.

She stood, ethereal, before him, her dark hair tumbling in the wind. Tears streaked her face, taking all his strength with a simple glance. He fell to his knees, weak and alone, crying out for her, the only woman he had ever lost himself to. He was running through a forest, chased or chasing something. His heart pounding, he fell again; this time, when he stood up, he realised he was holding a baby bundled in a green blanket.

The shock jolted him awake, and, noticing his limbs were twisted through his sweaty sheets, he stared scornfully at the moon. *What are you trying to tell me? Why can't you let me rest?*

The people in his dreams had the odd habit of appearing different to the way they actually looked, but he always recognised them. The woman he had seen was definitely a flame – the same woman he had dreamed about over and over the past few weeks.

She had appeared to him with much darker hair this time; her body tall and elegant, her eyes dark and starry, wet. She could have been an animation, drawn so seamlessly. So unlike the real person he once knew: the blonde girl who used to scribble all over her text-books and chew the ends of her pens until they broke.

The woman who had broken his heart like a shattered mirror.

He couldn't sleep, so he lay awake, thinking about her. For a while, in his youth, she had been the answer. She had filled the void he'd always felt, and then she'd left without properly saying good-bye, and the emptiness had only grown inside him, driving him deeper into his music in a vain attempt to find oblivion.

"Let the fun begin," Jimmy said impishly as they ascended the stairs that led to a very familiar studio apartment. Zane smiled back at him.

There was almost as much work in presenting and publicising an album as there was creating it. The record company took care of printing and advertising, but the band had to go through scores of interviews and expose themselves to the world. They also had to decide on the album cover.

More than ten years earlier, after their first album had come out, the four of them stumbled into a gallery opening and found the artist they'd been looking for. His name was Milton Johns, and he portrayed multi-dimensional images: people in all their layers of being, seas of psychedelic lotuses, patterns that took the mind on a journey in much the same way their music did. Since then, they had worked with him to create metaphoric claymation music videos and every one of their album covers.

Milton, a tall, lanky sort with grey shoulder-length hair, greeted them warmly like an old friend.

"Here it is, guys," Milton said, ripping a white sheet from a giant easel, revealing his latest creation. The band stood back to appraise it.

It was about two-by-two metres squared, but the design was circular. An intricately woven pattern surrounded it, but all Zane could look at was the centre: a void that seemed to expand and swallow him whole. He took a step closer, noticing the engravings that stood out in colour from the black that had been spread over the main surface. It reminded him of the crayon drawings he had made in kindergarten where he'd coloured the surface of the paper and then covered over it in black before scratching out a design that revealed the hidden world below. It made the image three dimensional. He stood starring at the centre of the painting, the void mirroring his own emptiness. Zane was transfixed, mesmerised by its depth. The more he looked at it, the more he saw.

"Dude. That's awesomely detailed," Baz began to say, pointing towards the edge of the artwork. "Remind me to let you design my next tatt."

It was only then that Zane realised the entire border was made up of tiny figures, amazingly life-like people in every stage of humanity, every expression and every position imaginable.

"That is trippy as hell," Mitch added. He and Jimmy were standing back. Zane joined them. From several metres away, against the black wall of the studio, the painting looked unmistakeably like a galaxy with a black hole in its centre.

It reminded Zane of a fractal: the computer-generated images that could zoom out until the pattern repeated exactly. He had always found them impressive, an allusion to the greater nature of the universe. He was willing to bet that if science advanced to the point that they could understand every aspect of an atom, they would find an entire universe inside each one and, at the same time, if they could fathom the end of the universe, they would find it protected by a magnetic field just as atoms were: a single building block in a far greater scheme.

Zane had spent all morning weaving lyrics through the music created by his band, finishing the final recording for their new album.

The recordings came out even better than he'd expected. There was a new depth to his voice that spoke to a greater pain than just his own – a collective human suffering. Zane couldn't help but wonder whether it was the dreams affecting him – the light-haired woman and the dark-haired women – like some kind of archetypal shift within him, like Jung's concept of the *Anima* – the feminine aspect of a man.

The band left the rest of the day's work up to the production team and strolled down the road to order celebratory tacos from Burrito King before retreating from the hot sun to their apartment building. Zane flopped onto a soft couch, Mitch stretched himself over two bean bags, raking his fingers over their corduroy material, Baz took up his usual chair by the tropical fish tank, and Jimmy lay on the floor, his fingers drumming the polished wooden floorboards to the beat in his mind.

"What's next?" Baz asked, running both hands down his sleeved arms.

"I vote we order pizza," Jimmy chimed, knowing his response was not answering the original question.

"No anchovies," Zane added.

"Tour," Mitch ordered, and the others nodded in agreement. They loved the magic of performance even more than food or their lazy Californian lifestyle. All heads turned towards Zane, who could command the rapt attention of a hundred thousand people. Zane's mind had drifted back to the last time they had played live on their European tour: the crowd, no more than specks of colour, flickering like television static as they rocked, hypnotised by the floating guitar, the deep throbbing heartbeat of bass, the thundering, primal drum-beat. *This,* he thought at the time, *is the new opiate of the people.* The crowd swayed in unison, drunk on the mass of energy that hung in the air.

Something, subtle as a dream, nudged Zane from the depths of his subconscious mind.

"This time..." he said, still staring into space, "I'd like to go home."

A strange quiet had descended over the apartment. When they had discussed their imminent tour, his bandmates were stunned at Zane's suggestion. There was a general unspoken recognition that something had shifted.

The band was a mishmash of nationalities; Jimmy was Californian, Mitch was English, and Baz was Mexican-American. Although they knew Zane's country of origin, even his most devoted fans did not. "Home" was not something Zane Strachan spoke about.

The Americans assumed he was English and the Poms assumed he was American. One article he had read claimed, to his amusement, that he was Chinese but raised in Iceland.

In his mind, Zane still regarded New Zealand as the most beautiful country in the world. The rich and varied landscapes were etched deep into his psyche, but he had not returned home since he first left, sixteen years earlier. He could not face the abandonment.

On this particular morning, Zane was reading Jung's autobiography and contemplating his dreams while the other band members did their own thing. It had been like this for days.

As usual, Baz was the first one to break free of the silence. He launched into one of his diatribes with the propensity of one in the midst of an argument already. Zane had a theory that the conversations began in his mind and expanded until there was no room left and they had to escape.

"We all have giant caverns in our faces," he began. The rest of the group, who had been loitering around the lobby in their usual places, almost jumped.

"Humans are born incomplete; we have these gaping holes here." He gestured to his own mouth, which happened to be tattooed blue, emphasising his point. "Is it any wonder babies need pacifiers? That's why people are always smoking and stuffing themselves full of junk with no nutritional value. We need to be filled, to feel whole."

Jimmy just nodded. He had that look that Zane recognised as: *You're finally catching on.*

"It sounds like survival to me," Mitch cut in, ever the practical one. "The urge to feed ourselves, all that kind of jazz." He was watching the neon bubbles at the back of the fish tank wall.

Zane didn't feel like joining the discussion today. He sat back and zoned out, wondering briefly which side would win out: Baz's unjust world or Mitch's naturalism.

Zane was not feeling charitable. The radio interviewer was just another naïve dumbass with a typical all-American voice, dripping with cheese and hotdogs, asking him about his personal relationships. He responded in a flat tone.

"A relationship is a social construct, differing from culture to culture, Steve. Essentially, it is a body of expectations." He couldn't help but feel smug at the silence his arrogant diatribe had commanded.

"So, Zane... Entered into anybody's expectations lately?" came the response, ripe with immature innuendo.

"Expectations are just ideas with attachments, often about the way things *should* be or will be in the future." Jimmy would have been proud.

The danger with expectations is that you are setting yourself up for a fall. His internal monologue filled in the blanks.

"Are you an expert, now?"

Zane ignored the jibe.

"If you are attached to one possible outcome, you may make yourself miserable worrying about things not working out, which may contribute to them falling apart anyway." Suddenly he was the commentator in some bizarre documentary on human behaviour.

"So your philosophy is not to expect too much?"

"No. Although people sometimes lower their expectations to avoid disappointment, this barely masked self-deception rarely works because people are secretly hoping for better."

"Are you saying you can't get any, or you just don't want to?"

It was Zane's turn to be silent. He wanted to put the broadcaster on the line. Nothing is worse than silence on-air, and Zane knew he was booked in for at least a few more minutes. This little stunt had lifted his spirits already. He listened as Steve Shapowsky scrambled to fill in the blanks.

"Well... tell us more about these expectations, oh wise one."

"Relationships in Western society tend to boast assumptions or expectations of monogamy, commitment, intimacy, emotional ties, dependency, attachment, particular acceptable and unacceptable behaviour in private and in public, and expectations around meeting some of each other's needs." Zane felt like he was educating a two-year-old.

"Wait – did you say there are cultures with no monogamy?" Steve chuckled, obviously entertaining the possibility of a nation of sexually free women. After a pause, he struggled, again, to fill the dead air. "So what happens when we don't get our – how do ya call it? 'Expectations met'?"

Zane sighed, feeling a little like a talk show psychiatrist. "Drama akin to a Greek tragedy," he responded, trying to keep his voice from cracking with amusement. "Or a daytime soap opera."

"Now that explains a few things… are you saying that relationships aren't real or just that they aren't necessary."

"I'm saying that people give others the power to make them miserable, whether the other person wants that power or not…" He was glad to be cut off as their time ran out.

"Well, that was Zane from the Nu-Metal band Wrench with his enlightening theory of relationships. All we've got time for today, folks."

Zane hung up the phone, wincing at the label his band was given. Maybe they needed to deviate more, do something more classical or folky. He hated being categorised and avoided it at all costs. The other band members, he noticed, were still in the room.

"So we've been put in the Nu-Metal bin again," Mitch groaned.

"I think it's time we gave up and got ourselves a label of our own," said Baz, a gleam in his beady eyes. "How about Medieval-Elvish-Rap?"

Zane was feeling frustrated with society in general and with mainstream media in particular. It was taking too long for the record company minions to organise their tour. He was getting impatient with them and fed up with the whole industry. He was sick of watching as other people zoned out and took in everything they were spoon-fed by the media. He was ready for a change.

The problem with having the world toned down and synthesised is that it warps our development.

He scrawled across the thick white pages of his leather-bound notebook. He recalled the crazy woman who stood outside their apartment block the previous day, calling them sinners and commanding them to repent in the lord's name. She was not so different from the scientists who argued that their theories were the only truths available or the politicians who spoke in absolutes. He was sick of people preaching their view of reality at him as if it were gospel. He was sick of people thinking they were right.

The mainstream holds its own religions: atheism, science, politics. People will always have their fundamentalism, with or without God. Whether we worship logic or Yahweh, it makes no difference. We claim to be right, to know, to scale down the world, to make it safer: the religion of science, closed, narrow, boring, whose wonders have been discovered and rediscovered so many times they've grown into dim facts, only proven through repetition and generalisation, only real in a lab, believed by the many with programmed imagination. An ancient art of discovery, broken down so many times, it has become meaningless to all but those blinded by its stability and certainty, the things people tend to crave.

There was so much more in the world that people didn't even think about: the bigger picture.

There has to be a progression. The most important part of the next step of human evolution is to realise how little truth lies around us: news, media, society. To explore our subconscious for the wisdom inherent in the universe, to gain perspective through observing our past lives, to seek a deeper truth, to experience enough to move to the next stage, whatever it may hold.

It was almost time for him to do something about it. This was the last album Wrench was contracted to make. They were all sick of selling out to their record company; they needed to break free of their corporate leash. *Next time it will be different,* he vowed.

9

LEA

The cigarette smoke burned up Lea's throat, singeing her lungs, provoking equal parts of revulsion and pleasure. Just like self-pity, just like any self-destructive indulgence. The part she liked the most was the damage she knew she was doing to her lungs, to her future.

She had heard adults talk about peer pressure, about just saying no. It wasn't *actually* like that. Sienna, who could pass for eighteen, bought them for her from the shop in town that didn't ask for ID, but it was always Lea who asked her to. No one had forced her to take anything. No one had dared her or coerced her at all. In fact, it was the defiance that made it appealing.

It was a rebellion against the person she was supposed to be, the person her mother and her teachers were trying to shape her into: someone wholesome and sweet and good. There was no point in deceiving herself; she knew she was none of those things. Someone like that would feel self-satisfied and content. Someone like that would follow all the rules and never question them. She would bake and watch movies with happy endings; she would choose to spend quality time with her family; she would have long curling locks in her natural hair colour. Lea couldn't think of anyone more opposite to herself. She was a failure in everyone's eyes, even if they hadn't given up hope that she would sprout dimples and start wearing pink lace. It was pleasing to think that these innocent-looking, white sticks could lead to her time on Earth being shortened, that they could reduce her sentence in this hell.

She watched the way the thin stream swirled slowly as it expanded, hanging in the air in defiance of gravity. She stubbed the butt out under her window ledge and then carefully pulled it closed. Still dizzy from the head rush, she bolted the latch quietly so as not to alert her parents. The moment was waiting in her mind to be captured as she reached for her notebook.

Smoker's Equinox
Senseless reams
Gliding ribbons
Opaque-transparent
Romantic mist
Silver-grey
Ageing moonlight
Refresh the mind
Scorch the throat
Poison the blood
Disintegrating the lungs
To silent music – Silent sentiment
Quickened thought – Quickened death
Ghost thought – Afterthought
Ghost life
Afterlife
In this timeless senseless
Tragic
Fatal dance

Lea scrolled through page after page, absorbing information like a paper towel, soaking up the knowledge available at her fingertips. Today, she had decided to focus on the occult. She ached to satisfy her thirst for depth, and this seemed mysterious enough to hold promise. She'd just finished reading about the Church of Satan, the irony of which was not wasted on her, when a little box popped up at the bottom of the screen, Erika had messaged her.

Erika: hi!!!
Lea: Hey, what's up?
Erika: i just got the email addys of all the boyz in my cuzins class!!!
U want them?"

Lea very much doubted that the emails Erika had acquired belonged to anyone remotely interesting, but she was getting bored, so she added them to her messenger app. Most of the names looked lame: big_cox13 certainly had something to prove, as did 3some_69, and some of the names looked like they had come straight out of an Armageddon convention: Gandalfthegrey1 and xanthian_destroyer.

She returned to her browser and looked up Wiccan rituals, most of which revolved around particular coloured candles and funny-sounding chants. Lea was reading a chant that encompassed an entire ritual, wondering if it was worth memorising in case she ever wanted to work some magic when another box popped up at the bottom of her screen *pessimistoblivion* was online. Lea was intrigued; at least this person, whoever he was, had a decent vocabulary. She would never have approached him in person, but loneliness tugged at her to begin typing. It was easier to be brave online than in real life.

Lea: Hi
Alex: Hey
Lea: I got your email from Erika, is that ok?
Alex: Yeah, whatever
Lea: So what are you up to?

He posted a link. It led to a chat room, the title flashed in bold red, lettered Atheist Forum. Lea was fascinated.

Lea: Is this where you hang out?
Alex: Mostly

Alex: What about you?
Lea: I usually just chat on messenger and google topics I'm interested in.
Alex: Fair enough
Lea: At the moment it's occultism
Alex: Heh. It's just another religion
Lea: I guess. I don't know. I'm not into satan or anything, but I like some kinds of paganism.
Alex: I don't believe in anything that's not proven
Lea: well, atheism is boring

It usually was, but the chat room was filled with arguments. Fundamentalist Christians would pop in just to be abusive and tell people they were going to hell for not bearing witness, whatever that meant. Lea was easily drawn into the arguments; it was quite enjoyable to watch clever people debate with idiots.

His name was Alex Cooper. *Alex.* Lea liked the way it rolled off her tongue with a sizzle at the end. She knew he had dark hair and blue eyes. She knew he liked the same music she did, not idiotic screamy metal, but the complex stuff with thought-provoking lyrics and intricate melodies, the music that drew her in and made her feel understood, and somehow, she knew he felt that way too. Their playlists were close to identical, and they shared an admiration for Wrench's lead singer, Zane Strachan, that Lea suspected extended to idolisation for Alex.

She knew he hated society, that he despised the government and was idealistic about anarchy, which she didn't believe would actually work.

She knew all these things, and yet, she didn't actually know him, not face to face. It was difficult to explain, so she didn't try to tell anyone else, but she did know him – even before hearing his voice – she could just tell.

For some inexplicable reason, he didn't have a webcam or a microphone, so she called him on the landline instead, nervous, doodling scruffily on the list she had written out in preparation, in case there were awkward silences.

The phone seemed to ring forever, and when it was finally answered, Lea heard a woman's voice, light and airy. She was taken aback momentarily but then remembered to ask for Alex, feeling her words crawl over her dry throat.

"Hello?" The voice was deep and velvety. The blood rushed to her head, leaving tingles in her tummy.

"Hi." Her voice was absurdly high. She wished she could take it back, but it was far too late for that. "It's Lea."

"Hey," he said, sounding pleased. She closed her bedroom door to avoid eavesdroppers and relaxed into the soft comfort of her bed.

She had a whole range of topics and questions written down, and she managed to cover most of them without sounding too much like an interviewer.

Each answer he gave came as a pleasant surprise, and she was increasingly mesmerised, intoxicated by the possibility that there was someone who might understand her. The feeling gradually built up until she had to say something. She hesitated because it seemed crazy.

"I know this sounds strange..." Her voice trailed off, and she hoped he would forget she ever began, but a listening silence ensued. "...because I've never met you in real life, but..." Then she said it because all the sensations in her body forced her to. "I think I like you." The confession left her dizzy.

There was silence for a moment, and then her words echoed back to her in his voice.

"I think I like you too." And she could hear his smile.

It was overwhelming for Lea. She had never quite felt this way – this drawn to anyone before – this gurgling happiness rising up through her chest and trying to burst through the pores of her skin. It was so much that she buried her face in her hands, waiting for her heart to slow down and normality to return again. It never did.

Lea was nervous. It was a chilly feeling in her spine. She had never met anyone off the internet before, and she knew it sounded bad. The news was full of horror stories of teenagers going to meet people they thought were their age but turned out to be perverted old people. But this was different. She had some idea who this guy was, he was in the same class as her friend's cousin, and she had spent hours chatting to him online and on the phone. She had to call him on the landline as he lived in the middle of nowhere without much cell reception, and they'd talked for so long that his mum had complained about them holding up the phone line.

They had a lot in common and conversation came easily: about the pointlessness and tediousness of school, about their problems with their parents, about their views of the world, their taste in music, movies, websites, everything.

She left school during assembly – there was no way she was going to sit through that contrite rubbish again – and headed towards town. It had been raining the night before, and the humidity made the day warmer than it had been in the previous frosty week. The overcast sky was reflected in blinding glare by the white cars and buildings she passed on her way, making her eyes water. The top of her forehead still burned from the dye she had used to transform the washed-out purple of her fringe into razzle-red while she re-dyed the rest of her hair black. She could still smell the peroxide emanating from her scalp.

The anticipation became overwhelming, and for a moment, she half-wished that he wasn't there, so she could avoid her own panic. That was when she saw him.

He was wearing headphones, standing in front of the mall where they had agreed to meet. More muscular than she had imagined, he looked slightly awkward. His black hair was short, roughly spiked; he was wearing baggy shorts and a grey T-shirt and staring into space. She almost turned away as the nervousness in her chest built up again, but she gritted her teeth and took the plunge, stepping right in front of him.

"Hi," she said, only to be caught off-guard by his grey-blue eyes.

It was awkward at first. They kept walking so that they didn't have to face each other, speaking into the street ahead and watching people dash around town. The business types in their dark suits and briefcases, the colourful, fashionable women, who were either on their lunch break or didn't have to work at all, the mothers pushing prams and towing toddlers along with them. Sometimes they commented on them but, mostly, they were in another world altogether.

Alex's mind worked fast; it delighted Lea. Although she barely remembered what they spoke about, she knew it had made her feel wonderful just to be in his presence, and if she was honest, more than a little high. It wasn't like smoking pot or cigarettes, although, at times, she did feel light-headed. It was a much stronger rush. The natural chemicals seemed to pulse through her veins, making everything slightly surreal. Her face was flushed, and she felt too big when usually she was too small.

She noticed a kind of electricity between them. She could feel Alex's hand near hers, although they weren't touching, and it surprised her. He seemed to be calm. How could he be? She tried to disguise the excited tremor in her hands. She wanted to express how she was feeling, but she didn't want to sound like a freak, and she knew it would come out weird. She wanted to talk about it, to make it real, not just something in her head. There weren't enough words in the English language to describe emotions, and no one ever seemed to talk about them that much anyway, so she guessed it worked both ways. Women were supposed to be too emotional, and it wasn't a good thing. She didn't want to fall into the stereotype. Not with *him*.

There was something vaguely familiar about his face, as if she'd seen it before in a dream. His skin was slightly olive, and his complexion was perfect, unlike hers, which was pale and patchy and always seemed to have at least one pimple. At the moment, it was in the centre of her chin, and she wished she could hide it.

When she asked him about his father, she instantly regretted it. His whole body seemed to tense up, and he only said that he didn't know his father. She accepted that, knowing not to push him further, and he had easily relaxed back into his normal state, although he seemed quieter.

As they passed people in the street, Lea smiled quietly to herself.

She knew they looked like a couple, even if it was too good to be true.

Lea had only known him a few weeks, but it seemed like forever. They spent almost every day together by the river, talking about everything, and every moment, she felt lighter and freer than ever before. They would often both skip school, and Alex would take the late bus home so he could spend more time with her.

At some point since first meeting him, her poetry had dissolved into sappy romantic rubbish that even she could not tolerate, but she didn't care. The spring sunshine felt magical and bright. It felt like she was somewhere in her mind she had never been before, and it was all because of him.

The second time they met, she had been braver. He had said he liked her over the phone, after all, so she had taken his hand casually, relieved when he accepted. She wondered if he was afraid to initiate contact, but he seemed so calm before and after touching her hand, and this motivated her to go further. She led him to her favourite place, under the pine tree where she had played as a child. It was dark and private. The tree's aroma filled up the space between them, and she took a step closer, slowly. She listened to his breathing as they leant towards each other. As their lips met, Lea felt the rush even stronger than before. It overwhelmed her. She felt unusually safe there, under that tree with his arms wrapped around her.

The next day when he met her, he casually commented that someone at his school has asked where he was going, and he'd said: "To meet my girlfriend". Her heart leapt. The official label made her feel recognised and accepted somehow.

She loved that his mind was quick like hers and equally cynical. They agreed on most things: politicians were liars, school was a waste of time, religion was stupid, although he didn't believe in spirituality at all, and she did; she just wasn't sure exactly how. She tried to explain to him that there was something else, some kind of meaning behind everything, but he just argued that she couldn't prove it, and he was right. It wasn't a prove-able thing. *But it must be something*, she thought to herself. *Something must have been keeping me alive these past few years.*

He was the first to admit his arrogance. He seemed to revel in it, and Lea somehow found this elating, as if being connected to him increased her value. He said his IQ was 178, and it sounded impressive, even though Lea knew that IQ tests were totally overrated because they only tested for particular things like memory or logic. Even *she* thought he spent too much time online, and that was saying something. He was always in that Atheist chat room; sometimes, she joined him there, but she often found it tedious. It didn't matter. It was so much easier to focus on him rather than her own problems, to bury herself in him, despite her better judgment.

She wished they were older, that they could have all the things a proper relationship could have: a home, a family, a future. Sometimes, when the infatuation bubbled up in her chest, she wished she could have met him later in her life. The realist in her somehow knew that it was unlikely their relationship could last forever, but the rest of her clung desperately to the hope that it would.

When she was around him, everything seemed to sparkle, and when she saw him appear online or first heard his voice on the phone, she got that same rush. When she examined the feeling more closely, it was like nothing she had ever felt before, almost a kind of pleasurable pain. He made her so happy she couldn't express it, so it burned agonisingly inside, making her wonder whether this was love. And still, there were times when she was alone at night or at school, or when he would rather play his stupid first-person shooter games or loiter in his chat room than talk to her, that she felt that familiar darkness creeping back into her, and she knew she was doomed. Whenever he said goodbye or when his words hinted that she might not be the most important thing in the world to him, she felt tormented, and she knew it wasn't rational or healthy.

Lea was baffled by his familiarity. She could pick him out of a crowd. She knew the smell of his deodorant and the way his body moved as he walked. She was preoccupied with him at school. At home, she hid in her room as usual, but he was always there, in her head. She couldn't have escaped, even if she'd wanted to. When she felt bad, she would re-play the highlights in her mind: the way his smile jolted through her, the way she almost flew out of her body when he unexpectedly showed the smallest affection, the touch of his hand, an arm around her waist, even a meaningful look.

They seemed to be in their own world, as usual, in the gazebo by the river. She held him as she watched the reflections shimmering on its surface, interrupted by leaves and twigs that cut through. There was something new today, an air of anticipation. She felt it when he kissed her, and it took all her effort to keep still, staring out at the trees on the opposite bank, because there was something burning inside her, not painful but exciting. She could picture the feeling as a red flame that emanated from the inside out, engulfing her.

When she turned to him again, she was swept up in it. She had the strong and surprising urge to tear his clothes off, and if society had permitted, she would have attempted it. The feeling was almost uncontrollable. Instead, they went for a walk.

They didn't need to speak of it, but they were both looking for the same thing: a place with enough privacy that they could be together. It took a while to escape the more public parts of the river walk, but eventually, they found it. Alex swept away a curtain of pale green vines to expose a cavern in the bank, just large enough for them both. He took off his jacket and covered the rough, stony ground, and suddenly, they were closer than they'd ever been before in the confined space. Lea breathed in the intimacy.

Their lips were locked as they fumbled clumsily with each other's clothes. Lea placed her cool palm against his warm, pale skin, admiring its tenderness, vulnerability. She was exposed; her papery skin freckled under the shadows of the vines. A twig dug into her back from beneath his jacket, and the discomfort split her attention from the moment, bringing worry with it. She forced it from her mind, focusing instead on the obvious. Then she was submerged in heat that crested like a wave and crashed over them, taking her out of her depth, and she was drowning in the unknown.

She felt a burning pain, and something inside her broke. 'Hymen.' The awkward word popped into her head, residual from some school sex-ed class. It seemed out of place now. She had known nothing even if she'd thought herself quite an expert before. This was uncomfortable, painful, yet somehow intoxicating. She could feel the tree roots tear at her hair as the motion propelled her back and forth. She noticed the beads of sweat forming on his brow, his shoulders tensed, his breathing ragged and an absurdly serious expression on his face. It made her want to laugh, and she might have if she hadn't been spending so much energy trying to endure this experience, trying to survive.

When the bus pulled up, she was still struggling to smooth her hair, which was unusually rebellious. She tucked it behind her ears as the bus driver waited for her ticket with a bored, dinner time expression on her aged face. Lea took the loneliest seat as usual and closed her eyes. It hadn't been a bad experience, at least she didn't regret it, but there was something inside her that had been permanently broken, or maybe, it had always been that way, and she had just been made more aware of it. The thing that concerned her most was the reoccurring thought that the pain had been pleasurable. She had to admit to being a masochist.

"The first time always sucks," Sienna said knowingly, twirling the drawstring of her hoodie around her index finger. "I'm just glad someone else in our group has lost theirs." She glared around at all the virgins, Maggie and Steph browsing a glossy magazine, Sarah sunbathing with her polo shirt tucked into her bra. Erika glared back from behind her sherbet stick. These were the girls Lea hung out with at lunch when she stayed in school, some of the least snobby students at Girls' High. Sienna had never liked her much, competing with her for Erika's attention, but now they seemed to have something in common.

"It's no big deal," Lea mumbled, just thankful her story wasn't as horrid as her recollection of Sienna's: blind drunk at a party, waking up next to a stranger, not remembering anything. Even the thought made her nauseous. Sienna smoothed her bleached, blonde hair and examined Lea closely.

"You know, I'm always here if you wanna talk about it?"

"Sure." Lea was being polite, trying to keep the newfound peace. *When hell freezes over.*

Lea spent the weekend at Alex's house. His mum didn't mind, but she insisted they sleep in different rooms, not that it made any difference. They spent all day wrapped up in each other, walking on the beach, letting the sea wind chill their skin and sweep chaos through their hair. There were moments she felt she had never been happier, when she could forget the torment that usually dominated her life, but even when they were together, the happy moments were fleeting, and at every turn, she had to confront her pain again and push it away, to bring herself back to the absurd joy she felt when he touched her, when she was the centre of his universe.

Their connection was sublime. Lea felt as if she had been separated from herself for sixteen years, and suddenly, the floodgates were opened, and her essence was pouring through, overwhelming, drowning her in bliss.

There is no truth, no absolute, no proof, and no set reality. There is nothing.

My entire life is an oxymoronic contradiction, but with you here, it makes the metaphysical burden of proof bearable. Thank you, Alex.

She looked out at the stars, so much brighter than in the city. She didn't feel the need for isolation with Alex because, with him, she was so comfortable and centred. He was her balancing, grounding stability. She felt as if he completed her, their insanity united.

As if hewn from the same stone, the same flame burning inside. If I ever find you, I find myself, if I ever know you, I know myself, when I think of you... I'm selfish.

She heard the stairs creak and Alex's heavy breathing as he crept downstairs to be with her.

Alex's mum was interesting; she liked to walk around the house in her dressing gown and seemed to always be in the process of making delicious food. Alex said she was writing a book on something new age and weird.

Lea helped her make dinner while Alex was on the internet. She liked the way Iris seemed genuinely interested in what she thought, not in the patronising way that most adults talked to her; she was more like an equal. All the wood in the house made it glow in the artificial light of energy-saving bulbs. They cut up the vegetables together for stir fry.

"Do you like it here?" Lea asked. She was not used to talking to an adult in this casual, friendly way, but Iris made her feel comfortable.

"Absolutely! I adore it," Iris said, smiling through a mouth full of carrot.

"Alex said Wellington was more interesting." Lea had disliked his sentiment.

"Too interesting! There was too much going on and never enough time. I'm surprised Alex noticed. The only time he ever left the house willingly was for soccer games, and he didn't want to play this term. He spends all his time in front of the computer screen."

Lea blushed silently, keeping her face locked on the chopping board and the broccoli she was clumsily decimating. She was often occupying his time, thinking of countless questions to ask him through the medium of her messenger program.

"I suppose it's good for him to have you," Iris said, looking into space. "He doesn't seem to do much socialising."

Lea nodded in response, remembering Alex saying so himself, his naked body wrapped around her, sweaty and sticky, on a bed of moist leaves, twigs in their hair. Her cheeks burned. She doubted Iris would still feel the same way if she knew what they had been doing on the couch the night before, at the beach, in the gully near the river. She swallowed hard and concentrated on stirring the onions that were beginning to caramelise in the bottom of the wok.

It was the kind of unbearably muggy day Hamilton was famous for. Lea had left school early to meet Alex, who was missing almost as much of his 'education' as she was. It wasn't like she learnt anything anyway. The only subjects that were bearable were History and English, and Mrs Milton, her soft-spoken History teacher, was revealing herself to be a little bit psycho. She was usually so sweet and calm, but occasionally, she would snap and start yelling at a student for the slightest thing. Last week she had berated Lea in front of the class because she had been slow to sit down after presenting her seminar, so Lea hadn't felt inclined to show up since.

English was better. She sat at the back next to Naida and had good conversations, most of which were scrawled on refill to avoid Ms Mitchell's scorn. Naida had at first been so quiet that Lea had pre-judged her to be one of those good girls who followed the rules and did their homework and had no opinions of their own. She was surprised to find her almost as opinionated and interesting as she found herself. But recently, all Lea wanted to talk about was Alex, and Naida stubbornly refused to admire him. Instead, she picked at his flaws and cautioned Lea not to get in too deep. It was far too late for that.

Lea sprawled across the couch with her head resting on Alex's lap. Her parents weren't home, so there was no one to complain about the music blasting through the living room.

The latest album by Wrench was smoother sounding than their last. Alex said they were slowly selling out, but Lea liked the way it drew her into a trance when she put her headphones on and tuned out the rest of the world. It was still just as political and controversial, she argued. They were developing their style, making it into more of an art form. She knew the words to all their previous albums. Her poetry was influenced heavily by the music she liked. *Take what you will from this world that we sell.* It was anti-capitalist. *Trade yourself piece by piece.* It was cynical. *Value by value, virtue by virtue, vice by vice.* It was derisive, cutting the edge between her and the rest of the world, separating her from the flock.

At times, she hated society. She hated people and the way they tried to conform. She hated the way corporations were exploiting the planet. There were other times when she was at peace with it, as though it was a movie she was watching, not real, not relevant. When Alex was angry at the world, which was often, they would complain about multi-nationals and ridicule idiotic politicians. Then they would debate the way the world should be run. They agreed about so many things, but there were a few issues they could not have been more divided on.

"Do you really believe in nothing?" Lea asked him, not intending it to be the challenge it came out as.

"I believe in reality…" Alex replied. "In what can be scientifically proven, things that I can see for myself."

"But don't you think other people might have different 'realities'?" She gestured with her fingers to emphasise speech marks around the word.

"That's their problem." Alex was dismissive. "I don't care if they're deluded. It's none of my business."

Lea took offence. "Do you think I'm deluded?"

"No, you can believe what you like, but you can't convince *me*."

Lea sighed, more than a little frustrated. "So, if you could see God or experience nirvana or enlightenment or something, then you'd believe?"

"I guess," he conceded reluctantly. "But it's never going to happen."

That was the end of the conversation as far as he was concerned, but Lea would keep pushing. It was unsatisfying to her, this limited view of reality that Alex seemed to enjoy. Her parents were staunch atheists, but something inside her screamed out for more, something deeper than the day-to-day tasks, schedules, and problems that often felt like a mediocre version of hell. She needed something to believe in; she just wasn't quite sure what.

The Goddess was her latest fixation. The internet had provided her with a myriad of strands from various origins: ancient civilisations, indigenous cultures from around the world and modern revivalists. Hera, Diana, Isis, Inana, Kali, Aradia. Each one seemed like a puzzle piece, a facet of something universal and endlessly powerful, the divine feminine. She had always had the inexplicable urge to pray, and now, she had something worth praying to. Each full moon, she would sit at her open window and imagine the iridescent silver energy flowing through her. It was her own sacred ritual and something she could never tell Alex about.

MRS EVERGLADE

M rs Everglade made her way through the gate and out into the world on her weekly trip up the hill to the supermarket. She felt alive and refreshed as the birds called through the crisp morning air. She chose to ignore the aching in her joints and focused her attention on the path in front of her with determination.

Halfway up the hill, she realised she had overshot her mark as the breath caught in her throat, making her rasp. She sounded awful and was thankful that there was no one around to hear her. She stopped to catch her breath, clutching at a nearby fence to steady herself. She noticed the veins showing through the translucent, wrinkled skin on her hands more vividly than usual.

Just a year ago, she had been able to stroll up the hill effortlessly; she even walked around the block for fitness every day rather than just this weekly trip of necessity. She continued on, but, still short of breath, she made her way more slowly and carefully.

The car park was crowded with cars and school children in blue and green uniforms. The girls in makeup looked insulted by her presence, as if her age was a contagious disease that they couldn't stand to be around. She ignored their disrespect and carried on.

All the necessities, it seemed, were either on the highest shelves or the lowest ones. She had to bend over, cursing her rheumatic joints to retrieve her favourite cans of soup, which weighed her down further when placed in her basket. The cheapest brand of canned tuna was on the top shelf, forcing her into the nigh-impossible task of finding an employee to help her retrieve it. After ten minutes of trying, she gave up and opted for the nearest can, one with a brightly coloured label and added flavour of teriyaki. She wasn't too old to try new things, and she had, after all, eaten teriyaki in Japan many years before with her sister.

She pulled her thoughts to the present, refusing to be one of those geriatrics who dwell wistfully on the distant past. She had enough on her plate without losing her precious energy to reminiscences.

There are many types of fear. Mrs Everglade burrowed her head under the covers, feeling absurdly immature, experiencing the acute variety. The kind the horror films thrive on. Her heart was racing. It was silly, really, that she had allowed herself to get so worked up over nothing.

The shadows in the trees had been temporarily transformed into demonic creatures when she went out the front gate to fetch the recycle bin, which had been emptied of its solitary milk container. She was sure she heard heavy footsteps as she fumbled with her keys to get back into the house. She had been in such a state she retreated quickly to her bed to calm her overactive imagination.

As her ragged breathing calmed, it struck her that this fear was worlds away from the worry one experiences over a loved one late to return home. It was even dramatically different from the fear she had felt when her survival was put into question, finding herself face to face with a lion in Africa, fifty or more years before. This was a darker fear, but just as instinctual. A fear of the unnatural.

A banging sound erupted, jolting her nerves. Her mind raced through terrifying possibilities faster than her body had moved in years: an intruder breaking in, a hooded figure at the door, a tree falling on her house. *How ridiculous.* She snapped herself out of it and, hearing the sound again, came to the dreaded conclusion: she had left the front door open. The wind was furiously whipping it back into the frame, hence the banging.

She plucked up her courage and struggled out of bed and into the hallway, towards the door, which was by then wide open. She felt a rising panic at the possibility that she was not alone in the house. She leant desperately for the light switch, and then she was falling, endlessly, into a peaceful void.

The bright light that assaulted her was uncalled for. The noises around her made no sense. The next realisation she had was that she was no longer at home, and then it dawned on her that she was in hell.

Mrs Everglade frowned out the window at the rain. It had sounded beautiful the night before. It had even made its way into her dreams, and she had imagined it washing away all her worries: her frailty, her tiredness and every weakness in her body. She had awoken refreshed to find the rain still drumming at the windows, washing away any hope she had of leaving the house that morning. Her doctor, a ginger-haired man at least thirty years younger than her, had warned her to stay inside by the heater through any cold or wet weather. The risks of pneumonia were too great, he'd said, and the last thing she needed now was another fall.

It had taken her hours, or it had seemed like hours, to drag herself up and crawl to the telephone to call for help. Her breath had been heavy and painful, and yet, she could think of no one to call. Finally, her stubborn will conceded, and she dialled the only number she could think of, 111, asking for an ambulance. It was nothing serious. They sent her home with a few packets of pills and a warning.

A year ago, she would have dismissed her doctor and gone about her business, but not now that her distant relatives had made it clear that they were all for locking her up in a retirement home and throwing away the key. They probably wouldn't think twice about selling her house. She would lose everything: all her china, her books, and her garden. She might have been ready for death, but she certainly wasn't ready for that kind of life.

Every now and then, it crept into her nightmares.

She was locked in a room with pastel wallpaper and elevator music. She tried to talk to the other residents, to the staff, to tell them she didn't belong there, but they were all lifeless zombies, glued to the television, watching infomercials that, perplexingly, always advertised yellow rubber-duckies. The smell of decay and disinfectant was overpowering. It made her feel ill. She needed to get out. She screamed and kicked, and they restrained her...

That was usually when she woke up, her sheets twisted under the eiderdown.

She shivered and brushed the memory from her mind. She would have a nice cup of tea and some toast and ask the cheerful, plump lady who brought her meal to pick up the newspaper and bring it in for her. She would enjoy the dismal weather, and perhaps she would have the neighbour's cat over to keep her company in front of the heater.

A beeping sound shocked Mrs Everglade awake from her dreams of home.

"Just the nurse," a woman's voice said. "Time for your morning pills.

"No!" Mrs Everglade said. "I can't be here. I fell, but I'm fine. I need to go home."

"Now, now," said the nurse. "You came here after your fall, remember? Your memory is playing tricks on you. Here, take your medicine, and you'll feel better shortly."

Mrs Everglade looked around at the pastel-coloured room. Everything inside her screamed out for escape. She wanted to be home with a cup of tea and the neighbours' cat; she even would tolerate the messy garden next door if it meant leaving this place immediately.

However, she had no choice. She opened her mouth and took the pills the overly cheerful nurse gave her, vowing to do everything she could to get out of this dreadful place as soon as possible.

11

MARCIA

M arcia flipped through the colourful pages of a home décor magazine as large white- and plum-hued magnolia petals rained down spurred by gusts of wind. A strange noise caught her attention and dragged her head up in time to see the most unexpected sight. A family of ducks was making its way across her deck. A blue father, a brown mother and a mass of yellow and black fluff that waddled as if the ducklings combined to make one organism. She wondered what on earth the ducks were doing so far from water.

Out of the corner of her eye, she caught Nui prowling towards them. She leapt up and opened the door, causing the father duck to flap his wings and take off in the opposite direction to his family. She growled at Nui, who stopped in his tracks. The mother duck quacked warnings at her as she ferried her babies into an overgrown corner of the garden. Marcia felt a sheet of guilt fall over her as she realised the possibility that she was responsible for robbing the ducklings of their father. She brought out some stale bread to feed them, treading on the mulch of magnolia petals beneath her feet. Drops of rainwater fell on her from the trees, but she hardly noticed. She watched the mother sheltering her young beneath her. She left them there to rest, catching Nui and imprisoning him inside with a saucer of cream as a bribe.

Half an hour later, she returned to the spot to find the ducks gone. She had unwittingly left the door open, and as she realised this, she watched Nui's tail disappearing over the fence. She called out and ran over to where he had launched himself into Mrs Everglade's garden. By the time she got there, he was on his way back with a limp looking fluff ball in his mouth. She chased him under the house and then gave up in exasperation.

She was sitting behind the house, mourning the tragedy of nature and trying to forgive the cat for following his instinct when she heard a tiny squeak coming from under the deck. She lay on her front and leant upside down to see what it was. Nui was following a yellow-black fluff ball out from under the deck into a flax bush. She snapped at the cat and dived into the bush to retrieve the duckling, which shivered silently in her palms. She admired its oversized webbed feet while she carried it next door.

12

MRS EVERGLADE

Mrs Everglade put on the kettle for tea. It had been days since she'd returned home, and her mobility was slowly returning back to how it was before her fall. She picked up her small steel teapot and rummaged in the canister for a teabag when something outside caught her eye.

Mrs Everglade peered out through the curtain netting to find the most unexpected sight. The neighbour girl, that Marcia, was walking in the rain in a *sundress* of all things! With her hands cupped in front of her as if performing some ancient religious right. She hobbled over to the door, turned the latch to open it and called out.

"Excuse me!"

The girl stopped suddenly like a child caught where she shouldn't be.

"The ducks," she blurted out.

"Excuse me?" Now, Mrs Everglade was perplexed.

"I'm sorry, Mrs Everglade. There's a family of ducks in your garden. I'm just returning a stray duckling caught by that cat." She turned to look over her fence, narrowing her eyes.

"It's alive? Well, that's something, I suppose. Poor thing." she mumbled.

"They're in the far corner by the gazebo." Marcia gestured with her cupped hands, and Mrs Everglade could see a fluffy head and little beak poking out the top.

"Well, don't just stand there, girl! Let's get it back to its mother." She pulled an umbrella from the coat stand and stepped into her gumboots. As she shuffled down the steps and across the wet lawn with the cool breeze in her lungs, she felt younger than she had in years.

A quacking sound was issuing from the bush behind her little white gazebo. As the women approached, it changed its tone as if shifting from a summoning call to a warning. The duckling in Marcia's palms began hopping uncontrollably. When she opened them slightly to check on it, the little bird took off in an impressive jump, landing on the grass in front of the gazebo. Answering its mother's calls in tiny squeaks, it hopped through the white archway and toward the trellis at the other side. Mrs Everglade held her breath as it looked unlikely the duckling could make it through the small spaces between the crisscrossing wood. It jumped at the gap and wriggled its fluffy body through, allowing both women to breathe a sigh of relief.

"I don't fancy my chances of catching something so small and full of life if it hadn't fitted through the trellis," Mrs Everglade chuckled.

"Neither do I," admitted Marcia.

They strolled back towards the house and the front gate.

"You'd better come in for a cup of tea," Mrs Everglade advised. "I'll get you a towel, and you can sit by the heater. I don't know what you were thinking, running outside without a coat in this weather…" Her voice trailed off as she reached the front door, left open in the flurry of the moment. Marcia had no choice but to follow her in for tea, a malt biscuit, and plenty of complaints about the Reed family's overgrown garden.

13

MARCIA

Marcia let the hot tap run until it had half-filled the large metal tub. She let her dressing gown slip off her shoulders and watched the pale, flowery silk pool at her feet before gradually descending into the bath.

The morning light was shining through a small window high up on the easterly wall of the bathroom. Marcia had often grumbled to herself that these old houses were built facing the road rather than the sun. She had wondered who in their right mind would build a dark bathroom in the sunniest part of the house. But today, she was grateful for the little window which allowed beams of light to fall from the morning sun, through the magnolia trees outside, and into the room, where it illuminated the steam that rose from her in swirls of silver organza. It reminded her of a fabric she had once worn to a masquerade ball, draped over an emerald gown.

The memory tugged up her grief, but Marcia finally felt ready to think about William.

She had felt like a princess in that costume. She remembered William in his top hat in the rain, offering his coat to protect her, bringing the car around so that her outfit wasn't ruined.

She had laughed when they were first introduced. William Wilton seemed a ridiculous name to Marcia, who had been tipsy on cheap wine and the social excitement of her friend Margery's Halloween party. She had been Snow White, her dark hair shining in ringlets. William, the pirate, with a gleam in his eyes, re-introduced himself in a terrible gruff Scottish accent as Billy-the-Devourer-Wilton. Later, he confessed he did just it to see her smile again.

Although she hadn't realised it then, that was the turning point. She abandoned her semi-nomadic life, sleeping on the couches of friends and taking temp jobs between trips to every corner of Europe, to 'settle down'. That was the moment she decided she wanted some stability, and he was there, offering everything he could give her. She never thought an accountant could have such a marvellous sense of humour or that she would find herself engaged after only a few months of knowing someone.

They had lived a simple, child-free life full of tasteful luxuries and social engagements.

Her old friends had hardly recognised that new Marcia. The domesticated princess who delighted in showing off her latest pottery piece was worlds away from the wild, untamed being she had once been. The years seemed to pass easily, and for a while, she held the illusion that this would be the status quo for the rest of her life. It had surprised her that she was happy with the thought.

The heat from the bath was so immense it spread right through her whole body. She hung her arms and legs over the side, thankful for the cool enamel-covered metal.

The steam that rose was stunningly beautiful; mysterious plumes of glittering spirals emerged from the bath and ascended. She lost track of how long she stared, entranced. Every movement of her body sent more gossamer clouds swirling upwards while the cooled precipitation descended slowly in an evenly spread curtain of shimmering silver.

Marcia lived for these moments of beauty so simple yet so magnificent she could lose herself in them.

A rolling sound outside disrupted her trance; the spring rain had arrived, bringing with it a feeling that ran through her entire body, electrifying, tingling, as if she were made of water and the heavy drops were falling through her.

She rose from the bath, sending steam swirling around the entire room, picked her towel off the cabinet and made her way outside. She stood at the open door, her body still boiling from the bath's heat. She let her towel fall to the ground and stepped into the rain. She lifted her arms and let the downpour wash away the past.

She felt reborn, fresh and alive. She sank to her knees under the old avocado tree, grateful that the foliage her parents had so frivolously planted offered such privacy, and then curled in a foetal position, as innocent as a baby.

Marcia made her way to the community house under a shower of tiny white petals, excitement rising in her chest. For the past month, she had immersed herself in the creation process, preparing material for the workshops. Seven people had registered and she was delighted.

She set up the room by arranging cushions in a circle on the floor. In the centre, she placed gemstones: clear quartz for a clear mind, amethyst for detoxification, rose quartz for harmony, onyx for protection, tiger's eye for truth, hematite for grounding. Around these, she scattered other things she had found or been given, river stones and shells. In the centre, she placed a small bouquet of October blossoms, picked from her garden that morning.

Marcia flicked through the name tags she'd created, each anointed with a small blossom; Aroha, Dora, Lizzie, Helen, Sam, Iris, Theresa. She watched as they began to arrive, most of them approaching shyly, uncertain, looking in all directions, some blushing when they asked if they were in the right place. She greeted them warmly, dispensing comfort with her easy smile so that they knew they were exactly where they needed to be.

"So lovely to meet you! I'm Helen," said a woman with curly red hair. "Is Sam here yet?" She looked around hopefully.

Marcia had assumed the attendees were all women. As it turned out, Sam was short for Samuel rather than Samantha.

"I made the booking for him. He resisted the idea, at first..." said Helen.

Marcia smiled, though she wasn't surprised Sam hadn't arrived.

"I know it will be good for him," Helen insisted, looking out the window as she waited for Sam.

"I see. Who are you trying to convince?" Marcia asked with objective curiosity.

Helen replied in a quieter voice. "I just want him to get over his *issues*." Her eyes were downcast, face shielded by her tangerine ringlets.

"For you or for him?" Marcia's voice was gentle this time, coaxing Helen out of her defences and into awareness. Behind them, the other women sat in the strained silence belonging to those who refrain from sharing their opinions out of politeness rather than choice.

"I suppose I have to let go of this urge to rescue people." Helen sighed.

Marcia smiled, and Sam knocked on the door.

"Sorry I'm late." His apology was slightly muffled through the glass.

They began with introductions. Aroha, a young Maori woman, introduced herself along with her tribal affiliations, her mountain and river and some of her ancestry. An older woman, Dora said she was hoping to expand her horizons with the workshops. Lizzie, a brunette girl who still looked to be in her teens, blushed as she merely said her name and gestured to Helen to take the spotlight. Helen seemed pleased to talk; Marcia had to pinch herself discretely to keep from looking bored.

Sam brushed his sandy hair from his forehead as he introduced himself and said he was happy to be there. Theresa said she was a mother of two. There was something oddly familiar about Iris who calmly stated that she had recently flipped her life upside-down. Marcia liked her instantly.

Marcia listened intently to the introductions, hoping she could remember the key details. "Thank you all for coming. My intention with these workshops is to approach the subject of holistic wellbeing by focussing on different levels of awareness in the body, and on energy centres."

"Are you talking about chakras?" Dora asked with a smile.

Before Marcia had a chance to respond, Helen interjected, "Oh, but isn't that cultural appropriation?"

Marcia took a deep breath feeling her chest tighten. In her more intense moments of self-doubt this was the kind of criticism she feared. She let the breath out slowly and focussed on staying present.

"Thank you for bringing that concept up, Helen," Marcia said. "It's important to think about, especially when it comes to spirituality. Understandings of energy centres and meridians in the body are ancient and found across a variety of cultures. There are many similar concepts found throughout different traditions including Hindu, Buddhist, Islamic, Jewish and even ancient Celtic belief systems." Marcia felt as if she was rambling, still knocked off balance by Helen's question. She would have preferred to have taken the lead in talking about the topic at hand, but she continued speaking, going over the thoughts she had aready rehearsed, hoping that things would become clearer. "Many people have heard of the Hindu concept of Chakras. I learned about these when I was travelling in India and this understanding helped me to reconnect more deeply with my own heritage. My mother's mother was Indian though I don't know where she was from. No one talked about it so the connection was severed in my family... however, I'm no expert on ancient Indian mysticism."

"So why would you want to focus on energy centres then?" Helen asked, then seeming to realise her abruptness, added, "I'm just trying to understand. You know, as a white person these days I'm always trying to figure out what's okay for me to do. It's changing all the time..."

Marcia shot Helen a patient smile that was echoed by several of the other group members.

"Sure, it's changing because minorities are finally getting the opportunity to call out things that have been a problem for a long time," Aroha said. "But the important thing is to listen. Marcia has whakapapa – ancestry – that connects her to some of those traditions, but she's also talking about a concept that is broader than any particular tradition."

"Thank you, Aroha," said Marcia, feeling more comfortable.

"Also, there's a difference between closed systems and open systems," said the dark-haired woman, Theresa. "Some traditions are sacred... they aren't supposed to be shared while others are open. As far as I know, there are lots of traditions with energy centres that are more open."

"This is all good context," Marcia said. "I don't want to appropriate cultural traditions. I want to focus on my own personal understanding of energy centres, which is a bit new-agey, with due respect paid to any cultural wisdom that may come up throughout the workshops. I'm not here to be dogmatic though. I want to encourage you all to come to your own conclusions and figure out what works for you."

She smiled at the group. "Energy centres have been depicted in so many different ways: as symbols, as patterns, as flowers. I imagine them in the colours of the rainbow: red, orange, yellow, green, blue, purple, and white. You can choose the colours that sit well with you," she said.

"Are we going to focus at all on the power of our minds in creating reality? You know, like *manifesting*?" Dora asked, brushing her greying hair from her excited eyes.

Marcia had been expecting this. There had been such a fuss about these ideas in popular culture over the past few years. Documentaries filled with scientists and motivational speakers had flooded the internet and spiritual stores. To Marcia, it was a simple truth among many.

"Is that something you would like to talk about?" she asked in a genuine tone.

"I would like to learn more about it, yes." Dora nodded as she spoke.

"Then we can talk about it. In my understanding, the concept that our thoughts shape our lives is just one part of a greater picture. The thing is... we possess not only the thoughts that we consciously choose but also those that we have been subconsciously taught." About half the group nodded.

"In my view there are many forces working in the universe," Marcia continued. "Some of them are noticeable, some indeterminable. If 'manifesting' were as simple as motivational speakers claim, we would all be driving luxury cars, holidaying in Hawaii for half the year, and living in enormous mansions because these are the ideals many of us have been taught represent true happiness. But even if we were in this idealised reality, we would probably find ourselves just as dissatisfied as before and longing for a world in which we had something else completely."

"I don't know," said Sam. "I'd be quite happy driving luxury cars in Hawaii."

The group laughed.

"You *might* be," said Marcia. "The problem with the idea that we can all have what we want - aside from being hugely consumerist, it that it risks placing blame on individual people for their circumstances. It's also... well there's this Western cultural pathology of always wanting more, the best the biggest – which totally dismisses the other side of nature, of letting go like the leaves in autumn. We need that too. The darkness and the rain are all part of a full life. Denying them does us all a disservice."

"Absolutely," said Aroha. "Thanks for saying that, Marcia. You've put into words something that I've always felt uncomfortable about with the whole 'self-help' movement... that never sat right with me, culturally."

"We are all in different places in our lives," Marcia continued. "With different lessons to learn. I can help you to understand where you are now. I can even help you to move to where you want to be, but first, you have to figure out what you really need."

The group fell silent but they seemed to accept her diatribe. The fear Marcia had felt about the workshops had vanished; even the memory of it was distant. She was able to proceed unimpeded.

"Today I want to focus on the physical world, our experience of material reality..."

14

IRIS

Iris lay awake, her breathing heavy. The nightmare she'd just had replayed over and over again through her mind. It could have been a typical thriller film, the kind she had suffered through in her youth and still sometimes watched when there was nothing else on TV.

A man stood, holding a terrifyingly large knife; the sound of scraping metal issued forth as he sharpened it. Abruptly, he held it to a woman's throat. Blood gushed out, leaving her lifeless. He was in the house, in the shadows, the knife was sharpened again before a second murder. Iris screamed. She could feel his eyes on her as she tried to escape him. Then she held up a baby. It was Alex as he had been almost sixteen years before, and then, suddenly, the man was there beside her, holding the knife to Alex's throat.

That was when she woke up. The panic must have done it, driven her back to her senses. She knew Alex was asleep upstairs in his loft. She knew he was fine, but she wanted to see him, to check his breathing as she had when he was a newborn. She couldn't bear to move from the fear. It coursed through her body, and logic did nothing to quell it. *I'm fine,* she told herself, *I am safe.* She searched for the feeling of safety; a memory of her father's warm embrace when she was ten surfaced and then blurred away into the fear, costing her more sleep.

The terror returned with the darkness the next night after a perfectly ordinary day. It was weaker now, and Iris had the opportunity to study it. It was a manifestation of fear itself: her fear. This aspect belonged to her, and yet, she wanted to cut it off. As she observed it, she was surprised by the impression that the fear itself was like a frightened child. The warmth of compassion trickled through her, dissipating the chill. It grew into a sweet chocolaty feeling.

It was her shadow. She knew it: the part of her she was afraid to face. It had surfaced because she had wanted it to. She wanted to resolve all of her issues, but when this one had appeared, she wanted it gone in favour of comfort.

Her shadow was made up of lots of little things. Times she had been hurt or afraid, times she had been told she was a bad person. Every time she had cut off an unbearable part of herself, it had lingered there in the darkness wanting nothing more than inclusion, wholeness. She imagined all these little aspects coming together, connecting like a puzzle. In her mind, it looked like these colourful pieces converged in the shape of a planet that resembled her soul.

Iris sat cross-legged in her purple tracksuit on the pumpkin-coloured window seat in the corner of the open-plan second story of the pole house in quiet meditation. She was trying to recapture the serenity she had experienced during the workshop. It had been run by a remarkable woman, Marcia. She seemed to possess ageless beauty and boundless wisdom. Iris was in awe of her.

The group had sat cross-legged on the floor like school children. They were mostly women and only one man, Sam. He seemed the sensitive sort. There was his do-gooder, red-headed friend, Helen, who had irritated Iris slightly, to begin with, but redeemed herself by being honest. Aroha was tiny, probably in her twenties, with a bright smile and extremely long, straight, dark hair. Dora was an older woman, tall with grey hair; she had a sensible air about her that Iris liked. Lizzie was young, maybe still in her teens. She was enthusiastic, but her eyes were those of a much older woman.

Theresa, with dark hair and rosy cheeks, had to leave early to attend to her three children. Overall, the group was lovely. Everyone seemed to contribute something, and Marcia had encouraged their shared learning through conversation. She taught in a way that inspired Iris.

She had taken them through meditation in her calm English accent, that focused on their physical body: the sensation of their breathing, awareness of themselves as physical beings. Bringing all her energy back to focus on her physicality had the unexpected effect of energising Iris to the point of rapture. She realised that the energy she was usually putting into her thoughts that she was sending out into the world, was being wasted on worries and to-do lists. She had been letting her energy drain away into unwanted things rather than enjoying the wonderful experiences of life.

Iris wriggled her legs around, making herself as comfortable as possible on the window seat so she could try to recapture the experience of the workshop in her meditation at home. The perfumed smoke of incense curled up, tickling her nostrils. Her body resisted this stillness. She felt aches tug at her back, her leg went numb. She focussed her attention on her breath, the sensation of breathing. She could not see the gorgeous forest greens behind her, but she was aware of the sound of the stream below, swollen from the late winter downpours.

Iris' mind wandered back to the workshop. With her eyes closed, she could see a murky red, the light glowing through her eyelids. She could hear a low hum, as if the matter all around her was subtly singing. She had listened to Marcia's voice guiding her to release the tension from her muscles, one by one, until she was completely aware of her body. She felt floaty, light and heavy at the same time, and each word flew right through her.

Imagine a vibrant red light shining through from the base of your spine
Right through to the front of your body
This is the root energy centre
The physical centre
Allow this light to illuminate any blockages in this area
Allow any physical burdens to dissolve

At the end of the meditation, Marcia had guided them to stand up and make their way out to the garden while holding their attention on their physical experience. The morning air had chilled her skin, and the sun had warmed her face. She was acutely aware of every sound, every scent.

She brought her attention back to her breath every time her mind began to wander, to sensation, the physical world to which her body and the path she was walking belonged. As her trance deepened, she became more aware of her body. Then the realisation spread through her: that all matter was energy vibrating at different rates, that all energy was really love.

The sensations she experienced in her body were just bubbles of awareness, popping, impermanent. There was only one force in this universe, the creating force: energy, light, love. This amazing force crystallised into prisms of awareness: conscious beings, able to take in this raw light and transform it into rainbows of colour, unleashing the potential that was there all along. This same force could form mirrors, reflecting back the reality that was revealed to them. She was a prism, taking in this divine light and forming the colours that she could see reflected in the mirrors of the world around her. Only perspective could portray life as anything other than perfect, and, as she had known all along, a shift in perspective was all it took to realign harmoniously, to recognise the beauty in everything.

15

MARCIA

After weeks of rain, the sunshine had finally returned, giving Marcia something to celebrate. Early spring always carried with it a free and magical feeling as new life awakened from its winter hibernation. The air was light and sweet with the scent of daphne. Magnolia flowers littered the deck; Marcia adored their soft, supple skin, as delicate, gentle, and fragile as human flesh. Even their bruises conceded a flawed beauty.

She could see Mrs Everglade ghosting through the garden next door, her thinning hair tucked behind her ears, her sharp stare piercing the morning light.

Marcia inhaled the sun-warmed air on the deck, enjoying the dregs of her plunger coffee. She had never been happier than in the two days since the workshop. Her body tingled as each cell rejoiced in its existence. She had never experienced this sensation before, as if she was finally living inside her destiny rather than chasing it or running from it.

She looked down; between the steps and the side of the deck, something was glinting. She reached down and dug it out. A coin marked 1972. It was a coincidence, perhaps, but this was the year she had left home. She pulled at a fist-full of tradescantia, and old concrete revealed itself beneath the wooden steps.

A memory came back to her of riding her bike on the grass beneath where the deck now stood. She carried on weeding until she had uncovered the original steps that led to the house, and below them, she noticed a different kind of plant. It looked like a dead twig, but closer inspection revealed tiny buds that hinted at something familiar. She searched her memories.

There had once been an old washhouse here, a metre from where she stood, and an enormous grapevine which had grown up its side and right across to the roof of the house. She remembered the sweet and sour taste of the grapes and how their purple bunches adorned the back of the house for several weeks every year before the large green leaves withered and fell off, leaving the twisted woody vine naked. She remembered the vine being cut down when she was ten years old and how she had mourned its loss. To comfort her, her father had promised more vines would grow in its place, and when they did, he promised to help her train them to grow in an orderly fashion.

The baby vine had light green leaves which stretched towards the sky, and Marcia had watched as her father had broken off twigs and twisted stems, and in the process, he snapped off the original stem.

The fifty-five-year-old Marcia recalled this, along with the anger and frustration she had felt at the time. She had buried so much resentment for her father, and she could feel it smouldering in her chest. She knew she needed to let go and set herself free of this. She continued to pull at the weeds surrounding the precious plant. He had been trying to help her with the grapevine. He had been doing his best. Even when he had screamed at her countless times, called her insolent, lazy, selfish, called her a bitch, a whore, a slut, hurt her over and over again without even realising the damage he was doing. It was his failure he was angry at, his loss of control, and in his rage, she was less a person to him than a scapegoat.

The vine stood alone now. She had freed it of the choking weeds and given it light and room to grow. There could be no better metaphor for hope than this, and she would see that it flourished.

Rain assaulted the windscreen, and powerful gusts of wind almost sent the little car sailing sideways over the wet tar seal. Marcia wondered whether the second-hand Toyota she had bought for $3000 on the side of the road was suited to this kind of abuse.

She had awoken to spring thunder and had not been able to shake the urge she'd had all morning to drive to Raglan. Another inside day would have given her a serious bout of cabin fever, she had reasoned. Even if the West Coast weather wasn't any nicer, it was better to be out and about, and this certainly felt like an adventure.

The snake-like stretch of road that crossed the hills mid-way between Hamilton and Raglan called the Deviation aptly described Marcia's divergence from her inner calm. She struggled with the tight corners as she accelerated up the hill and rode the break all the way down the other side, where she was rewarded with mercifully straight stretches of road.

Marcia was invigorated by the storm but relieved to reach her destination. The simple Raglan of her childhood had been transformed into a trendy town, boasting cafes, surf shops, and artsy boutique stores. The town had grown but not as horrendously as she had dreaded. There were, thankfully, no chain stores or fast food outlets. She was surprised to find most of the car parks had sixty-minute parking signs, and her inner child had a giggle at the throngs of motorbikes parked outside the old hotel. She made her way through each shop, admiring the local art, of which there was an abundance. The herbal dispensary was of particular interest to her, and she explored its shelves with relish. As she approached the counter laden with incense, nettle tea, immune-boosting elixir, and alfalfa seeds, she noticed a familiar figure.

Iris's frizzy blond hair and intense concentration were easily recognisable as she browsed the natural cosmetics stand. Marcia was contemplating whether or not to disturb her when Iris turned, and recognition flashed across her face.

Iris smiled. "Lovely weather for the beach," she said. "You don't live out here, do you?"

"Just visiting," Marcia replied. "Better here than at home, sorting out the garage."

"I love this place," Iris gestured around. "I spend hours here; my son thinks I'm a crazy hippy."

"That's nothing to be ashamed of," Marcia laughed. She happened to be wearing a flowing aubergine skirt and a teal, tasselled blouse.

"Aren't those toxic?" Iris asked, gesturing at the alfalfa. "I read something about them the other day…"

"Only if they aren't sprouted properly," Marcia informed her in her gentle voice. "All seeds contain substances that protect them from being destroyed, but usually, these are used up in the sprouting process. Once the alfalfa sprouts have two little green leaves, they're safe."

Iris nodded, smiling with a hint of admiration in her eyes, and Marcia was aware of herself becoming a little bit proud.

"Could you recommend the best place for coffee?" she asked.

"The Shack is my favourite," Iris responded. "The staff are friendly, and they make a killer latte."

"I'm sold. Have you eaten?"

"No, I'd love to join you." Iris beamed, childlike.

"That would be wonderful; I could do with some conversation."

The coffee was superb, the food was slow but satisfactory, and the service was pleasantly casual. Marcia had nothing to complain about. She enjoyed hearing Iris talk about her teenage son and her daily struggle to get him out of bed in the morning and delighted in the description of her home.

"We used to live in Wellington," Iris said. "But the hecticness of it all drove me insane, and I quit my job on a whim." She snorted. "It turned out to be for the best, though; I can't remember ever having so much peace. I can't even imagine going back now. I don't know what I was thinking all those years."

"You were probably just trying to make it through the day and meet your needs, and your son's," Marcia said sympathetically.

"That's just it," Iris replied, absentmindedly toying with the foam on her coffee with a spoon. She looked Marcia in the eye.

"I was just *surviving.* That was my focus, like an animal. I was trying to put food on the table and pay the bills, and no matter how much money I earned, there was never enough because that was how I was thinking. Every dollar was spent before it came in. We were always upgrading things in the house, and Alex always needed new clothes and shoes. It was actually just like life when I was growing up. I was subconsciously turning into my parents, and I had no idea." She shrugged. "Things are so different now, and it's blissful. What about you? I'd love to know what your life's like."

Marcia wasn't sure where to start, but once she did, everything came spilling out: her life in London, her husband's death and the shock it was, coming back to New Zealand for the first time in decades and sifting through her childhood memories as she repaired the house she grew up in and worked on the sprawling garden.

"It has been an incredible journey," she said. "Life is like that. I dreaded coming back here, and that is exactly why I knew I had to. There were too many loose ends to ignore, and I couldn't run from them anymore. I didn't even realise I was avoiding the past until my comfort blanket was ripped away from me." She sighed and took a sip of her long black.

"The workshops almost came into being of their own accord. It was like I was following fate. It still seems mysterious to me."

Iris had been listening intently. "I know what you mean. When I quit my job, I had no idea what was going on. My friend Ariki asked me what I was going to do, and without thinking about it, I just said, "I think I'll write a book", and it made sense. Now I've written several chapters. I don't even know how it happened. It was almost like I was typing words that were already written in the blueprint of my life like I was following a plan I couldn't even see. When I re-read the words, I can't believe I came up with them. It's as if they fell into place all by themselves. I was just the messenger or something."

Marcia nodded. "Perhaps it is your higher self, and you are finally surrendering to it. That is how I sometimes feel when I know I'm on the right track and everything seems to be working. It is a magnificent feeling, like I'm floating and being pulled by a divine current."

"That's beautiful!" Iris exclaimed, clapping her hands together. "Can I borrow that metaphor for my book?"

"Of course. What is the book about?" Marcia smiled.

"I guess it's a self-help book," Iris blushed. "It's about the ways that spirituality can benefit people's lives. I must admit, your first workshop was invaluable to me; it's exactly what I needed."

"That's exactly what I was hoping to provide people," Marcia said, and her eyes sparkled. "What's your inspiration?"

"I have to admit, I get most of my ideas in the bath," Iris confessed.

16

LEA

Lea, forever cynical about romantic movies, flicked through the television channels in disgust. All that was on Saturday afternoon was some lame 80s romance and a tacky soap opera. This evening, she could be riveted by a blockbuster crap-fest, starring the worst actors in the world. She already knew how the story would end, but she had no other entertainment with the internet malfunctioning and Alex out of town. It wasn't his fault, but she blamed him anyway.

There was something else on her mind, something she had told him about online before he and the internet connection both left. He had barely commented. It wasn't that big a deal. It was just a late period. That sort of thing happened all the time, and they had been careful, so they had nothing to worry about. It was no big deal.

She scowled at the screen. She hated clichéd Hollywood plots and obvious scripts, but secretly, she enjoyed the feeling of watching people in love. She liked the way they seemed to float, even when they were just acting, even if they weren't even acting well. There was something thrilling in the connection, something exciting in the tension. She had always yearned for something like that bliss, and now she had it, and it was just as magical as it was in the movies. Only, it was hers.

The thing she disliked the most about it was that she could not control it. She couldn't bring the feeling back when it deserted her, when she was frustrated at Alex for having bigoted views or when he would rather play stupid computer games than talk to her. Because of this, she knew she couldn't trust it. It was just as elusive as the Disney happy ending that never happened in real life.

Life goes on, she thought sullenly, although she wished it had ended in the perfect moment of bliss when she had fallen in love. She wondered if all relationships started in such a wonderful way, full of hormones and chemistry and then fizzled into nothing or were replaced by arguments. Even her parents might have been 'in love' once upon a time, although the thought was somewhat disturbing.

Love wasn't real. It wasn't as meaningful as everyone and everything made it out to be. It was just a fantasy that felt good, even though Alex still brought her waves of delight just at the thought of him. The only love that she could even conceive to be real was not even in the same league. It was not romantic; it was spiritual: devotion to a higher cause, to the divinity of creation, and the sanctity of nature.

Lea nervously scattered the rose petals in a circle. She watched them flutter to the ground in the mid-morning air. She had to stop herself from looking around to see if anyone was watching.

Alex would literally roll around on the floor laughing if he saw her now, wearing *flowers* in her hair, in her paisley dressing gown, performing a ritual, but she didn't care. Her parents were out at the boys' rugby game, and she had picked the most sheltered part of the garden to protect herself from undue attention.

She walked around, making a circle under the cover of camellias, their late blooms dropping like corpses, and the freshness of cherry blossoms. She scattered salted water around the circle and then waved the burning incense she had found in her mother's drawer called 'spring fling'. It was the best she could do with the resources she had.

When the circle was cast, she lit a candle and whispered the chant she had memorised.

"Isis, Astarte, Diana, Hecate, Demeter, Kali, Inana."

She closed her eyes and felt the air thicken, sending slight shivers down her spine. She filled the wine glass with tropical fruit punch and toasted the goddess; then, she was unsure how to proceed. Beltane was a tribute to spring, to new life and new beginnings, and she wasn't sure what blessings the future could possibly hold.

17

ZANE

Zane was sick of all the publicity. The last few weeks had been full of interviews and public appearances. He hated the record company games; all he wanted to do was make music.

Finally, the band was on tour. First America, then the world. He put aside his frustration at the newspaper reporter he had just had a teleconference with and let his excitement build.

Their first gig was San Diego, which, to Zane's utter disbelief, was hotter in early fall than a Los Angeles summer. The dry easterly wind was almost unbearable. It swept the essence of the Arizona desert over him, and he could taste it, dry in the back of his throat for the brief time they were exposed to the elements as the band clambered between the air conditioning of the airport, limo, and hotel lobby.

They only used limos because it meant they could sit comfortably and have decent conversations while they were being transported. Zane usually liked to experience more of the scenery than this. He hated being a tourist, not getting to see what the place was really about.

He often found himself anonymous in strange bars, with drunken strangers telling him their life story. He had wandered into service stations and been invited back to barbecues by friendly locals. One of his favourite pastimes was performing stand-up comedy in any dive that would have him, but it must have been a hundred degrees out there. He wondered for a moment what that would be in Celsius, the way the temperature was measured in New Zealand and most of the rest of the world. *Thirty-something*, he estimated.

Zane could sense the impatient frustration of the waiting crowd. He hated festivals for this reason. The unfulfilled energy was vacuous. It moved tensely, sought out and consumed everything. It was everywhere, not just festivals; it plagued people in their relationships, their jobs. It grasped needily and destroyed all that could not satisfy it. It snarled at his throat in the morning, the only thing that got him out of bed, this void seeking to be filled. Food only masked it, temporary satisfaction. Completing meaningful work brought about a warm, sunny feeling that satiated it until the need arose again. Zane often wondered if the reason so much calculated crime was committed was because of it. Drug abuse, murder, rape, molestation. *Maybe if we were taught to deal with unfulfillment from a young age, we would manage it before it turned into a consuming obsession.* Shopping, plastic surgery, diets. He was so lost in thought on his walk to the backstage entrance that he hardly noticed the journalist in a red blazer with dark brown hair pulled tightly into a bun. She proceeded to block his path, shoving a dictaphone at him as if to stave him off.

"Mister Strachan," she said in a serious voice, then for a moment, she reverted to an expression Zane recognised from the awestruck teenage girls who occasionally stalked him.

"Yes?" He tried to sound polite despite his time constraints.

"There have been reports that a youth involved in a public shooting last week in Amsterdam was a fan of yours. Do you have any comment?" He was liking her less every second.

"Not really," he shrugged, raising his eyebrows in question. "I think that's his or her business, not mine."

She appeared taken aback by his casual response but recovered quickly.

"Could your music be the cause of this behaviour?" she asked, but Zane was already pushing past her to the door.

"Don't you have a responsibility to your fans and the youth of today?"

Zane heard her call out as the door closed, leaving the preposterous accusations behind him. He had written darker lyrics that expressed anger at society, but he sure as hell hadn't given anyone the mandate to take life and death into their own hands. He tried to squeeze his feelings of unease over the encounter into the back of his mind as he took to the stage.

The atmosphere was thick with anticipation. The band paused, waiting for total silence before beginning their intro. The guitar started gently, a riff that reminded Zane of tropical rain. He watched the crowd sway in unison, rippling like an organism. The base came in heavy and took over, then the guitar came back with a vengeance, and Jimmy's gigantic gong sounded as he broke into his signature thundering drum rolls.

The lyrics rose eerie, in sharp melodic contrast to the dreary, dreamy accompaniment.

The boogie man's coming to swallow your souls
Don't stray too far, stay close to the fold

When Zane performed, he felt like he could feel the pulse of the world.

His audience was united in a profound experience, this was the closest thing to religion Zane had ever believed in, and in concert, he was the messiah.

The ratings are dropping, let's start a new war
Look this way, don't notice the rot at our core

He felt the song climax as he was brought to his knees.

In his mind, they flashed again – the two women from his dreams, their eyes full of pain and rage. Zane couldn't fathom what it meant, but he was determined to find out.

MARCIA

The twigs beneath her feet induced a bearable pain as Marcia gardened in an old, white, cherry-printed sundress. She hadn't felt, or dressed, this light or frivolous since she was a child. She returned to the house to sip refreshing peppermint tea, cooled by a night in her antique floral teapot. After re-hydrating, she walked around to the back of the house and looked out over the overgrown mess, which she hadn't quite gotten to yet. She had done her best to make the front garden presentable, although it was far from finished. She had her vegetable plot in the sunniest spot, facing north, but she hadn't had time to attend to the least visible part of the garden.

As she walked along the deck, something bright and unusual stood out. The little grapevine's buds had opened into fingers of apple green with veins of cherry showing through, the beginnings of leaves. Marcia was immensely proud of them.

Marcia had kept her maiden name because she liked the way it sounded. Reed, like a wild water plant. It was the one thing her father had given her that she wanted to keep. To her delight, when she had combined it with William's surname, it ran like a stream. Reed-Wilton. It was this she was pondering as she sat cross-legged on the blue-green carpet in the main room of the community house, waiting for people to arrive. They trickled in, acknowledging her with shy nods, still not sure about the social protocols of the workshop.

This day was about the second energy centre, the level of need, survival, and desire, she explained to them, each one listening intently.

"Too often, this is the level that relationships are based on," she said, looking around at each one of them so as not to single anyone out.

"These are usually the kind of relationships where power and control are central. Where each person looks to the other to meet all their needs, a task that is impossible, to say the least."

"Excuse me," Helen piped up. "Are you saying that it is a bad thing to need someone else... emotionally, I mean?" She blushed and looked down at her hands.

"Not a bad thing, no," Marcia said, looking directly at Helen with her warm eyes. "It just doesn't work in a healthy way. Both people are competing for each other's energy rather than creating their own. Eventually, the supply is diminished. People often start out in mad infatuation that feels wonderful, like a drug, and it is addictive too. It becomes harder and harder to get a fix, and that's often when people try to get control, and the relationship becomes a power struggle. It is only when people are able to enter into a relationship as two whole beings, able to maintain themselves, that the relationship can be nurturing, healthy and sustainable."

Helen nodded, and Marcia could see that she was trying to take this information in.

"It's just that I don't see how it can be a relationship without needing one another."

"A different kind of relationship, perhaps," Marcia offered, and her enthusiasm seemed to quiet Helen's qualms as she continued with her description of the second centre.

"Each one of us is blessed and cursed with an inner child; a needy, demanding, emotional angel that can be sweet or cruel, and this is where she or he begins to emerge." She gestured to her navel.

"This is the home of gut feelings, of digestive problems, of lust, passion, and greed. It is where your umbilical cord once joined you to the placenta and life-blood of your mother. This is the sacral centre. On this level, we are instinctual animals."

"When you are ready, close your eyes. Experience the sensations of your body like we did last time. Become completely aware."

She paused, allowing them a few moments to become conscious of themselves.

Now… Take a deep breath
Exhale and go deeper into awareness
Focus on the area around your navel
Your belly
Right around to your back
This is the area governed by your sacral energy centre
Take a moment to completely experience the sensations of this area
From your navel, right through to the other side of your body, there is an energy centre
Imagine orange light radiating through it and out into the rest of this area
As you imagine this light, notice it becoming clearer and more beautiful
If you encounter any blocks, allow them to melt away
Now, as you focus on the centre of this energy…
It is going to take you on a journey into yourself.

Marcia let go of her link with the group for a moment and delved into her sacral centre. She felt the connection, her need for survival. She felt a pulling sensation at the umbilical cord, a feeling that she could not differentiate between emotion and physical pain. It was probably both. Her sacral centre was playing up again, as it did whenever she had almost forgotten her past.

Sometimes it is not the things that are forced upon us that hurt us most. It is the choices we make ourselves when we become the people we cannot abide. It was as if she was there again, in the white room, the strangers around her, staring at her, giving her orders as she endured the most intense sensations of her life. It wasn't the pain that hurt her the most; it was the conflict, the discomfort, the feeling that there was no way out. And then it was over, and she heard him cry, a sound that rang through her nervous system, and she knew she wanted him more than anything. She needed him, but he was already gone. She screamed, more than she had in the entire labour, but they held her down, and then there was a prick in her arm, and she was floating away, somewhere else, where nothing was real.

19

IRIS

It was most definitely getting warmer. The sky was overcast, making the atmosphere ever so slightly humid. Iris felt as if the gentle mid-morning air was cuddling up to her body like a blanket. It was the most pleasant sensation as she strolled through the little township on her way to her usual café. She noticed from a distance that something was amiss; the doors were closed. To her astonishment, a sign on the window read, "Closed for soundcheck. Live Jazz performance tonight: *Meeting Marcia*." A bubble of delight burst through her as she watched fate play out. Surely there could be no coincidence; this must be a sign.

The cherry tree was in full bloom; its tufts of baby pink floated lazily on the branches while dandelion seeds adventured from the confines of their nurseries to surf the breeze as Iris disembarked from her station wagon, a little dizzy from the hour drive. She stood in the driveway, not knowing quite what to do. Marcia had given her an open invite, but would arriving out of the blue be too much? She didn't have long to hesitate. A colourful figure emerged from the side of the house with a shovel in tow. When Marcia noticed her in the driveway, her eyes lit up, relieving Iris of her concerns.

"The tomato plants can't wait, I'm afraid," Marcia said in mock apology. "I told them I'd plant them last week, and they are impatient little things."

"Do you always converse with your plants?" Iris asked, bemused.

"Of course," Marcia said matter-of-factly.

"This may sound strange…" Iris said, following her to the garden bed where zucchinis bloomed and basil was generously spaced in neat lines. "But I think I was supposed to visit you today. Let's just say I followed the signs."

"That sounds cryptic. Did you get out your pendulum?" Marcia asked thoughtfully as she dug little wells in the soil between each of the basil plants. Iris was unsure if the question was a joke or genuine.

"Much more mundane actually; the sign was on a café door."

"Well, in any case, it's a nice surprise." Marcia's smile was warm and illuminating as always. She carefully extracted tomato seedlings from their trays and gently tucked them into their new homes. Iris automatically got onto her knees to help, letting the damp ground soak through her jeans. It struck her that this was a very sacral centre thing to do. There was something intimately carnal about it; hands buried in the earth, planting vegetables, a symbol of survival.

October yielded spectacular sun showers, heavy raindrops that fell like jewels through the evergreen leaves that surrounded Iris's dwelling, an obvious blessing for the natural world. Iris wondered why people did not often treat themselves as they would actually like to be treated, not just by avoiding unpleasantness and hiding from the world, but by doing the things that really made them feel wonderful.

She recalled distant memories of the way her heart had leapt like a child's on a swing when she found "I love you" notes where she had least expected them; in her handbag, the desert bowl she reached for in the cupboard, sticky-taped to her toothbrush. She became caught up momentarily in the feeling of being loved by someone, of always knowing she was in his thoughts while he was in hers. There was no reason someone couldn't love themselves as much as anyone else.

She wrapped her arms around herself in a tight hug, dipping her chin until it embraced the soft, warm skin of her chest. She was tired of people expecting others to meet their own needs to feel valued and special. There was no perfect person out there who could take all that self-responsibility away; there was no reason one couldn't satisfy one's self in the same way. She hastily typed out lists of advice.

Allow your mind to clear and visualise yourself as a newly born child, in awe of the amazing new world around you, innocent and pure. Allow yourself to realise that all the guilt, resentment, and regret you have felt is not natural or necessary. It is merely something you have been taught. Free yourself of these burdens by acknowledging your innocence.

Iris paused for a moment. She knew what she was trying to get across but was unsure of her personal direction. She took a moment to centre herself, experiencing the parameters of her body, this vessel she was ordained within. It came to her momentarily. *I choose love and light, acceptance and openness, the universe, agape, benevolence, bliss – This is what I want between myself and any other. This is what I want to be.*

The two energy centres they had covered so far had stretched Iris. The physical and carnal levels of life she sometimes indulged but often dismissed now re-emerged as intrinsic aspects of overall spiritual growth. She thought of the monks she had once admired in a new light, for their strict vows seemed limiting; the devotees who shunned the flesh, barely taking in sustenance in order to focus on a higher dimension. She had once felt inferior, but now there was no such thing. Every level of existence was just as important. The physical world, her body, and its interactions were setting the stage for her life to play out. It was her choice how much she took in. The lessons she had learnt through the emotional afflictions that had plagued her at times were now more obvious. They belonged to the sacral energy centre. Addictions to people, dependency on chocolate, work, television; these were all manifestations of trying to satisfy the cravings she had to feel safe, to feel wanted and accepted.

Life had always seemed to her like a journey: a slow climb, discovering new realities, gaining perspective, letting go of her weight and excess baggage in order to attain more wisdom. The difficulties she faced in her daily life were no longer bad things; bad and good were, after all, merely human labels. She could see abstractions while recognising the many complex perspectives. *Only by letting go can I experience life fully; holding on is hiding, blocking progress.* From time to time, she found herself stuck in stagnation. When the only thing that gave her the foothold she needed to get out was blind optimism. *I can do this; I can break these patterns and learn as much as I can from this life.* She needed to lose control to gain perspective; control was only a trap, a pattern forged in fear. *Just be, as I have chosen to be; here, now, at this moment, every moment, one moment; everlasting love.*

When Iris entered her bedroom, she instantly knew there was something out of place. It gave her the strange feeling that her space had been invaded. It made her shiver ever so slightly. The room looked normal, but she was sure, so she inspected it closely, checking her bed first, which seemed to be made the way it was that morning with her rose-coloured duvet. Then she took stock of her nightstand. Every bottle of lotion seemed to be in place. It was only when she opened up her closet that she noticed what had been disturbed. A clean white edge stuck out from the pile of correspondence she kept there. She fingered it for a moment, wondering what it meant. She retrieved the letter in question and mulled over its contents.

It was a draft. The final copy of a letter she had sent to her mother before Alex was born, when he was still a squirmy presence in her belly. She had been full of doubts and fears. *I don't know whether I can do this*, it read. *I know I'm putting my career on hold, possibly jeopardising it, but this is the way things are.* Her mother had been the one who had been most concerned about Iris' career, having given up her own to raise a family. *I know you think I'm making a mistake in keeping this baby.* Did they? She struggled to remember.

Alex. It was surely he who was responsible for unearthing this piece of her history. What had he taken from reading these simple lines scrawled in her untidy handwriting? Could he have interpreted her youthful uncertainty, her attempt to communicate with her mother, to gain her understanding, as something else? Had he even read the last paragraph that admitted that she had wanted him all along, that she had even deceptively planned him, that she felt she was driven into this situation by destiny itself?

She had no way of knowing how such incomplete information might affect him, and he kept his guard so close that she was afraid even to mention it. She decided, as she always did, that if Alex wanted to ask questions, he was welcome to.

The humid November wind picked up as they walked; the two women, revelling in the electrifying atmosphere that could only mean a storm was brewing. Invigorating gusts swept over them, tousling the trees. Branches and leaves littered the ground.

Their friendship had grown to the point where each could speak candidly without fear of offending the other. Iris admired the way Marcia looked then, with the weather swirling around her, elemental, ethereal. She envied the way her friend could fit perfectly into any natural scene, not in the background, but as the centrepiece, as if her surroundings were made to compliment her. The light rain caught in her hair could have been deliberate adornments. When drops landed on her skin, they glistened meaningfully.

"I wouldn't peg you for fifty-five," she said into the wind. "You could easily pass for thirty-eight."

"I have to say I resent that." Marcia's tone was playful, as was the glint in her eyes. "I've earned my years, thank you very much. Each one of my wrinkles – they make me who I am."

Iris smiled to herself until her attention was sabotaged by the emergence of fears from her subconscious.

"I'm worried about Alex," she admitted. "He doesn't really communicate with me anymore. He just keeps to himself. I don't know how he can live like that."

"You remember being a teenager. It's a difficult time. Your personality is fragmented, and you become so... insular. It's a developmental stage." Marcia's voice sounded reassuring.

"It's strange. He's really not like me at all. I don't think he's even much like his father. He's this conservative, atheistic pessimist, the total opposite of me. Where does it come from?" Iris waved her hands in the air in exasperation.

"That's funny. I've often wondered if spirituality skips a generation. My grandmother was very spiritual. I never met her, but apparently, she believed in pyramids having mystical powers and that sort of thing. My father hated it. He thought she was a quack, and here I am, believing in energy centres and other invisible things."

"Maybe it sometimes moves to the side," Iris mused. "My grandparents weren't spiritual, although they were religious. They went to church, but it was just fact to them, not faith. My parents aren't spiritual either, but my aunt Esther is a member of the spiritualist church, and I always wondered if it somehow came from her or whether it was a recessive gene or something. Who knows? We're in the most agnostic country in the world. If spirituality doesn't come from our parents, it must come from somewhere."

"I like to think of it as evidence of something that can't be proven," Marcia said. "It must come from somewhere... it must be something. It's just impossible to measure."

They walked on in silence, taking in the pre-storm atmosphere.

The gale picked up, and something sharp smacked into Iris's leg. She picked up the twig that had offended her, pushing both ends towards each other.

"This is what happens when we resist nature," Iris said as if in awe.

"We get windswept hair?" Marcia joked.

"We break," she said as the twig snapped cleanly in half.

It was one of those moments when she just knew she was right, where everything made perfect sense in its existence. She enjoyed the feeling of being present, aware of the wind sweeping over her frame, pushing her back into herself. It was a rare and precious experience. Universal truths always revealed themselves to Iris in this way, in this state, and they were all interconnected and perfectly obvious. *Resistance can only go so far before it is forced to give, one way or another. Simple physics but also true on a personal level.* If she had said something like that to her former colleagues or even to Alex, they would have given her that look: slightly concerned, slightly frightened, and heavily out of their depth. Her own son would gladly hand her over to a psychiatrist; she had no doubt about that. But Marcia understood. She just nodded, smiling vaguely to herself, and Iris didn't need to explain.

20

LEA

I t was the only thing that made sense: if they thought in the same way, they should be together. So why had Alex sent that text message?

Lea, I don't think we should see each other anymore.

At first, she was in shock. There must have been a mistake, a misunderstanding. He couldn't possibly do this, not to her. He had told her he loved her. He had said she was perfect for him.

She spent all morning in bed, pretending to be sick. She didn't have to try very hard. Her pale, gaunt face was convincing enough for her mother to leave her home alone with some Panadol and a large bottle of water.

The shock had quickly transformed into anger. *How could he? How dare he? Had he been lying to her this whole time? How could he possibly be so evil?* Then the tears came.

I want you, Alex. She thought. *I want you to die.* She quickly took it back, reproaching herself for wishing him harm. She cared about him too much, despite him obviously not giving a damn about her.

The schism was torture. She felt she had been spliced in half. He wouldn't answer his phone. She had sent texts, becoming increasingly desperate. Nothing. Could he possibly be this cruel, this selfish, this arrogant? She already knew the answer to that.

She couldn't escape the feeling that something had been torn from her unjustly. She folded her arms, digging her fingernails with their chipped black nail polish into the flesh of her shoulders. She hated him for his arrogance, believing he was always right. *When will you learn?* she thought. She dug her notebook out from the gap between the wall and her mattress. She re-read the words she had written on the cover with a metallic bronze pen and varnished over with clear nail polish.

There is no one truth. No absolute.

The words echoed through her mind encountering no obstacles. *So why do I feel so awful? Why is my perspective so painful?* She could not find a boundary between self-pity and the understanding she had that reality was subjective.

It must have been her fault. She must have done something wrong, or he wouldn't have cut her off like this. She caught a glimpse of herself: puffy eyes, light brown re-growth evading her dyed hair. She would dye it all black, wipe out the red, erase the past and start again with nothing. A blanket of darkness. She hated herself more than ever. She turned the page and began to write again, ignoring the tears that soaked splotches into the paper, smudging the ink.

The face in the mirror.
So familiar.
You've always been there.
To stagger the pace.
To rob me of my rightful place.
Betrayed by the closest one.
Overshadowed by the Sun.
My reflection is my shadow.
I've been running from you all my life.
I've been dying all my life.

21

MARCIA

G *uilt is like ivy*, Marcia thought as she plunged into the midst of it, dragging at the vines which threatened to engulf the old oak tree that grew in the very front of the garden and often terrorised the power lines. *As it grows, it penetrates through boundaries, digging its little roots in so tightly, its clinging strands determined. It will never relinquish its hold. Just like the ivy, it is useless to let go of guilt because guilt won't let go of you. There is no hope without intervention.*

Intervention for her meant facing the things that most frightened her, the things she felt most guilty about.

Marcia had almost worked up the courage to knock on the door, but instead, she chose to walk past the 1950's cottage with its newly painted exterior and well-maintained garden. It was clearly Anna's house; she always had to have everything just so.

As a child, her dolls were lined up on their shelf in order of height, and her bed was always perfectly made, in contrast to her older sister, who left her clothes in piles on the floor of her room. Everything else ended up there, too, making it impossible to walk in without first clearing a path or jumping between the rare open spaces where the carpet was visible. Marcia had been a messy child and a disgusting teenager.

She hadn't seen her baby sister in almost forty years. She had been sixteen when she left home, and Anna had been six, her golden hair falling in ringlets. Her dimples and rosy cheeks bore no resemblance to Marcia, and neither did her personality.

Anna had been sweet and placid as a child. Their mother had been so in love with her youngest that it was hard for Marcia not to feel resentment, but now she was the one who needed to apologise. Family was supposed to stay in touch. Blood was supposed to be thicker than water. It was not a bond that could or should be broken, although Marcia had done as much as she could to sever the connection.

Anna had been innocent. She wasn't the one who neglected Marcia or yelled at her or hit her. She probably had never even noticed that the family she had grown up in, with a loving mother and proud father, was worlds away from the one that had raised her older sister to be damaged and rebellious and reckless.

As Marcia began to walk away, the sound of thunder broke through the clouds, bringing with it a sudden downpour. Marcia was instantly drenched, three kilometres from home, without an umbrella. It struck her that the weather was conspiring to force a reunion whether she liked it or not.

Anna answered the door, serene in a cream turtleneck. She appeared initially surprised at the stranger who sheltered on her porch and more so when she spoke.

"Anna." Marcia looked into the pale golden eyes of her little sister. The same eyes she remembered from the pieces of her child-hood that had not been torn apart, the memories that were still intact. They were the same eyes, but they were older, tired and worn. She did not respond for a moment, and then, tentatively, she nodded.

"I know this is... unexpected. I haven't seen you in such a long time... I..." For once, her words failed her. There was nothing she could say that could bridge the divide she had intentionally created to separate herself from her pain.

"I'm your sister." It was the only thing she could say that explained anything, but it had no guarantees.

Anna looked as though she wanted to close the door, but she

remained where she was, steadying herself against it. Her eyes flicked to the rain outside.

"You'd better come in," she said reluctantly, as though she knew it was the right thing to do – not the thing she would have preferred.

They sat at the kitchen table. Marcia examined its new, light-coloured wood. It looked like it came straight from a catalogue. The room was in perfect order. Marcia would have expected no less. The colour theme was neutral: cream, eggshell, beige. Family pictures sat on the mantelpiece. Prints of Monet and Renoir hung on the walls.

"I came to see you because..." *I'm sorry, I'm a terrible sister. I have no other family.* "I'm back in New Zealand."

"I know." Anna's voice was low. She looked at her hands. "The lawyer said you'd bought the old house." She looked up into Marcia's face as if searching for something, an explanation perhaps.

"I thought you hated that place, I thought the reason you left..." Her voice became high as it trailed off, the voice of a child.

"I did, well, not the house. I hated..." *Our father? Our family? My life?*

"I know it was hard for you... what you went through."

Marcia was surprised. What had Anna known as a young child? What had she been told?

"I have my own family now," Anna said. The exclusion hit Marcia in the chest.

"Children?" The word caught in her throat, acrid. She looked back to the photographs on the mantle, taking in the little blond cherubs.

"Three." Marcia knew from her guarded tone that it was not Anna's intention for her to ever meet them.

"That's wonderful, Anna." Her enthusiasm wasn't quite genuine. "I'm happy for you." *Am I really?*

She got up from the table, regretting the wet mark she had left in the pale suede seat of the dining chair.

"I better get going. The rain has slowed down now." Anna didn't question the statement, although the rain clearly hadn't. Distant thunder rumbled, and the sound of rain deepened as Marcia retreated to the door. Her presence did not fit in this calm suburban paradise. She paused at the sound of Anna's voice.

"Are you looking after it?" she asked. "The house? It needs lots of TLC." She smiled at her abbreviation, and Marcia recognised the buoyant spirit of her sibling. It was a relief she was still there inside that otherwise vacant shell.

"I'm doing my best." It was a plea, more than anything.

22

IRIS

I ris's third energy centre was burning a hole through her chest. This was where her control issues were. This was where her middle back pain and the tension in her shoulders came from. This was where her arguments with Alex started. The level of control seemed to be where all of her issues developed. She would have gladly cut it out and gone about her life, but unfortunately, it was here that she could learn the most, and she knew it. Marcia's words from the third workshop danced through her mind.

The solar plexus is the home of the conscious mind, that which seeks control.
It is here, in the solar plexus, where one feels tight-chested.

Her conscious mind was indeed running rampant through this meditation. Her crossed legs felt uncomfortable. Her posture was bad and constantly needed adjusting. It was as if her consciousness was deliberately fighting any improvement, any change. In the discussion prior, it had been on the tip of everyone's tongue, but only Iris had the guts to express it.

But what if I don't want to accept. I'm not a doormat. What if I need to fight something?

The answer was as clear as day:

You can accept and still ignite change. It is only through accepting that you can free yourself enough to do your cause justice.

It made sense. Fighting was wasting energy, struggling against a wall. It felt good to express the frustration, but it rarely did any lasting good. Something inside her wanted to feel important. She wanted to single-handedly change the world in all its devastation. Again, Marcia was a guiding light.

The ego will always have its tragedy. One can always see the cycle through to its obvious conclusion.

Which, in this case, was letting go and letting her energy shift from focussing on the evening news and all that was ever wrong into support for what was right. Concentrating on the things that brought her hope and joy. She delved deeper into what felt like knots in her chest, inner conflict.

She wanted to help Alex, to teach him, but just as she was as a teenager, she found him unwilling to listen. It was his journey, not hers, and she could no longer carry him like she did when he was a baby, wrapped close to her heart. There was something troubling her, something going on between him and Lea that she sensed was not what it should be. Just as she began to dwell on all the hideous possibilities, Marcia's voice broke through again.

Imagine the yellow light growing brighter;
So bright it expands to fill your entire ribcage.
Become aware of any blockages in this area;
This is your opportunity to accept and let go.

This was exactly what Iris needed to do. She felt her body relax slightly.

Allow acceptance to trickle through you like a running stream;
Accept what you cannot change.
Let it spread into a river;
Let go of what is not yours to control.

There was so much she couldn't control, but worry would not help these situations. It only made them worse.

Let it wash over you
Accept the longings that linger
Ghosts of the past
All the baggage
It is what it was
Accept and let go.
Even if you don't understand it
Take what you have learnt and move on.
Accept all the unfairness
The injustices of the past.
Accept the pain
Let it remain in the past.
Accept the anger
And let it go.
Accept the fear
And move through it.
Accept yourself
Your whole self.
As each thought or memory comes to you
Accept it and let go.
Allow yourself to embody acceptance.
Allow this feeling of acceptance to spiral out...
Into the entirety of your life.
Now you are free.

Iris watched as her words flowed effortlessly into place. She wrote about abundance and growth, about cycles and universal truth, about love. She was happy when she wrote. It occurred to her, as she sat in the warm caress of mid-morning sunlight, that her life was like a perfect day. Taken by the moment, she released a barrage of affirmations.

I write easily and clearly.
I write beautifully.
My writing is inspired and inspiring.

I compile my written work with ease.

This took care of the present, so she moved some of the energy, paving the way for the future she wanted.

I write best-selling books.
I am a renowned author.
I receive wonderful, positive feedback about my writing.
I am successful.
I am published.

Everything was perfect.

Romantic relationships were far too important to leave out of the book, but since becoming a mother, she had experienced so few of them. She hadn't the time or the inclination. Occasionally, someone she knew from work had persuaded her to go to dinner with him or to have an after-work drink. But Iris wasn't entertained by small talk, and she found these encounters tedious. She preferred her own company.

Now she was trying to give other people advice about something she hadn't had in years. She chose to do it in an abstract way. She remembered going through periods in her youth when she had been so disillusioned with relationships that she had said to herself, over and over again, "I don't want to have a relationship."

Strangely enough, this mantra had landed her almost immediately in a relationship she did not want. It took her a while to work that out. When she did, she realised that it was a negative affirmation. She was putting energy into something she did not want, and it was manifesting right before her eyes.

She re-phrased the thought to, "I enjoy being single," which was true, but it did not eradicate the concept of relationships from her mind. She found herself in a position where she needed to ask: *What is the ideal relationship?* She knew her parents had compatible dysfunctions; her father was critical, her mother emotionally distant; he was a bully, she the victim. This pattern was not something Iris wanted for herself.

She had to go through the process of deconstructing the concept of "relationships" in her head. She found that even the idealised movie relationships were not something she wanted. She didn't want to be clingy, to need someone, to focus all her energy on them to the exclusion of everything else. It was just too exhausting. She didn't want the kind of relationship Marcia had brought up in the second workshop, the co-dependent kind or one based on power and control.

She wanted to live her own life, and if she was to have intimate company, she wanted it to be equal, mutually beneficial, and somehow independent. Bearing all this in mind, she had followed the advice a friend had given her and written a detailed list. She wanted a partner who was creative, caring, exciting, deep, philosophical, articulate, critical (but not too negative), and attractive to her, someone she could enjoy spending time with, whom she could trust with her innermost thoughts. Her intention was that she would not enter into a relationship with anyone unless all the criteria were met.

To her utter amazement, it happened in a matter of weeks, but, to her consternation, even the perfect relationship was still hard work.

23

LEA

Lea's tears had dried up, leaving her tired and dazed. She took her notebook to the window and looked out at the night garden.

I hear the dial tone, my chest reams with cynical suspense brought upon me by your constant apathy. Pressing those buttons, hearing that sound, almost a tune, music to my fading heart. But as soon as I have dialled those familiar numbers, any optimism is snatched from me by your voice telling me you are not there. I retreat to my nervous state that cannot avoid you; you swim through my mind like a trapped eel.

What made matters worse was that her period was still late. Coupled with the suspicion she had that this was Alex's impetus for breaking up with her, it was a dreadful combination. She pulled her top up and studied her belly, smooth, cold, and luminous under the faint orange glow of the street lights. It seemed so normal, so inno-cent. Of course, it was too early to tell, but she wondered how people found out they were pregnant. Did they just know, even before they took the test? She remembered Alex's words.

"I never want to be a father."

His father probably didn't set a good example – not bothering to stick around, even to meet his child. There was a spark of hope when she thought about it. Even if she lost Alex, maybe she would gain someone, some part of him, someone who would love and accept her and ruin her life and inevitably grow up to hate her. It was only a spark, after all. In a damp, dark place where it had no chance of igniting anything.

It was almost an eerie feeling: that there could be a parasite feeding off her, a hybrid of her DNA and Alex's. Some kind of monster, or genius or idiot, because as clever as she liked to think herself, she was stupid to have become so dependent on him and stupid to put herself in this situation. She was groping around in the dark, and her light had gone, leaving her double-blind. She felt a gnawing sensation in her abdomen.

is that you?
growing inside me
in that unspeakable silence
that I dare not name

is that you?
churning my stomach
clutching my throat
pounding on my chest in the dead of night

is that you?
pretending I don't exist
pretending you're all that matters
believing you are affected the most

is this me?
suffocating your privacy
nagging at your attention
draining your mind

I'm dying in your arms…

this is my fault

She put down her pen and relaxed into the night air. The creepy feeling was out in the open, but instead of freeing her, it made her feel trapped. If it was true, she had no choice. She would have to abort. There was no way she would make a fit mother, and she was humanitarian enough not to inflict herself on an innocent being. She was assaulted again by the tormented feelings. Then they faded and she was hollow.

Lea knew it was stupid, but she still had hope. It glowed inside her, in contrast to the deep red of pain and the darkness of despair. There was a chance that she could make him see that they were meant to be together. It was her only chance, and it was all she could think about.

It was what drove her to lie to her mother and get on the 5pm Raglan bus after wandering the streets of Hamilton, trying to make up her mind. She watched the country flash past her, green and overgrown. The barns painted a typical barn-red, the dilapidated sheds and weather-worn farmhouses, the peaceful cows and nimble young sheep. Rural life had never appealed to her more than it did now.

She knew it was crazy, showing up at his house uninvited. Her mother thought she was at Erika's. She hoped Iris wouldn't mind too much. When the bus slowed to a stand-still outside the Raglan information centre, it was getting dark. She couldn't help the feeling of dread. How would she travel the ten more kilometres to get to his house? She started walking past the cafes which were closing up along the road that would eventually lead her to him.

Hitch-hiking scared her. Her mother had drilled her full of horror stories as a child, but she had no alternative. Walking would take her all night. She eyed the passing cars suspiciously and then tentatively stuck out her thumb in front of an innocent-looking blue Honda. To her surprise, it pulled over.

"Can I give you a lift?" The voice was high and wavering. It issued from an old woman with curling grey hair.

"I need to get to Whale Bay." Lea's voice was small and uncertain.

The woman smiled and waved her inside.

"We live just around the corner from there."

Lea relaxed into the seat, inhaling the new car smell. She pretended to listen politely to the woman talk, although she didn't really hear any of it. She wasn't in danger, after all, at least, not yet.

Their driveway looked just as chaotic as it had the last time she had been there. She had to walk for ten minutes before she got to the steps and then will her tired legs to climb them. She seemed to become heavier the closer she got to the door. Thousands of doubts crowded her mind as she knocked on the glass. She heard movement, and then Iris was there with her beaming smile.

"Lea!" She sounded pleased. "This is a surprise; Alex didn't tell me you were coming."

She felt the guilt creep up. "Well, actually, I wanted to surprise him." She didn't sound convincing.

Iris examined her closely, no doubt taking in her school uniform and the circles under her eyes. "Does your mother know you're here?'

"Of course," she lied, enthusiastically nodding her head in the hopes that it was more convincing.

"Great. Well, Alex is upstairs on the computer, as usual," she sighed in mock exasperation. "You know how he is."

"Yes, I do." At least, she used to think so.

"Would you like some dinner? You must be starving."

Lea hadn't really thought about food much, not for the past few days, not since her life had disintegrated into nothingness. She had barely existed. Having made it this far had cemented her hope. Although she couldn't get Alex off her mind, it seemed rude to sneak upstairs when Iris was so nice and chatty.

The bowl of spaghetti bolognese Iris produced was more delicious than anything she could remember eating, and Iris seemed to pour out happiness as she spoke. She wanted to know how Lea was doing at school. Of course, it was the question all adults asked, but the way Iris said it, it sounded genuinely interested. So Lea told her about studying the Russian Revolution in history. This was apparently the perfect topic because Iris seemed passionate about it. They theorised about Rasputin's influence and what his real agenda was and lamented the execution of the poor royal children. Lea didn't tell her anything that was really going on, and to her relief, Iris didn't ask personal questions.

It was dark as she climbed the stairs to Alex's room. He had his headphones on, so he hadn't heard her arrival at all, staring at the screen, flicking through websites that Lea didn't recognise.

"Hey," he said when he saw her movement. If he was surprised to see her, he didn't show it. He had the decency to remove his headphones, but his face was locked on the computer.

"I needed to see you." Her voice cracked into obvious tears. She paused, but he didn't reply, so she went on.

"Will you please just talk to me?" She sounded as desperate as she felt.

"Sure," he said, but he didn't move.

"Alex, I love you." He didn't so much as blink. "I thought..." Her voice trailed into sobs. "I thought you loved me too."

"I thought so too." His voice was cold, hard, unrecognisable.

"So, you don't anymore?" It was unbearable. "Is that why you did it?"

"I don't know," he said evenly.

"What changed?" she said. She reached up to touch his shoulder. He stayed still as a statue. "What happened?" she asked again. The silence was awful.

"I don't have an answer for you."

The tears were streaming down her face. Contorted in agony, she collapsed onto the floor between his chair and the bed.

"Did I do something?" She turned the blame on herself.

After a torturous pause, he finally answered. "Not that I can think of." The same bland tone. He was giving her nothing.

"Is there something wrong with me?" It was the obvious conclusion. But what? The pain pushed more tears out.

"No."

"You said…" It was an accusation. "You said I was perfect for you."

"I'm going to bed." He was almost casual. She sat on the floor, crying until she was empty, until the computer was off, and he was under the covers. Her eyes burned dry, and there was nothing she could do. She was absolutely powerless.

She knew he was still awake as she got up and crept under the blankets. His body was rigid, uninviting, but it still felt good to be close to him.

"You know, you could give this another chance." She knew he was still awake.

"I could." She nestled her head into his shoulder, where she knew it fit perfectly.

"Would you?"

"Maybe."

It was enough to keep her breathing, to keep her going, to allow her to get up the next morning and go back to Hamilton with Iris, without making a fuss.

24

ZANE

On a mild evening in early fall, Zane felt like taking a walk alone. They were having a break between their national tour and the impending international one. He let himself out of the apartment block and took a left towards Hollywood Boulevard. Zane let his thoughts run free as he passed gothic boutiques and cheap souvenir shops. It had been so long since he had been alone. He'd been so caught up in his band and preoccupied with promotional pandemonium. He wondered briefly if fame had affected his identity. Then his mind flicked over a familiar pattern.

Zane had tried to shut her out of his mind, out of his life, but some people were impossible to escape. His birth mother was always going to be there somewhere. He had been through the usual drama as a kid. Whenever he needed another excuse to be upset, it was always something to cry about: his own mother had discarded him. She obviously didn't think him worth her time. He was worthless.

He got over that along with adolescence. He figured she probably had her reasons, and he knew the usual sob story: teenage girl gets pregnant, and her family forces her to secretly adopt, so the neighbours don't talk. He figured it was something like that, and at any rate, he had been pretty lucky. Compared to the millions of children in the world with no food or running water, the children who live with a day-to-day threat of land mines or domestic violence, his parents were charming.

They had their flaws. His father was the strict religious type. His mother was a gentle doormat, but she was loving and sweet. She had gone to all his soccer games and tucked him in at night. Yet despite the bedtime stories and packed lunches, he had always wondered about the missing piece of his life. Some connections were just too strong to cut, though the wound was deep.

He wondered later, after the love of his life had suddenly deserted him without so much as a 'goodbye', whether the pattern was stuck to him, whether it was something about him that made them leave. The pain of separation was too much to face, so he decided not to get too close. He kept his lovers at arm's length emotionally, letting them play but not linger. His close friends, his band, they were the ones he turned to for advice, his chosen family. They consoled him even with their cheap jibes and witty sarcasm. It was nice to know they cared.

As he approached the old Hollywood cemetery, he noticed the twinkling of lights. Thousands of tealight candles adorned the graves, which were also decorated with flowers and photos, even food. Zane watched as the Hollywood community celebrated the Mexican day of the dead, Día de Los Muertos. He remembered Baz and Mitch discussing it a few years before. Mitch thought it was morbid, and Baz tried to convince him it was just a different way of looking at death: as a natural part of life, as something to be celebrated. Instead of contributing to the conversation, Zane had jotted down some words that remained etched on his mind. He had come up with the idea of focusing on seasons as the theme for songs, maybe even albums.

Autumn falls into oblivion
Vermilion, gold, okra,
The night stretches on
We shed our pasts and merge in mourning,
We burn our chains to let go the past
We face the brutality of nature
Through chilling rains, we are purged

We go forth without fear
To make our peace with death

It didn't have a tune yet, just an undulating rhythm. Unlike his usual writing, this piece was calm, accepting, lacking his trademark cynical angst. He wondered if it meant he was turning over a new leaf, and the metaphor seemed fitting. After all, this was a time for change.

MRS EVERGLADE

Mrs Everglade peered over her glasses at the tray of grey pureed food. *Unsatisfactory*.

She was disgusted to find herself back in the geriatric recovery hospital after another fall.

She despised the pastel wallpaper and the plastic cups. *Disdainful*. She detested the nurses and their polite smiles. *Ingenuine*. She abhorred her nieces for locking her up in this horrible, disinfected place, where everyone was trying, without her permission, to keep her alive. *What's the point?* she thought. *It doesn't help them. It doesn't help me. I'd be better off dead.* Her existence had never felt more futile. She lay in her uncomfortable hospital bed, day after day, watching mind-numbing infomercials and soap operas. Her only comfort lay in knowing she couldn't be much longer for this world, whether or not something appealing lay in the next.

Rex was her favourite orderly, although she gave him an ear full about the bits of metal he'd had purposely gouged through his face. He had a handsome face, not unlike her Albert, but he insisted on wearing that awful ring in his nose, the spikes in his eyebrow and the bauble under his lip. *Labrette* he called it, but a fancy French-sounding name did nothing to improve it in her mind. She had been to France once, years ago, and none of the French men she had seen had worn such piercings. In her day, brassy women drove needles through their ear lobes at home, but good girls like herself wore clip-ons. She still had drawers of them tucked away somewhere at home. *Home,* her little cottage, the place she'd much rather be than here.

She liked Rex because he spoke to her as if she was a person rather than an object, rather than a child. She hated to be patronised. He would lean casually on her dresser and tell her about his weekend's activities: the bands he went to see, the girls he met.

Mrs Everglade did not doubt that it was not her scene. She knew she would hate his kind of music and think the girls he talked about under-clothed and under-mannered, but she liked to imagine them anyway. It was much better than staring at the walls. She would sometimes put her own spin on his stories, imagining them in a different time. The dances of her youth where the girls wore pretty dresses and the boys asked them politely to dance. Even during the Great Depression, they'd had the gayest of evenings.

It had been at one such occasion that she had met Albert. It was a cold winter evening in 1938. She and her sisters were at a dance in the town hall. She had seen him across the crowded dance floor and knew at once. That was how she found out what love was. It occurred to her in that moment that she was sure. She had worn her yellow dress because her favourite lavender one had become unravelled just as she put it on. He said the yellow brought out her eyes, and it quickly became her favourite colour.

September, it was. She remembered that clearly because exactly one year later, war broke out when Germany invaded Poland. She was seventeen, he was eighteen, and that meant he was old enough to enlist when the call came. New Zealand, in loyalty to the British, had declared war on Germany. Because they were engaged, she insisted they be married before he left to serve his country: that way, at least, he would still be hers.

Even at that young age, she had known the risk. Her father's older brother had died in the Great War. The grief had made him ill and ultimately killed him at a young age. At least, that was what her mother had said. At his funeral, she had heard an aunt mutter the word "suicide." She had only been thirteen, but she understood that it was something sinister, something to be ashamed of.

Looking back on the memory through the lens of her many years, she envied her uncle's freedom to end his own life. If she had the energy and opportunity now, she would do the same, if only to escape the retched tedium of daytime television.

IRIS

I ris had decided to take an overgrown path through the bush.
She was unsure of where it would lead, but she felt the prospect
of adventure swell inside her, lifting her up.

She knew she still had patterns of victimisation. She was still
sometimes the protagonist of the drama of her life. *These may take a
while to break, but I will break them,* she vowed, snapping back the
branches that obscured her path.

As she waded through a mess of native fern leaves, she realised
that being bullied by her father, siblings, and teachers in her childhood helped to forge defence mechanisms, but Iris refused to think
of them as bad things. She chose to think they were created in the
most perfect way for her to experience and learn from her life. *I must
learn to trust myself, in the decisions I have made to get here.*

At present, she was unsure of where exactly "here" was. The
path she had followed seemed to become narrower and more overgrown with every step she took. Fears and insecurities rattled at her,
about the future, about money, about her son. They made her want
to hide, but she was too busy avoiding the nasty prickles of a gorse
bush. *Now I can choose to trust the universe and myself for getting this far, for
choosing a purpose,* she thought, bringing the ball back into her court
as she made her way up a steep incline, hoisting herself up with the

help of kanuka trunks. She wondered who on earth would have made such a path and whether it was a path at all or just a natural coincidence until she spotted the remnants of some steps composed of rocks and wood. She longed for the asparagus she planned to have for dinner, fried in butter, not boiled soggy the way her mother made it.

She carried on, noticing the afternoon was quickly fading. *Without purpose, there is no meaning, no motivation; stagnation and apathy prevail.* She wondered whether she would be able to find her way home in the dark with only the pale half-moon already mid-way through the sky to guide her. She smiled up at it to curry favour. *My soul's purpose is probably too broad to grasp, but fragments reveal themselves.*

Up ahead, she could see what looked like a dead-end where the path met a wall of trees. *Purpose creates impetus.* She got closer to investigate whether her journey had been a lost cause. The path in front of her opened up to the sea and sky in a magnificent vista. To her left, she noticed a peculiar anomaly. The green park bench looked quite out of place in the middle of the forest, but it was placed in perfect view of the sunset, which was now stretching lazily across the sky. *My fears teach me about trust.*

Iris wondered who would go to such great effort just to appreciate one of the most spectacular views she had ever seen. The thought made her laugh. She took a deep breath and closed her eyes, shutting out the brilliant tangerine and gold. *Only through fear can we know trust.* She heard it as if it were a whisper. Her eyelids opened to take in more beauty and realised it was true. Without darkness, people wouldn't recognise light. Without sadness, happiness wouldn't be so vivid. She wondered what kind of things people might possibly be experiencing constantly and yet be blind to them because they had no comparison.

27

LEA

He was online when she logged in, and she braced herself. The bubble of hope she had depended on was obviously a delusion. She knew now that he could hurt her and that he probably would, but she still clung to it.

Alex: Hey Lea
Lea: Hi
Alex: About the other night

She knew it was coming. She held all her muscles tightly to resist the impact.

Alex: I don't think it's a good idea if we see each other
Lea: I thought you might say that

Surprisingly enough, it wasn't so bad now that she was ready for it. It was almost amusing. She had been right. She could see something else in him. It was a weakness, and it made her feel stronger.

She was relieved that the school year was nearly over. It couldn't possibly get much worse.

"We're going out." Sienna's voice was firm.

"Out?"

"You're coming. Don't try and argue." Erika had her arms crossed.

"But…"

"No. You're always arguing. Stop it. You're coming with us. I'll pick you up at seven. Tell your mum you're staying at my place."

Lea wasn't feeling wonderful but was excited by the possibility of a distraction.

"Where are we going?"

"You'll find out."

Lea felt nauseous as Sienna's aqua Ford Anglia wound around the darkening corners on their way to the middle of nowhere. It wasn't the car's fault, but Lea cursed it all the same, even though she was terribly jealous of the classic Sienna's dad had re-built for her sixteenth birthday.

"Where are we going?" Lea knew she wouldn't get a decent response as she hadn't the million other times she had asked. But to her surprise, the car began to slow down, and Sienna pulled off into a lookout point.

"Here." She said, pulling up the hand brake as she opened her door.

"Where the hell are we?"

"Don't be difficult!" Erika yelled in mock exasperation. She pulled a bottle of wine and a corkscrew out of her handbag.

"We're in heaven," Sienna said, her voice issuing from the distance. When Lea caught up to her, she was already leaning against the wooden railing, looking out into the cavernous black of the valley below. There were no houses for miles. Lea could see a few timid lights in the distance, but everything else was covered in darkness. She looked up into the sky and gasped at the brilliant milky-way.

"Here." Erika handed her the bottle. "You'll forget he ever existed."

Lea had the strange sensation people were standing around her talking, but when she opened her eyes, everything was quiet. She could see the dawn light through the car's windows and hear Sienna and Erika's slumbering breath as they slept in the reclining front seats. She tried to move her head, and the pain in the base of her skull brought everything back. It was only then that she realised she had forgotten Alex, even if it was just for a minute. But with the blinding pain, the tattered state of her life was all she could think of.

"Erika?" Lea probed.

Erika grunted a response.

"My period is still late."

"What?! Seriously? What are you doing drinking then? Have you taken a test?"

Lea wasn't sure why, but at that moment, a lie flew out of her mouth, so small that she didn't realise until it was too late.

"Yes."

Erika was wide awake now, her eyes gleaming with excitement. "And...?"

Lea wasn't sure why she said it, but it was a choice now, and she so wanted it to be true.

"Positive." The word had an alarmingly pleasant sound to it, like the tinkling of silver bells.

"Oh my god." Erika's response brought Lea a strange sense of satisfaction, as if she mattered somehow. She was brought back down to reality with Erika's next demand.

"You have to tell him," she said.

The pain must have started while Lea slept because she woke, feeling as if her dreams had been full of suffering. Her back and abdominal muscles had twisted themselves into an impossible knot, and the sensation was as if a blunt, rusted instrument was being driven through her.

Her mind was foggy, but there were two thoughts that chased each other around her head. She had her period. At last, the long wait was over. But the relief was bittersweet when there was a possibility of what she might have lost. If she had miscarried, she could have unintentionally squandered something infinitely precious. Her last link to Alex, her last claim on him, and a perfect being in its own right. Her chance at redemption.

It was ridiculous to think it. She turned around, wrapping herself in her sheets, trying to adjust to a position that hurt less. There was no baby. It was probably just a late period. It was probably nothing at all, regardless of what she had told Erika. She felt a pang of guilt at the reminder of her lie.

She wasn't sure what was worse, losing something or never having it in the first place. Either way, she couldn't know for sure.

Her hands dialled the number automatically, and Erika's voice answered.

"Hello?"

"Erika."

"Lea, hey, have you told him yet? You know he has a right to know if he's going to be a father."

"He's not." Lea noticed the defeated tone in her voice. "I've got my period."

"Oh." Erika, always one for a good scandal, was, of course, disappointed. Lea almost felt sorry for her.

"Well, I think I do. The pain is much worse than a normal period." She wasn't sure if she wanted to talk about it, but Erika pressed her for details and came to a conclusion.

"You have to tell him," she implored. "It's not just about you, he's just as involved. If you miscarried, then he still has a right to know. If you don't tell him, I will."

Lea had forgotten that Alex was on her messenger contact list too. He had commented once that she was an airhead, and Lea had laughed. Her best friend often came across that way.

Even the thought of telling Alex made her sick. She put down the phone and made her way slowly, wincing all the way to the bathroom. She had been sure she would throw up, but the nausea faded, and instead, she took the opportunity to inspect the discharge. There was no doubt it was different, thicker and darker than usual, but that could be explained by the extra eleven days it was stuck inside her. She took double the usual dose of Panadol, hoping it would help ease the agony.

He was online, as usual, probably being his insolent new self. She didn't bother with formalities. There was no point, and she wanted to go back to bed and sleep off the cramp.

Lea: There's something I have to tell you
Alex: Yeah?
Lea: well, you know how my period was late?
Alex: yeah

Leah held her breath as she typed.

Lea: I was pregnant.

Lea finally exhaled. That was that. She couldn't take it back. She felt a surge of guilt. She had lied. Or had she? She didn't know. She could have been pregnant; she wasn't now. Either way, it was done. Alex didn't reply, but she didn't care. If he had a problem... well, it was all his fault anyway. She had enough to deal with. She crept back into bed.

28

MARCIA

The garlic bulb on the windowsill was now something of a marvel. Marcia had meant to do something about it when she first saw the little green shoots pierce through the white papery skin, but, by and by, she kept putting it off until the sight of it intrigued her. The grassy spears had begun to twist in their growth towards the evasive sun; unbeknownst to them, they were mirroring the suburban wilderness surrounding the house.

When Marcia left home all those years before, the trees seemed to be growing in a normal, if disorganised fashion, but the lack of sunlight brought about by too many large trees like the towering redwood, which had now cracked the concrete garden path, caused the smaller trees to adopt bizarre shapes and angles. The skinny kowhai underneath it grew at 90 degrees, while a plum tree, weighed down by the burden of its unripe fruit and shaded by a rotund phoenix palm, slumped in an arch so that its tips almost touched the grass, which had not been mown for several weeks.

Of course, she blamed her father for the bothersome nature of the garden, but it had also inherited his eccentricity in its verbose eclectic state. The natives planted with old-fashioned flowers, the loud phoenix palms, and overgrown magnolias. Marcia remembered him wearing caftans and bandannas in the 60s, a turquoise bootlace tie with his shirts. It would have amused her if she had not been dying from embarrassment.

Her father had been so arrogant and quick to anger. Marcia did not miss him at all. Try as she might to let it go, she still held onto her hatred for him, like a hot coal in the palm of her hand. It continued to hurt her no matter how she tried to heal from it. Her mother, on the other hand, had always had her pity. Marcia had never understood why a woman so quick to embrace feminism would stay with an abusive husband.

Marcia had always missed her quiet, sensible mother, even though she could never forgive her. If her mother had one unredeemable flaw, it was her inability to keep confidence from her husband. Every time Marcia had confided in her, she had run to him with the problem, as if he were the only one capable of solving it. Marcia should have known better, and her deepest regret was tied up in this knot.

Her thoughts of the past, as they had often done over the years, sent her attention spiralling into the future. She was in the mood for answers, but as things weren't set in stone, she would settle for clues. She unravelled the silk scarf that nurtured her tarot cards, enjoying their cool, smooth surfaces. They possessed a rather unlikely porcelain quality. She shuffled the deck loosely, allowing her eyes to lose focus as she went into a light trance. *Not my intent.* She told herself and the deck. *Just show me what's really there.* It was too easy to influence these things. She didn't have a particular focus, and the reading would inevitably be vague, but it would keep her mind away from the things she didn't want to think about.

As she laid the cards out in their familiar pattern, she forgot almost everything, including what each position meant. The first three lay in a triangle. The High Priestess: wisdom, the internal, sacred feminine. The Sun: self-actualisation, celebration. The Devil: resisting temptation, her own darkness.

The cards were self-explanatory, marking elements of her current situation. Four of Disks came next, depicting quiet time, reflection, claiming sacred space. Its place in the spread indicated its significance to the root of the situation. To the left was the past, the Ace of Wands: her baptism by fire, the phoenix, taking the action that led to her current life. At the top sat the Priestess of Wands, overlooking the reading with her creativity and insight into the interconnectedness of all things.

Then there was the Shaman of Cups, placed in the near future: the alchemist brewing an elixir of life. This puzzled Marcia. Was this an aspect of herself? She suspected it was someone external. Someone significant who was about to appear in her life at any moment and turn things upside down. A shiver of fear and anticipation tingled over her skin, raising goosebumps.

The final resolution card was the Ten of Disks. It showed a family and community coming together to provide support for the birthing of a child. Marcia knew it could symbolise any kind of creation, and she wondered briefly what in particular she needed this support for.

She sat back and examined the spread, tracing the connections between the cards that mapped her present life. It was possible it was all a coincidence. Even if it was, she would remain satisfied. Life was just as colourful and complex as her cards, and she liked to believe in meaningful coincidences.

29

IRIS

I ris had done all the dishes, swept the floor, and folded all the laundry. Alex's job was to put the rubbish out, and as it was a two-person household and getting him to do anything else took more effort than doing it herself, she ended up burdened with the rest of the necessary chores. She was on her way up to Alex's room with his pile of laundry when an unfamiliar noise made her stop. At first, she thought he was talking to someone, perhaps on the phone, and then she recognised the sound. Sobbing.

It struck her that she had never seen him cry, not when he'd injured himself while playing soccer, not when he'd left all his friends behind in Wellington. Not since he'd been a little boy. Lea must have done something to prompt this rare emotional display. It was the only plausible explanation, but Iris was not angry about it; if anything, she was relieved.

She didn't know when exactly it had happened, but it had become obvious. Lea had stopped calling for her son, and he had retreated into his hermitage. Thinking back, the last time she had seen Lea, her shoulders had looked more slumped and her eyes were darker, as if the light had gone out of them. Iris connected the dots; Lea's unexpected visit must have been around the time their relationship had ended.

Iris retreated down the steps, leaving the pile of clothes on the bench near them. She wanted to comfort him more than anything, but she had the feeling he would reject her. He would be embarrassed, even angry. There was no way of knowing what happened between them, but she had the feeling that it was Alex's choice. He felt power in keeping his distance; he had always been that way: untouchable. It was his way of controlling his world, and she tried to respect that.

30

MRS EVERGLADE

As the days progressed, Mrs Everglade found herself spending more and more time in a vaguely dream-like state. The things that bothered her became less important. She left the television off and enjoyed the silence. The staff came and went. Even Rex held little interest for her. She understood that she was detaching from reality. It was obvious in her dazed moments, and she questioned it in her more lucid moments. People came and spoke to her, and she did not respond. Not because she couldn't, just because she lacked the inclination. There was nothing much to hold her attention.

Detached was the word and in such a pleasant way. She had been dreading the vegetative state inevitable to those who stave off misfortune in their early life only to have it catch up with them in the end. She'd had the idea that this would be painful and boring, but the truth was far from it.

It was like an early morning dream, the kind in which time did not quite exist, at least not in any normal sense. Days slipped by her. She stopped counting them. She didn't need to keep track. She didn't seem to have any needs at all. The food that the patient order-lies spooned into her was irrelevant, unnecessary; she didn't mind either way.

At times, it seemed she was not in her body at all. She would float up above, she would circle the room, and then she would wake up to find herself being bathed or fed or spoken to. It was odd the way these moments of clarity were the only things that broke up her day, the only indication time passed at all.

LEA

L ea tore the piece of refill paper into tiny shreds, but it didn't help. Erika wasn't talking to her. Steph had given her the note at lunch and then ignored her for the rest of the break. She could hardly believe it as she read:

You're a lying bitch! I can't believe you would do this to Alex. You don't deserve him. I can't believe I trusted you.

It tore at her, but there wasn't much more damage the betrayal could possibly do. She was already beyond repair, a write-off. The rumour was that she had faked a pregnancy, that she had lied to Alex to try to get him back. In a girls' school, gossip spreads like wildfire. It was only a matter of hours before she would be a social pariah. Pregnancy was one of the most abhorrent things a girl could lie about, second only to rape.

The other problem was that she wasn't sure if she had lied or not. She knew she had lied about taking the test to get Erika off her back. She just wasn't sure if she had been pregnant, and it was too late to tell. She grappled with her conscience all morning.

It turned out that Erika had been chatting to Alex online, and this damning conspiracy theory had been spawned, making her the culprit. For once, she wanted to argue her innocence, but there wasn't a shred of evidence. She might as well have made it all up. Maybe she had. It seemed to go round and round in her head, never reaching a satisfying conclusion. Either she had lied about the test but had been pregnant, or she had lied and had not. Each situation was just as dismal, but if she had been pregnant, maybe she would be slightly more innocent.

"I don't care," Sienna had said when Lea had tried to tell her side of the story. "I'm not getting involved in this." Lea had been grateful. Losing her best friend on top of everything else that had happened was bad enough without everyone else thinking she was evil incarnate.

In history, Erika sat on the opposite side of the room next to the girls she usually mocked behind their backs, the girls who called themselves the 'A' group', as if it would clinch their popularity. Lea avoided her gaze because it burned.

"Why does she think I lied?" Lea asked Steph in maths. It didn't make sense.

"Because you can't miscarry until you're three months pregnant."

"What? *Really?* I don't think that's true." She didn't know for sure, but it didn't sound right.

Naida was more sympathetic, as Lea knew she would be. She knotted her hair, which was naturally a peculiar shade of burgundy, between her fingertips while she listened to Lea pour out the same story she had already shared with Erica, adding the new twist at the end that Erika was now spreading the malicious rumour that Lea had made it all up in a desperate plea for attention. Of course, she left out the one small detail that would damn her for sure: that she had lied about taking the test.

Naida's response was simple: "He's an asshole! I'll beat him up!"

Lea was shocked. Her friend had always seemed so quiet and self-contained. The outburst was a characteristic she'd never seen.

"You'll what?!"

"I used to in primary school," she said, matter-of-factly. "I used to beat the boys up when they were being dicks."

Lea glanced incredulously at the small frame sitting next to her, but the fierce look in Naida's eyes left her with no doubt that this was true, as preposterous as it had sounded.

"I don't think that would help, and anyway, you're out of practice." She smirked at the ridiculous nature of the conversation.

"Well, those girls are shit-heads, they're all stupid, you know that," Naida continued.

Lea nodded. It was true. She may have hung out with Erika a lot, but it was mostly a friendship of convenience rather than one of great conversation.

"Just don't listen to anything they say. Don't take it on board. You're much better than that."

At least someone was on her side in all this mess. Someone believed her. Lea wasn't sure that she deserved it, but it reassured the part of her that doubted her own validity, her own sanity, the part that wondered whether it was all just in her head, test or no test.

32

ZANE

It had been the clichéd whirlwind world tour: Paris, Moscow, Berlin, with Hawaii, Tokyo, and Sydney still to come. If Zane didn't love it so much, he would be exhausted.

Baz was getting his German eagle tattoo touched up. His back looked like the cover of Mad Magazine. He collected them as souvenirs, one from every country he visited. Mitch had seated himself at his favourite bar, chatting up the girls who would give him the time of day. Jimmy was meditating at the local Buddhist centre; later, they would walk the streets together and take in the atmosphere.

Columbiahalle was packed out but surprisingly silent. It was a more intimate gathering of 3,500 people compared to the tens of thousands that crammed into their stadium gigs. There was more of an awed murmur than a roar as the band emerged on stage. Zane signalled to the band to play their new song, and the crowd hushed. He spoke into the microphone, cupping it with both hands and enjoying the way his voice rang out and echoed around the walls as Mitch began picking a watery tune.

Each one of you has the potential to be a murderer
Each one of you has the potential to be a saint
This is what it means to be human

The base sounded to Zane like the low deep clanking of nautical chains. It was rhythmic and numbing. His voice was a spoken whisper, quick like falling rain, anchored by a matching drum beat.

Do you pray for the predator as you pray for the murderer, worse still the Jew, the atheist, the homosexual? Who decides what is natural? The murderer violates the sanctity of life. It is our choice to kill, but how free is the will of one who has been so deeply wounded they eschew their own emotion? How free to never be given the choice? People who kill others or themselves do not see a choice. If you lock them up, they are still inside you. It is time to face your own demons. The demons inside.

The crowd was swaying slightly like leaves in a breeze, taking it all in but zoning out at the same time. The music became denser, heavier as it headed into the chorus, painful and passionate.

You're in the mirror, watching them, full of disgust, of hate, of envy
When will you see through yourself?
I'm in the mirror, watching you, judging me
I am you, you are me
We are what we most despise

It was a message to society in general, although he doubted they would get it. His delirious, rapid whisper took over again.

The evil one violates you. He shits on your altar, washes his ass in holy water and has the nerve to be honest about it. He knows who he is; he doesn't pretend to be beyond rebuke. Do you hate the faggots, the Nazis, the Jews? Homo, hetero; black, white; politically correct. There is nothing so vulgar as the hypocrisy of violating one's own principles, arrogance in the face of humility, judgement in the face of forgiveness. Jesus didn't go to church. Buddha dismissed ceremony. Mohammed was a feminist. How can such beautiful compassion be worshipped by such ignorant dogma?

33

MARCIA

Marcia was restless. The group watched as she circled them, impatient to express herself. She was thinking of the phone call she had made, the inquiry. The one that she had been both dreading and dreaming of for years. She wanted to explain something to them, something she was only just coming to understand herself.

"We all go through cycles, much like the seasons. We have summers, where everything flows wonderfully. We become carefree and joyful. Then autumn comes. It sends us into a period of re-conceptualising. There are things to let go. There is always the temptation to fight the change, to keep things the way they were, but the more we resist, the harder life becomes. The winter is a still time for reflection and quiet understanding, but for some, it is dark and terrible. Sometimes we try to hold on to the past, to the comfortable and the known, but that only blocks the cycle and causes more misery. If we allow it, new light dawns. Spring comes, bringing more change in order to right the balance. We complete the cycle."

Marcia was breathless after her rant. Iris was eyeing her eagerly, with the expression of one wishing she had brought a pen and paper.

"Now," she said once she had gathered herself together. "Let's get into this heart centre."

IRIS

I t was the first time Iris had actually seen the energy centre colour. She had always tried to imagine the red of the root centre, the orange of the sacral, and the yellow of the solar plexus in her mind's eye, but the heart centre had revealed itself in dazzling emerald light. She marvelled at the beauty of it: unconditional love.

"This is the centre of pure love," Marcia had said. "Not to be confused with infatuation; it is in no way confined to the romantic. It has no limits."

Iris could feel herself opening up; she could feel the blockages melting away under this vibrant green light. She was no longer hearing Marcia's words; she was feeling them, experiencing the subtle shift in her body's energy with each one.

Take a moment to enjoy this state of openness,
This state of pure connection,
Of compassion.

From this place, you are able to understand everyone;
From this place, you can empathise with any perspective.

Now, if you are aware of any tightness, any blockages,
Allow your mind to focus there;
Feel around the edges of the blockage;
Now, gently allow yourself to enter into it,
To understand it.

This may be related to a past experience,
To a person or people;
Allow yourself to become aware.

Release anything that needs to be released.

Relax and let go of any unnecessary tension there.

Allow any wounds to heal.

You are whole.

Iris considered the contents of her mind as she sat on a large drift-wood trunk, watching the surfers twist and turn on the break below her house. Marcia's workshops had brought her a new wave of inspiration. The seasons that she had merely tolerated for most of her life were now obviously an intricate metaphor for the cycles in every person's life. She jotted her ideas into the pink flowery book she carried on walks because it fitted easily into her jacket pocket. Summer was the time when things bloomed and ripened, when life was joyous and sweet. Autumn was the time when the trees let go of their leaves, shedding baggage, preparing for their descent into winter, which was dormant, a time for resting, for peace, but also stagnation. Spring was the awakening, the new ideas, change for better or worse.

When she got home, she was still surging with a new kind of energy that the New Year seemed to have brought in. Her jubilation was overwhelming, and yet, she struggled to find the words to express it.

The English language is often inadequate for describing the complexity of emotions, but the words that we do have can be used as tools to improve our emotional state.

Here are some ideas of feelings to foster:
Love, Faith, Gratitude, Acceptance, Harmony, Serenity, Tranquillity.

Take each of these words, one by one. Turn it over in your mind. Speak it aloud to yourself. What does it conjure in you? What colour is this word in your mind? How does it feel/smell/taste/sound? How does its presence affect you? What image comes to mind? What does it mean? Can you invite it into your body? Absorb it? Experience it consciously?

What other words would you add to the list above?
How can you bring these concepts into your life in a meaningful way?

From another angle – next time you realise you are feeling good, find a word to represent the feeling.

There is beauty in simplicity. Elaborate words can clutter and complicate things and make a gaudy mockery of simple universal truths.

Having a single word as a cue can be a powerful tool in enhancing your life. When the feelings you want to experience become mentally connected with the words you give them, you can use the word to call on the feeling any time you like.

35

LEA

The internet was down, so she had no way of finding out whether what Steph and Erika said was true, so she turned to the nearest font of adult wisdom. Her mother was baking muffins for the twin's cricket fundraiser. Lea was sure it was something she had never done when *she* was younger. She sat on the breakfast bar in the immaculate kitchen and swung her legs the way she always did without thinking, in chairs that were too high for her feet to touch her ground.

"Mum?" she asked, unsure how she could possibly extract this kind of classified information without her mother knowing anything.

"Yes, darling." She wasn't really paying attention. She was too busy measuring baking soda into the blue ceramic mixing bowl Chad had bought her last Christmas.

"When you were trying to have the twins with IVF, did it always work?"

Her mother's interest was piqued. She scrambled for a way to put some space between the question and herself.

"My friend… Natalie." She doubted her mother knew more than two of her friends' names, so she assumed she wouldn't notice the made-up one. "Her parents want to have a baby, but they're old, er… older." Her mother went back to her mixing.

"Well, it did take a few tries, Leanna — Lea." She got some points for the correction. "We had a few disappointments."

"Miscarriages?" Lea asked. The word stuck to her tongue, metallic and harsh.

"I suppose so. They were quite early on in the pregnancy, so we weren't too… attached. I think it is much worse when people are used to the idea that they are having that particular baby. Then they really lose something." She brushed a brown curl from her forehead.

"So, you had miscarriages?" It was the first time Lea had heard about it. She wondered whether her mother had cried, whether Chad had. The thought was half amusing, half appalling. "How long after you knew you were pregnant?"

"Well, you must know we tried to do things… naturally before." It was obviously an uncomfortable topic. "But we never made it past a month. It was devastating at first, but then we got used to it. We were prepared for it."

So, they could happen before three months. As if in answer to her thought, her mother added, "Miscarriages usually happen in the first three months. The doctor said we shouldn't count our chickens before the first trimester was up."

Lea was relieved. She had been right. Erika was totally wrong. She got off the stool and made for her bedroom.

"Lea?" her mother called. "Tell your friend that it isn't a sure thing, but she can tell her parents to be positive – it helps."

"Thanks, Mum. I'll do that."

36

IRIS

I ris watched Alex devour his breakfast. It was entirely unappetising to her: Coco Pops with raspberry cordial. She had tried to convince him to eat something more nutritious, something other than pure sugar, starch, and food additives, but he had demanded the right to eat what he pleased and when. This particular recipe was a staple snack as well as a breakfast food. He ate silently, starring down at his plate. Her son: a human island.

Alex had never been a particularly curious child. Other mothers had complained to Iris that their children never stopped asking repetitive "But *why?*" type questions, but she had a son who would sit quietly and take it all in. She was ashamed to admit that she had taken advantage of his disposition.

He had never asked her much about his father, about how he came into the world or why he'd only ever had one parent. She had told him bits and pieces when he was younger: that they had met at university, that his father had dark hair like him, and that she hadn't seen him in a long time, but Alex had never demanded the full story. He had seemed content with his lot until he became a typical teenage boy who grunted in response to questions and occasionally sprayed deodorant on his T-shirts instead of showering.

Even with this change of disposition, he never asked questions, and so it was easier not to tell him. He barely spoke to her these days, and she had a suspicion that he was depressed. He had hardly surfaced since the summer holidays began. He spent more time than ever in front of the computer screen and rarely spoke to anyone. Iris had noticed that when he did speak, his voice had developed a slight lisp from lack of use, and this disturbed her, but when she suggested anything – sunshine, exercise, getting out of the house, socialising, seeking professional help – he would do something on the scale between rolling his eyes and ignoring her for days.

It had been her secret for so long that she was afraid to let it out. She told herself it was to protect him from rejection. She reasoned that she couldn't risk breaking their fragile relationship, but underneath this internal argument, there was also a strand of guilt. She knew he had a right to know about where he came from, the right to know both his parents. She knew she ought to provide him with the chance.

There was something else that held back her tongue. It was more of a feeling than a reason, and she knew it was steeped in selfishness.

37

LEA

L ea was relieved the school year was over. She had barely scraped through. She had a funny feeling that she had failed English, the subject that came most naturally to her, because she hadn't completed some stupid poster assignment that had nothing to do with language at all. She could blame Alex for her low grades. She had been so wrapped up in him at first and then so messed up after he dumped her, but she knew it was her own fault.

She was the only one responsible for passing or failing, for everything in her life. There was no point in feeling sorry for herself. There was already too much to feel, and she wished she didn't have to experience any of it.

Suppressed emotions
Seeping through
Bloody footprints trail along whitewashed memories
Concrete barricades secure the mind
The feelings can never break free
Temptation lurks beneath the stone
The core is molten, liquid sin
So warm within
To betray the mind is too great a task

The weeping crows shrouded in mist
The surface frozen, numbed
No pain, no life
Never again
Never again
The soul's echo bleeds
No rhythm, no harmony

"I can't deal with all the pain." Lea clutched the phone, feeling its cool, smooth plastic against her cheek, her lifeline.

"You can't block it out either – it's not healthy." Naida's familiar voice was comforting. She didn't feel so alone.

"I want to." Her voice sounded small. She didn't know if she could shut out all the emotion she felt, but it seemed like a bearable solution.

"It's part of life, you know. It makes you stronger," Naida encouraged.

"I'm not strong enough. It's too much. I'd rather be numb."

"If you suppress it, you know it will always be there, under the surface. You can't, you can't be like him. It's inhuman."

"I don't want to be human if it means feeling like this." She knew she was insufferable.

"Look, you'll get through this. He's a prick. He doesn't deserve you. You deserve much better." Naida's voice sounded slightly frustrated. They had been over this so many times already.

"I'm sorry you have to deal with me. I should go."

"It's alright. I just want you to get better."

"What should I do?" Lea felt utterly hopeless.

"Write. I love your poetry." Lea silently accepted the compliment, but it didn't resolve anything.

"If there was some way for me to block it all out, I would be better. I could just get on with my life."

"You wouldn't really be living. Life is full of pain and every other emotion. That's what makes it interesting and sad and beautiful."

Lea marvelled at her friend's wisdom. It always surprised her when everyone else seemed to be so stupid, herself included.

"You're right. I guess I'm just trying to find an easy way out of this. I guess I'll just have to learn to live with it and hope it gets better," Lea sighed.

"It will," Naida promised.

She wished she still had the memory of Alex, that it was preserved perfectly in her mind, but it was gone. The loss was piled on top of everything else, overwhelming her again.

"That bastard," she muttered to herself, hating how weak she had become. "Fucking bastard." The anger was easier to deal with when she let it out.

Shattered are the memories of our souls joining,
of our communication being almost telepathic,
of our understanding, seeming so extraordinarily uncommon
Torn are the very wings that brought my spirit to its home in your heart
Suffocated is the hope that I can let go without losing you completely
Faded are the joyous feelings I can barely remember
Tainted are the minutes, hours, days I spent with you while you promised me the world and meant nothing.

MARCIA

The pre-Christmas rush was driving Marcia insane. Crazed women in pastels swarmed every shop in town, with toddlers in tow, indulging in the capitalist spirit. Red, green, and gold were getting tediously common everywhere, and the cheerful, repetitive music made her cringe. An oppressive, muggy heat hung over Hamilton, and she had to escape.

Escape. That was the word. It was essential. It sparked a memory, which replayed vividly in her mind. Many years previously, on one of her forays around Europe, Marcia had the good fortune of meeting fellow free-spirited travellers: an exuberant woman called Estari with a mixed accent and colourful dreads and her quiet, gentle, fair-haired boyfriend. The pair had recently been to New Zealand. They had spoken with awed voices and starry tears in their eyes about a truly magical place. Marcia remembered the description as if it were yesterday, and so, with sufficient curiosity and more than a little Christmas-inspired desperation, Marcia booked tickets and prepared to journey alone to a place she had only ever heard about.

Tucked between Motueka and oblivion, Marahau was quite obviously the most beautiful place on earth. The turquoise waters and golden beaches were so tranquil they radiated peace. She had caught a flight to Nelson and been picked up by local farmers almost straight away. They were happy to drop her off in the minuscule settlement, comprised of an art gallery and two cafés.

She arrived at sunset with no idea where she would stay or what she would do there, but her feelings of insecurity melted as she inhaled the sun-warmed evening air. Music floated towards her. She investigated and found its source: a small caramel-coloured building with a crooked iron sign above it reading *Hooked on Marahau*. The round wooden tables outside indicated it was a café, and the music came from a long red-haired boy playing the guitar. She stood, listening for a while as the tune lulled her. He looked up with bright, friendly eyes that smiled. His gangly limbs reminded her of a wood nymph.

The locals were so welcoming, Marcia soon found herself at home at a table surrounded by people of various ages. Dylan, a dark-haired girl with flesh-tunnels in her ears who looked about twenty, passed Marcia a joint, and she politely passed it on, preferring to enjoy the evening through sober eyes. They were all very concerned about capitalism and the few invisible figures at the top who controlled the world.

The women at Atamarie wore bells around their ankles and yoga pants. They grew their hair long and seemed, to Marcia, to be forever smiling. It was a lovely community: an old farm, turned commune, tucked away in the forest, yet close enough to the ocean to hear its swish in the background. She had been invited there by Isaiah, the guitarist at the cafe, who often wore a curious expression when he wasn't in the possession of a cheeky grin reminiscent of a fairy-tale dryad.

He asked her about her current life, and his questions became more and more particular as he zeroed in on her past, trying to figure her out. It should have made her uncomfortable, but there, sitting under the patchy shade of the ancient pohutukawa tree flamboyantly displaying its fuzzy festive-red flowers, with the cool breeze blowing gently over her, it was impossible to feel anything bad.

"What were your parents like when you were growing up?" He seemed to wonder the question to himself. It made it less intrusive.

"My father was, well, he was abusive, emotionally and physically, and my mother..." She remembered the early greying hair that hung limply around the ever-tired face, the dull eyes that had already given up. "She just put up with it."

Isaiah nodded as if it was a story she had told him many times before. Marcia was humbled by this boy who seemed to possess wisdom well beyond his years, clearly an old soul.

"Do you plan to forgive him?" he asked it as if he was inquiring whether she planned to get up in the morning. It seemed inevitable somehow, as much as she tried to resist it. Even if she could forgive her father for his angry outbursts, his negativity that bore into her spirit, for all the times he had raged at her, leaving her physically and emotionally damaged, there was one thing she could not forgive him for.

In a Gestalt counselling workshop she had attended a year before, she had visualised herself sitting around a bonfire with an imaginary support person.

"It can be anyone," the instructor said. "Fictional or not, someone you have or have not met." She had been surprised that hers turned out to be Joan Baez. The idea was that she would face her parents in this fabricated situation, that she would express the way she had felt and say the things she was unable to communicate at the time.

She had imagined talking to her mother, telling her why she couldn't trust her, how she had needed her so badly. Tears had poured down her cheeks, and she had been grateful for the feeling of release. By the time she got to her father, she had nothing left to say.

Isaiah sat beside her, silently leafing through her tarot cards, turning each one over to admire the painted artistry. He held them out to her sheepishly.

Marcia absentmindedly cut the deck. Her card left a shocked

expression on his face. Marcia examined the card, the goddess Kali, skulls adorning her, expressing her dark power.

"Death," she said casually. "It doesn't mean I'm about to kick the bucket."

Isaiah relaxed. "It's just a bit…"

"It's transformation," Marcia assured him. "Great change. That's where I'm headed."

39

IRIS

The room was dusky red from the street lights that shone through the scarlet curtains. She could make out the curves of his body, the satisfying muscles of his abdomen, his ribs, his collar bone that stretched across those wide shoulders. She lunged playfully, taking control, enjoying the dizzying feeling of the moment. From her position, she had no concept of where he was. She tried to bring herself to climax, but the dominant part of her awakened, wanted to maintain control, so she receded enfolded in his arms. He rolled her over. She was overcome with a carnal need, red, emanating from her, arachnic. Pulling him closer, engulfing him. She finished in starry black oblivion, cathartic, waiting for him to come. As she lay there, she felt the inner hunger she had been unable to satisfy. A need that was bound up in her physical nature, in her very being.

The guilt took over as she remembered her contraceptives sitting in the bottom of her bag. The same pills she had chosen not to take for days because it seemed the only way to get what she wanted.

Iris awoke with that same guilty feeling she had experienced in her dream. It was quite possibly the strangest one she'd ever had because it was an exact memory, repeating in her mind with no interruptions, no cryptic bananas or symbolic lampshades. It had been so clear in that it could have been yesterday's memory, but she knew, as she came to her senses, that seventeen years had elapsed since, and she was not that same naïve girl. She now realised her actions had come back to haunt her.

When Iris was eight months pregnant with Alex, swollen and sweaty, she had arrived on her parent's wisteria-laden veranda with a backpack. Her doting father and anxious mother took her in and waited on her hand and foot despite her resistance. She was forbidden from hanging laundry or helping with the milking. Her mother bought her women's magazines filled with tedious gossip about celebrities and made her cups of tea while she scoffed at the way the sensationalist headlines masked thin stories with watery evidence.

It was a couple of easy and mindless few weeks as her body gradually became more and more difficult to manoeuvre, and she was bored stiff. She spent the last few agonising days before her due date, hoping the baby would be early. Unfortunately, he had different ideas.

It was three very slow days later that it started: a strange ringing pain in her tail bone woke her from a heated dream. It was still dark outside, and suddenly, she was wide awake and relieved that change was finally happening. Fifty contractions later, each one progressively more intense, her body took over, and through its own organic vibration, Alex was born.

He was the strangest thing she had ever seen, pink and slimy, and surreal. He cried from the moment he was born and hardly stopped except to eat and sleep. Despite her sleep deprivation and shattered emotional state, she left her parent's house three weeks later.

She knew being a solo mother was going to be hard; she had expected it, but the expectation didn't make it any less difficult. Every day, she gave up and buried her head in her hands in desperation, and every day, she smiled at his tiny curling toes or his sharp little fingernails. She worshipped his soft, tender skin and looked into his blue-grey eyes in a staring competition that he always won.

She wondered about the kind of person he would become, and she never regretted the decision she had made.

Sixteen years later, she found herself standing on that very same veranda with a teenager in tow. Her parents had asked her and Alex to celebrate Christmas with them, even though it was her turn to host, because they didn't want to travel the extra couple of hours to her new residence. This turned out to be a fortunate coincidence because the owners of Iris's house had requested its use for the two weeks around Christmas and New Year's. Alex had wanted to stay home with his computer, but there were some family occasions that even he couldn't escape.

Her parents rushed out to greet her. The joy in their faces didn't stop Iris from noticing that her mother, in her lilac twin suit, was limping slightly and her father's hair had become completely white. It must have been a hard year. Iris looked down as her mother hobbled over to her.

"Oh, it's nothing, dear, just a little arthritis. Don't you worry."

They both marvelled over Alex's height, claiming he had grown a foot. Iris estimated it had actually been a few inches, but she allowed them to fuss over him.

They sat around the old oak dining table from Iris's youth. When she was younger, her mother had guarded its polished surface with her life. The children were forbidden to let anything come in direct contact with it, but over the years, it had been marked by the reality of family life, and it now stood unprotected, bearing its many scars for all to see.

"So you're still working on the... book?" her mother asked tentatively. Iris knew her parents had disapproved of her sudden lifestyle change, and it was still a touchy subject. She smiled politely.

"Yes. I'm halfway through it, actually."

Her father, who was usually a tolerant man, had only a few things that he was truly bigoted about. "And it's about what? Crystals, was it? Or fairies?"

She knew he did not mean to insult her; anything spiritual was just beyond him, and he had no time for it. He shook his head.

"It's about ways of thinking that make life easier, Dad. I want to teach people to change their perspectives so that they are happier."

"Huh, well, whatever makes you happy, Rissy," he coughed. "I'll believe it when I see it," he muttered under his breath.

He had grown up in a generation in which the rules were dictated by science alone, and anything that was unable to be proven was automatically dismissed.

Iris sighed, remembering why she didn't visit her parents often. It was exhausting. She took refuge in the platter of juicy watermelon her mother had set on the table. *Why is it...* she thought. *That no matter how much you love the people who raised you, they are always impossible to live with?*

40

LEA

Lea escaped her family Christmas when tipsy Chad started to sing old Beatles songs. It was too embarrassing to endure. She wasn't in much of a mood for festivities. She was in mourning. She still struggled with her guilt and pain on a daily basis – over Alex, the baby question mark, and the lie about the test. She took refuge in her usual way by writing the poetry that made her feel worthwhile. She could admire the words, the way they flowed together, the rhythm that made more sense than the swirling, sinking thoughts that crowded her mind. Poetry allowed her feelings to tumble out, mingling with her tears, staining the white page. It seemed to make more room in her mind for herself.

Track me down
Through the anonymous whispers of my mind
Draw me out
Of the deep recesses and echoing abysses of my core
Aim as though we were the only beings to ever exist
Pull the trigger
Destroy your only hope of resuscitation
For what you fear most is your freedom.

I can't let go of the ledge, the crumbling pillar, the remains of something beautiful, the ruins of our relationship. Splinters of the glorious chandelier sparkle around me, taunting me with the memories, the light that you reflected, from unseen windows, the happiness your love brought into my life... I need to move on, but my eyes are still closed shut, my teeth clenched. Nothing is really here... it is all a state of mind.

Lea hated that it was like some kind of soap opera. *When the one you love can't love you and you can't love anyone else.* She had spent the last week doing the bare minimum, hoarding her energy. Perhaps it was laziness, as Chad always accused her, but she also hesitated to throw anything else away, to release anything. Like an animal born to captivity, she wanted to stay in her cage, her comfort zone. She couldn't risk losing anything else. She wished her parents would leave her alone. She wished the world would let her be.

41

MRS EVERGLADE

Mrs Alice Everglade felt as if she were exactly one inch above her body. It was an odd feeling because she was particularly lucid. She could hear the birds outside, the murmurs of conversation echoing from the rooms around her. She was perfectly aware, and yet, the room seemed dark. She could barely see beyond the light her body was omitting.

The sensation was as if she were burning up in the brightness, becoming lighter and lighter. Suddenly her body tightened, grasping at her, a stranglehold. She couldn't breathe, and the pain was agonising. She could hear a loud panicked beeping, the sound of the nurses' shoes brushing the carpet as they ran in, their frantic breathing and decisive voices. Then in a flash, she was free. The body had relaxed; it lay beneath her, no longer hers. She reached out and immediately floated up above the building, so vast that nothing could contain her. Wonderful. She had no more attachments to that place, to that body that had burdened her for so long.

But there was one place she still wanted to be. One last time.

She could see everything much more clearly now, even clearer than before her cataracts had clouded, making her world dim. She could observe every drop of dew glistening around her in the early morning light, hear them as they fell from leaves to meet the earth. She could feel the presence of every chorusing bird, every insect. It was more than just an enhanced sensory experience; she could feel everything inside-out, every atom, and she was connected with it all.

She was overcome by sudden joy, and an idea occurred to her. Her invisible form drifted down to the level of the grassroots. She lay there, sensing the essence of every blade, looking up at the perfect newborn sky in ecstasy.

42

LEA

It was New Year's Eve. It seemed to Lea that neither she nor Alex cared. She had persuaded her parents to let her bring the computer to the beach house where she was to be trapped with her family from Boxing Day to sometime after New Year's. She wished they would have just let her stay home rather than ruin the celebration with her dark mood. Fireworks interrupted her train of thought. She looked up to see them glitter over the sea. It was pretty, she supposed, but that didn't change anything. She looked over at the side of the coast that disappeared in the darkness. Somewhere in that direction, Alex was sitting at his computer, ignoring the world.

She loathed the boredom associated with dial-up internet, but it was all she could get out here in the middle of nowhere. She eventually gave up. What did it matter if Alex was online? He didn't bother to reply to her anymore, and the pages just took too long to load. There wasn't any point. She picked up her notebook instead and sought a quiet place outside.

She settled in a corner of the deck and noticed that the natural world was still as peaceful as it always was. She could see the glorious moon above her. It glinted off the waves, which she could hear as they crashed in the background, oblivious to this ridiculous human celebration. She could hear gleeful shrieks from down below.

Her terrible twin brothers were far too excited. It was just another day. She decided she might as well do something traditional anyway; she had nothing else to write about.

New Year's Resolutions

This year I will get over Alex
I will be my own person
I will make a decent attempt at school

She wondered briefly whether these were true, then decided that New Year's resolutions weren't about being reasonable. They were supposed to be idealistic.

I resolve to be comfortable with myself
To value my own opinion
To love myself

It seemed perfectly simple, yet perfectly impossible. She knew it was what she was supposed to do. How could anyone else love her if she didn't love herself? But she had put so much effort into self-loathing that it seemed an insurmountable task to undo it all. She felt exhausted, so she looked out at the midnight blue sea and the stars that speckled the sky. She inhaled deeply.

This year I want

A fresh start
Inner peace
Hope

43

ZANE

Zane had always liked Hawaii. It was slightly too warm and just a tad too humid, but the air seemed to be eternally sweet, full of the scent of tropical fruit or flowers. The rest of the band was out at the Aloha Flea Market. Baz was looking for the Tattooist who had inked a frangipani lei around his wrist, and Mitch and Jimmy were hungry. Zane could imagine them sitting outside a caravan, eating burgers, Mitch commenting on Hawaiian women while Jimmy made enlightened remarks about life, having the same conversation on completely different levels.

The temperature made him so comfortable that he was in an almost dream-like state as he entered the air-conditioned apartment block where his old friend lived. The artificial cold seemed to wake him up a bit, and he was pleased to find that Mike had his balcony doors wide open, letting the charming warmth back in.

"Hey, man." Mike hugged him. "So good to see you. It's been ages."

"Two years too long," Zane responded warmly. Pleased to be in the familiar company of one of the few people he felt entirely comfortable around.

"What's up?" Mike asked casually, but his eyes were more serious.

"You know, the usual... Making albums, touring the world," Zane bragged. "What about you?"

"Just working on this new zine."

Mike had started out as a nobody, a little fish in the big pond of the comic world, but his bizarre storylines and quirky sense of humour had paid off. His comic *Duran the Gay Umbrella* had gathered an underground following. He had followed it with titles such as *Grandma's Sexy Demon Teapot* and *The Washing Machine that Swung Both Ways*. Now he had a handful of regular strips, several graphic novels (emphasis on the graphic) and a couple of quarterly themed magazines. He filled Zane in on the newest one: a magazine catering to an audience in the distant future.

"So, it has its own sci-fi universe!" His enthusiasm was infectious, and Zane found himself smiling animatedly as Mike showed him some sketches.

"I have reason to believe," Mike said, half-serious, "that there is something that has been bothering you of late." They were eating sliced star fruit and doughnuts for brunch.

"How would you come to a conclusion like that?" Zane was only slightly defensive.

"My spidey-sense tingled when you walked in, and I saw the expression on your face."

"It's nothing. Everything's fine."

"Yeah, right. I know you better than that, man. Spit it out."

"Well..." There was something, but Zane wasn't sure exactly what it was.

"I knew it! It's a girl," Mike exclaimed rapturously. Zane was puzzled.

"There are no girls."

"Not at the moment? Well then, it's *that* girl." Zane knew who he meant, but he played innocent anyway.

"You know damn well who I mean. Shit, I knew this was going to catch up with you sometime. You can't leave stuff like this in the past; you have to deal with it."

"She was the one who stopped talking to me."

"Did you ever wonder why? Maybe she had a good reason."

"I didn't do anything."

"Well, maybe that's your problem."

Zane felt defeated.

"Or maybe…" Mike continued. "Maybe the situation was just more complex than you realised."

"What are you? Some kind of psychic?" Mike always surprised him this way.

"Well, I have been called all-knowing, all-powerful and godlike before." He batted his eyelashes.

Zane balled up a doughnut wrapper and tossed it at his friend's face. "You didn't see that one coming, did ya?"

44

MARCIA

Marcia settled into the old duck-down duvet she had been lent and looked around at the oppressive paisley wallpaper, laughable in gold and red. It was now closing in on her. She often got peculiar feelings in old villas such as this. This one had the misfortune of being redecorated in the most garish part of the 1970s.

Marcia had sometimes wondered about ghosts when she'd had strange feelings in darkened hallways or when she was alone in unfamiliar rooms. At times, she had seen movement out of the corner of her eye, but she reasoned it was just her overactive imagination. Strong winds shook the house, making the old wood creak.

She had been sleeping in the top bunk of the 'guest-room' at Atamarie. Other travellers had come and gone in the week she had been there. Violet, an effervescent girl with wavy, honey-coloured hair, had staked a claim on the bed below her, but for the moment, she was out, probably still around the open fire, chatting with the guys who spent night after night rhythmically beating their drums. Marcia strained to hear their tribal sound that usually drifted over to the house, but the night was silent.

The room had a feeling as if it were watching her. It was stronger now that she was alone in this place that was yet to be familiar. What she felt was not fear so much as a feeling that she was more intimately close to something *unknown* than she was comfortable with.

She had a few theories about ghosts. She didn't think it was very common at all that an actual human spirit would be trapped on this earth, captive. She had a feeling that only the most tortured soul would want to torture themselves even more with the memories of their awful time here, for surely, the afterlife was a much easier place to be.

Rooms held emotional residue from the living. It was the same energy that most people could sense if they walked into a room full of fresh conflict or of joy, and that energy didn't just vanish into thin air. Energy is not easily created or destroyed; it simply changes form. Old houses were full of emotional history, and it was this she felt exposed to: the remnants of hundreds of strangers who had come and gone.

The walls seemed to be closing in around her, their patterns warping in a sinister way. Although she knew it was irrational, the fear built up, such a dastardly emotion. It crept up her chest to her neck, threatening to choke her. She couldn't move; she didn't dare try. Every shadow was an enemy, dark and malevolent. Her rational mind became so frustrated, she started to ponder the evolutionary reason for such a ridiculous manifestation of emotion. Thousands of years before, the dark truly would have been a dangerous thing. In the wild world full of unseen predators, every shadow could have held potential death. The adrenaline pumping through her body would have protected her if she were alive back then, but now, it was nothing more than a hindrance to a good night sleep.

At precisely the wrong moment, she realised her bladder was full. She wouldn't be able to sleep until she did something about it, but she was paralysed by fear. She lay awake until her bodily urges overcame the counter-productive emotion. Then she dragged herself up. She felt her way along the walls of the dark hallway, through the front door and crept carefully over the uneven terrain between the old farmhouse and the long drop that sufficed for a toilet; the little wooden structure that supported a toilet seat over a deep hole in the earth. Her way was lit only by the crescent moon's light, and crickets jeered at her through the warm night air. Even in daylight, it was a horrid affair, an intimate reminder that she was not cut out for such simple living. She held her breath for as long as possible, grateful that these people invested in toilet paper, even if it was the unbleached, recycled kind that broke up too easily. She dipped her hands in the bucket of tea tree water outside to disinfect them. Feeling peace and sanity return, she was grateful.

The hallway seemed much tamer on the way back. She scolded herself for being so easily frightened. Her self-flagellation was interrupted by a creaking noise which jolted the fear back into her reality. She stood stock-still until the moment passed. It could have been something carelessly balanced, finally falling down in the kitchen. She continued, more carefully this time, and then hastened as the fear caught up until she smacked right into something hard.

"Ow!" The object seemed enraged.

"Oh, sorry." Marcia was secretly relieved that it was a person rather than anything scarier.

"Marcia?" The voice sounded gentle now.

"Isaiah?" The familiarity was calming. Everything was black except for the glint of his eyes reflecting off some distant light source. She realised his hand was still on her arm, and he made no attempt to let go. Something mischievous stirred inside her. She leaned in, mostly out of curiosity. She felt the air fill with intimacy as their energy mingled. Her logical mind erupted in a barrage of accusations. She was too old for this. She was a widow. He was barely an adult. What would William think? But all thoughts vanished when he stepped closer and the side of her face came to rest against his warm, bare chest. His energy was older than his body, still and calm. She drank it in, and it was enough for a moment, just to be there, not alone.

His other arm wound its way around her waist, and the stillness was interrupted by instinct. She could feel something orange and fiery stirring inside her, something carnal and unfamiliar to her solitary existence.

She let him guide her, almost carry her, to the nearest bunk. The springs squeaked embarrassingly under their weight. It wasn't too late to stop. His skin was warm and supple, so young compared to hers, which she had noticed becoming more papery and speckled as the years progressed. It was so wrong, too wrong, but there was a part of her that rejoiced in the freedom of doing something she shouldn't. It was a strong urge, too exciting to resist.

She let the feelings wash over her as he wrestled with their clothes, overwhelming her as the barriers between them were removed. She let her mind go blank.

45

LEA

The pain she couldn't control was unbearable; the pain she could control was delicious. She could empathise with the girls she had seen at school with scars right up their arms from cutting. Lea was slightly jealous of their bravery. She didn't have the guts to pierce her own skin, not for lack of trying. It was apparently the latest teenage thing, according to the documentary ad her mother had shuddered over. Lea had caught her mother surreptitiously checking her wrists − checking up on her without trying to make it obvious. The fact that she couldn't even work up the nerve to kill herself made her feel even more pathetic. It would be better for everyone if she wasn't around to rain on their parade.

All conversations with Alex seemed to go around in circles. She would try to pick his mind apart, to burst the bubble of insolence, to find something that resembled the way he had been.

Lea: you're so apathetic!
Alex: I am aware of that
Lea: but if you don't care about anything then you can't change it, you can't do anything at all, it's pointless, it's stupid
Alex: heh. I suppose
Lea: so you admit apathy is stupid?

Alex: sure, I guess
Lea: that makes you stupid
Alex: in line with your reasoning
Lea: but you hate stupid people
Ales: yes, I do

She seemed to have won something, but she didn't know what, and although it gave her some satisfaction, it hadn't done anything to change his state of mind, which was what she really wanted to do.

46

IRIS

I ris had been feeling out of sorts since she returned from her
parent's house. It wasn't the severe summer heat—the sea breeze
took care of most of that—it was the feeling of loneliness. She
hadn't made many new friends in Raglan, and she missed always
having someone to talk to at work. She found herself pining for a
social life, and her mind would circle around the only good friend
she had made in the last few months: Marcia. She was probably
back from her holiday in the South Island, but Iris didn't want to
pester her.

It was a strange feeling; a little like homesickness, a little like
addiction. Iris would find herself thinking of Marcia often, in childlike obsession. It was something she hadn't experienced in years, like
a childhood crush or youthful fixation. The pattern was so circular.
Iris pondered it every time it came up; she found herself writing
little emotional poems or contriving songs in her head, distin-
guishing her boundaries and her needs. She loved Marcia dearly,
even worshipped her a little, but it wasn't as if she needed more
from their friendship.

One evening, as she was taking a sunset walk, it struck her that
this was exactly the same pattern she had dealt with years before,
around the time she met Alex's father, the same mental circles and

longing sighs. It was an emotional problem she needed to heal. *I am open to this healing. I am open to being whole.* She retraced the threads of memory. *What did I do last time?* It was obvious. *I am independent.* It was as if a key had been turned in a lock. The affirmation made her feel lighter, more herself. She could feel all the energy that had been leaching out return to her. Every time the lonely feelings returned, she reminded herself: *I am independent. I am whole.*

47

LEA

Lea left school early because there was no point in staying for science. There was no point in anything, really. Missing classes in the first week was a dangerous precedent, but she didn't care. Escaping the oppressive institutional atmosphere made her feel lighter. For a moment, she forgot the horrible state of her life, but only for a moment. She crossed the road into the park where students often smoked before school and nestled into a shady spot in the small clump of trees in its centre. She pulled out her notebook and lit a cigarette.

For the first time in this lonely existence, I thought I had found someone who could understand me. I guess I'm just deluded. Maybe I deserve this, maybe I did something truly awful in a past life and this suffering is some kind of penance. I wish the Goddess could absolve me. I wish I could dissolve into nothingness. Anything would be better than this torture. When I talk to him, it's like he's not really there, like there's a wall between us that I can never breakthrough. Maybe it was all in my head. Maybe I was made for darkness and despair.

Her friends had all had enough of her lamentations. There wasn't anything they could do. She didn't bother to talk about it anymore, but it was the main occupant of her mind. The person she had fallen in love with was gone. All that was left was a shell, and it haunted her. She tried everything to bring him back. She had pleaded and begged, she had threatened and even insulted him to no avail. She had spent hours in the stupid chatroom he loved so much, bored out of her mind, waiting for an opportunity to get through to him. Nothing. It only frustrated her more. She wished she didn't love him. Life would be so much easier. She wanted to move on, but she didn't know how.

If she had access to better drugs, she would be a junkie by now. Pot seemed just to numb her senses while it made her head spin repetitively. Cigarettes made her feel dirty, not that it stopped her from relying on them for a moment's distraction.

Her mother had eyed her suspiciously when she came home, smelling like an ashtray, but she insisted it was from someone standing next to her at the bus stop, and her hands feigned innocence, thanks to the fake flower smell of the syrupy, public toilet pump soap.

"Lea?" It was the edgy voice her mother reserved for interrogations.

"Yes, mum?" She wondered what she'd done this time.

"You listen to that band they talked about on the news, don't you? It's named after a tool, a spanner or something?"

"Wrench?"

"Yes, that's it. They say that they're leading young people astray, giving them terrible ideas like with the high school shootings."

"Oh… Weird," Lea said. She hadn't been expecting that one. "I thought people could think for themselves."

"Leanna – don't speak to me that way," her mother snapped. Then her voice softened from guilt. "I'm only concerned about you; you haven't been yourself lately."

"Well, I'll try to remember not to take a gun to school or commit any violent acts. Mum. Really, you have nothing to worry about, it's just music. They don't even say anything *that* bad." Her mother looked unconvinced, but she managed to drop the subject.

MARCIA

The bowl of cherries sat invitingly on the kitchen counter, a tribute to New Zealand produce if Marcia had ever experienced one. It was the first thing she had arranged upon her return home. She had placed the succulent stone fruit one by one into her favourite green ceramic dish, feeling jovial. They were such a deep red, almost black, and when her teeth broke into their crisp flesh, the juice was a darker, thinner blood. She ate them one-by-one, enjoying the juicy meat as it orbited her mouth, the sweet, erotic fullness of their flavour that quenched the back of her throat, the satisfaction that lingered under her tongue. It was such a sensual experience it almost left her feeling slightly guilty.

There was so much to do. Marcia began by toiling with the weeds, pulling out stubborn grass by the root, the summer heat bearing down on her. The garden was drying up, and it seemed unfair that these weeds prospered in the worst conditions. Given a chance, they could outgrow her tomatoes in a few weeks, and she had been away almost that long. She rested her head in her hands, moistening them with sweat. She could hear the lawns being mowed next door, and the scent of newly-cut grass drifted over the fence in the hot, humid air.

She returned to her work. The tomatoes were yielding bright-red fruit, juicy, sweet, and tangy. The birds had gotten to a few of them, but there were plenty more to come as long as she watered the drooping plants and took care of the weeds. It gave her a satisfying feeling, collecting the produce that was ready for harvest. It was, quite literally, productive.

As she trotted back up the garden path, laden with the luscious red orbs, she heard the lawnmower cut out and a voice called to her over the fence.

"Excuse me, Ma'am." He was tall and wiry with bristly, greying hair.

"Yes?" She felt slightly ridiculous, clutching the tomatoes to her chest.

"I was just wondering… I've always wondered about the owners of this house."

"It belonged to my parents," she said. The words tasted metallic, rusty on her tongue.

"Oh, it's just that these two properties…" He gestured back to Mrs Everglade's fairy-tale garden. "They would make a great investment."

One of those people, Marcia thought. She had ignored the real-estate brochures and letters, responded bluntly, and hung up on the phone calls. She politely rejected the women in high heels and heavy makeup who had braved the potholes of her driveway to ask if she would consider selling.

"It's a *family* house," she said, emphasising the word and wondering who could possibly fit into this category with her.

"Oh, I see," he said, looking down. "I didn't mean to offend you. It's just that with Mrs Everglade passing away… I wondered."

Marcia could feel the blood drain out of her face as she paled.

"Passed away? She…"

"In the home – two weeks ago, I think." He was solemn. "I've been mowing these lawns for twenty-odd years. Her nieces asked me to keep mowing them, at least, until they decide what to do."

Marcia just nodded, too stunned to speak.

As soon as she was back in the safety of the house, she dropped the tomatoes. She watched them roll away from the careless gesture. Her neighbour, who had seemed just as ancient in her childhood as she did when Marcia had returned home, who had seemed like a permanent fixture over the fence, was gone.

Marcia had not seen her for weeks, possibly months, but that was not unusual. Mrs Everglade spent a lot of time inside, watching loud television, but as she came to think of it, Marcia had not noticed the muffled sound of talk shows for a while. How could she have been so ignorant? They were two of a kind: both lonely women, both self-sufficient, both strong. Now it seemed, Marcia was destined to the same fate: to die alone in a rest home, watching rubbish on television, with no one to visit her, no one to care.

The emotion spiralled into tears, which burst uncontrollably from her eyes. The injustice of it. That poor woman, who loved nothing more than her garden, had to leave her home and be amongst strangers, with no privacy, with no trees or flowers or birds.

She shook as she cried. It was the kind of uncontrollable sobbing she thought only children were capable of.

They were both gardeners, both widows, and although they'd hardly spoken to each other and they could not be considered friends, Marcia felt a kind of kinship with this other solitary individual.

Now the quarter-acre section next door, the biggest property other than hers in the entire neighbourhood, would no doubt be sold to developers who would strip it of all its beauty and replace it with ugly townhouses.

It was then that she realised that there was a far greater amassment of grief inside her. She had shed tears since William's death, out of frustration, out of anger and fear, over leaving her home, over her childhood, but she had not cried like this. She was surprised that she had not noticed this endless well of loss; she had wrapped it up so tightly and then ignored it. It was almost a year since his passing, since her life changed so completely. She had hardly dared to think about it.

That poor woman. If Marcia had only known, she could have at least visited her. She could have taken her home to the garden for a little while, so she didn't have to spend her last days in a holding cell for the soon-to-be-deceased.

She felt as if she had been crying for hours. She had lost track of time when she finally felt the comforting brain chemicals kick in, the ones that lulled upset children to sleep. It was only then that she was aware of the relief her neighbour must have felt, finally free of her decrepit body, and Marcia knew exactly where she would go. She began to chortle with hysterical laughter as she imagined the ghost of Mrs Alice Everglade prancing around the flowerbeds next door.

49

ZANE

It always confused Zane, crossing hemispheres. He had expected Japan to be on the verge of winter, the persimmon trees with their naked branches and plump orange fruit stalked by sinister birds. But of course, the season he had left behind was the opposite of the one he was entering into. Winter was long gone, and the summer air was thick and hot.

"What the hell is this? A paparazzo convention?" Baz was commenting on the crowd of journalists milling around their Tokyo hotel entrance.

"Looks like you're finally famous, man. It's what you've always wanted," Zane teased in a voice full of false emotion. As successful as they had become, being ambushed by reporters was not usually a part of their daily life. This must have been someone else's welcoming committee.

"Whoever it's for, they've drawn an international circus." Jimmy was commenting on the BBC and CNN vans parked on the side of the curb. These journalists weren't just Japanese; they were from all over.

As their limo pulled up, the faces looked their way, eagerly trying to get a peek at who was inside. Zane didn't want to disappoint them. After all, they were only a band, not a global embezzling businessman or the British royal family or billionaire mass murderers. As they got close to the lobby, a dozen dark-haired men in black suits emerged and formed a kind of tunnel between the limo and the front doors.

"This is weird," Mitch said. "It's like we're in a film or something."

Zane was overcome by the feeling of wanting to stay in the car. The whole situation gave him a sickening feeling. But he had little choice; Baz was already opening the door. The crowd stirred expectantly.

As they emerged, Zane realised how wrong he had been. They were assaulted by hundreds of shouted questions and bright camera flashes. He only caught snippets of the words as they were pelted at him.

"...influence on young people..."

"...committing violent acts?"

"...school shootings?"

"...teen suicide?"

It was a barrage of accusations, thinly disguised as journalism. The bolshie reporter who had ambushed him months before had been barely an aperitif compared to this banquet of blame.

"Fucking Socrates, all over again," Jimmy said, but his voice sounded more pleasantly surprised than angry.

"So, a bunch of kids in America, the country, which has the worst gun record in the *civilised* world, kill themselves and others, and everyone blames a band?" Baz was perplexed.

Zane laughed. "Since when did you expect the media to make sense?" It was, of course, a rhetorical question.

"It seems like this one's been brewing for a while." Jimmy was as thoughtful as usual. "It's just all coming up to the surface, and we happened to get caught in the middle."

"Yeah, is it our fault that young people like our music?" Mitch's temper was starting to flare. "Maybe we should stick to gooey love songs and themes like rainbows and ponies from now on. Maybe we should be censored just because we dare to voice the things that other people think but are too afraid to say out loud. Those fecking vultures are trying to destroy us for their own selfish benefits, and the politicians and parents are just looking for someone to blame so that it's not their fault."

"You should write that down, man. It would make great lyrics." Zane was always more impressed by Mitch's opinions when he was angry.

"So, what do we do?" Baz asked sheepishly.

"We wait," Jimmy said simply. Unlike the others, he was perfectly calm. "We carry on with our business, we don't fuel their fire, and we wait for it to all blow over as all insubstantial things do."

Zane's mind was racing. Society's idiocy was always the perfect fuel for his creativity. He shut himself away in his hotel bedroom with a pen, paper, and silence.

Interesting, how we deny all that we fear; death, decay, destruction. The other side of the cycle; the leaves rust and fall leaving the trees naked in mourning, annuals wilt into nothingness. Sometimes the plants you love die unexpectedly, converted into grotesque skeletons, beyond your control. It is all over the news: murder, loss, unfairness, like baby birds fallen from the nest too soon. We find them when we don't want to, plastered to the pavement.

Tragedy. We hide it away. We hide from it. We pretend we are absolved, inno-cent. We are good; they are bad: murderers, rapists, criminals. Them, these cats, who bring us presents of misfortune, unwanted corpses at our back doors... We find a scapegoat for our own evil. We ignore our own potential for such obscene acts, but the corpses are rotting all around us. We can always blame someone else. In truth, we all possess these potentials. They are facets of humanity; if they were truly beyond us, we would not see them at all. Pretending not to see only makes us liars.

50

IRIS

I ris was relieved that Alex was back at school. At least, it guaranteed that for most of the day, he wasn't sitting in front of the computer monitor. With him gone, the house seemed to have a more open atmosphere. She felt a bit more comfortable and a lot less worried. This freed her mind enough to let her writing flow. She settled down in front of her laptop with half a papaya and a spoon, scooping the sweet flesh into her mouth between bouts of typing.

Forgiveness can be challenging. If someone has hurt you badly, from that injured place, you may feel that they do not deserve your forgiveness. After all, they were in the wrong. This may be a reasonable, logical thing to think, but holding on to past pain will only make you suffer more. Your anger may or may not affect the other person. They have their own life to live and their own lessons to learn.

Forgiveness is not necessarily about letting someone else off the hook. I see it as a way that you can set yourself free of your pain, to acknowledge that whatever transpired is now in the past and that you are willing and able to move on into a better, brighter future.

This may be easier said than done. Many people get to the point where they feel they would like to forgive and move on, but they feel unable to get beyond the

*anguish of their past trauma. Knowing something intellectually and actually
living it are two very different things. In order to forgive, you must accept the past
and let it go. If you are able to summon the feeling of acceptance, this is a step in
the right direction.*

*Think about the person or people associated with the pain you still feel. Now,
begin to consider this person (or people, one at a time). Think about where they
learnt the hurtful behaviour that you experienced from them. It is likely that they
had a painful childhood. You may know about this already; if you don't know
much, allow your mind to guess. Every person on this planet was born innocent
and perfect, full of openness and love. Somewhere along the way, they learnt that
they could be hurt, and from the people around them, they learnt ways of
protecting themselves. When we hurt other people, it is usually while trying to
protect ourselves from further pain. As you begin to understand the person who
has caused you pain, you can begin to feel compassion, and from that compassion, you can allow yourself to feel love. In the spirit of this love, you can accept
and let go. This may be a slow process, but it is a healing one. If you allow
yourself to feel love and compassion instead of pain and resentment, you will
become healthier and happier in all aspects of your life.*

Iris took a moment to reflect on the words she had written. Even
though it was all true, she struggled with some parts. It wasn't easy.

As she was growing up, her older siblings seemed to take great
pleasure from teasing her. They took advantage of her emotional
sensitivity and seemed to revel in her tears. Her parents ignored
them, for the most part. *Kids will be kids.* Sometimes her father even
joined in, and her mother did nothing, making Iris feel that a
terrible injustice was being done to her and the people who were
meant to protect her were actually hurting her more.

It seemed trivial to look back on something like this in her childhood. She usually dismissed it as such, but that did not disperse the
pain. Compared to other people, she'd had a good childhood. She
hadn't been physically abused, she'd rarely been hit or shouted at,
she was always well-fed and clothed and kept safe. But even in
acknowledging all these things, she still held tightly to the injustices

that had occurred. She hardly had any contact at all with her two brothers and one sister, and there was a definitive emotional distance between her and her parents. She hadn't created this intentionally, but perhaps she had subconsciously.

She shook herself, willing herself to be rational. Following her own advice, she tried to understand her family. Her siblings had always resented her status as the youngest child. They had probably learnt from the other children at school how to tease and bully her and also learnt this from her father. He had always enjoyed seeing other people hurt themselves. This was something that Iris had never understood. His childhood had been a hard one. He had told her stories of sharing a bed with five of his ten siblings. They had all competed ravenously for their mother's kind attention. His father had been a violent alcoholic. Iris could imagine the darkness in that childhood, the fear and pain, and never having enough. The empathy seemed to burn right through her, painfully stripping away her indignation. She could understand him, the poor little boy who never had any lunch at school, who was teased by the other kids for being dirty. She could understand how his pain had caused her pain. The sadness she felt was strangely beautiful. Tears welled up in her eyes, and she could feel love instead of the anger and pain that once dominated this aspect of her childhood.

She accepted it and let it go in a wonderful rush of freedom.

51

MARCIA

It was too hot to go for a walk, and Marcia knew this, but she stubbornly refused to listen to reason. She was drenched in sweat but sick of the summer inactivity. The dryness in her throat craved the cool cucumber sitting at home in her fridge as she trudged through the neighbourhood. She turned into Miranda Crescent, the street that once won all the garden awards for its neatly trimmed hedges and magnificent floral sprays. The gardens looked neglected now. New people busy with their careers had probably moved in as the time-rich generation of elderly couples and stay-at-home wives had moved on. She scrutinised the dismal lawns, browned by the dry summer and edged with mediocre ornamental shrubs. She passed a modern Japanese-style garden with bonsai trees and neat bamboo fences, admiring the water feature that looked like a miniature temple. Some people, at least, had time to make their garden beautiful.

What could have been a breeze but felt more like a heatwave blew into her, bringing with it a familiar smell. Her mind was blank for a moment, then she remembered. Gardenias.

William hated gardenias…

… the wave of grief hit her, but this time, she was ready to think about him again.

After William died, the phone had kept ringing. Voices had bombarded her day and night, although she barely heard them. His relatives, their friends, colleagues, people she hardly knew, all suddenly spoke to her in gentle, intimate voices. They all asked how she was. Most of the time, she barely responded, nodding at the receiver dumbly as if they could see her through it, staring at nothing. The funeral director had materialised out of thin air. She was unsure how he was hired. He spoke to her about coffins and songs and clothing. He asked her who would speak and what kind of food she would like provided. Every time he called, he asked her to come in when she was ready. She didn't think she would ever be ready.

In the end, William's nephew James took control and made the arrangements. She couldn't have cared less. It was over. All of it. He was gone. What did it matter if his lifeless corpse was wearing a blue tie or a red one? Every decision he made, James respectfully checked with her in a quiet voice after handing her a cup of hot tea to replace the cold one that she had left untouched. She could barely respond.

"I asked the florist for a traditional arrangement," James said with his head bowed slightly.

Flowers, Marcia thought. *What does this have to do with flowers? What do flowers have to do with anything?* Images of bouquets passed through her mind, and then a memory flashed. William complaining about gardenias at his father's funeral. He hated gardenias. "No," she said. The word sounded much quieter in her ears than it had in her head. It was the first time she had spoken in days. "No... gardenias," she said. James nodded, and her mind was blank again, immune from any thought that she could have been misunderstood.

Everything at the funeral seemed surreal, bright, and big, and strange. She barely heard the music or noticed the many people who greeted her, hugging her, kissing her cheeks. She wondered why she was not the corpse in the box instead of him. She was just as lifeless. She felt like she was overhead, watching.

Is that where William is? she wondered. *Is he floating between the ceiling beams, or has he moved on?*

Halfway through the service, she felt something unsettle her. There was a strange sweet perfume in the air. She looked to her right to find a bouquet of small white flowers: gardenias. Appalled, she looked up to find the source of this injustice and realised the coffin, too, was covered in the pestilent blooms. Outrage spread through her as she realised the whole room was adorned in the flowers William had despised. She was fuming, and in that state, she noticed that everything was wrong. The coffin was oak, not cherry. William's tie was entirely the wrong shade of red. The music even sounded *religious*, although she had missed most of the words. The body in the coffin was all wrong. It looked small, pale, and waxy, nothing like the man she'd loved.

William should have been beside her where she needed him, to guide her through all this insanity. She glared at the bunch of flowers next to her, wishing they would shrivel up or burst into flames rather than looking so serene while her world was being ripped apart. Her glare was interrupted by laughter so vivid she looked around in surprise to see where it was coming from, but all she could see was tear-streaked faces, bowed in sadness. She turned back to the front and felt a warm, comforting hand on hers where she knew there was none. William's hand. She didn't dare look down and spoil the illusion. She let his presence embrace her as she tried to re-capture the laughter, his laughter, at the absurdity of her anger.

"It's alright," he seemed to say as if he was speaking in a voice made of pure, uplifting light. "I was with you for a while, looking after you, but you don't need me anymore." And although a moment ago, she wouldn't have believed it, she knew it to be true. "There is more for you here, on this Earth. And we will meet again... We always do."

She had returned home from the funeral in a state of inexplicable and silent joy. The phone rang, and she picked it up automatically to hear an unfamiliar voice. "Marcia Reed?"

This phone call seemed so ordinary, and yet, it instigated significant changes in Marcia's life.

"Yes." Her name sounded odd without the hyphenated 'Wilton', but she supposed she was no longer married, so it fitted somehow.

"We have been trying to locate you for some time now. I represent the Coulter-Hartley Law Firm. We have some unfortunate news." Marcia laughed. There was no way there was any news in the world worse than what she had just been through. It seemed absurd.

The voice cleared its throat.

"What is that?" she asked, gaining composure.

"Your parents have passed away." He paused, gauging her response.

Marcia also wanted to know how she would respond and waited for the pale reflection in the hallway mirror to show some kind of emotion. Her expression remained unchanged, and she began to examine her own unfamiliar face. She had not seen her parents in almost forty years, nor had she desired to.

Taking her silence as response enough, the voice continued. "It happened three months ago. Your mother had a severe stroke, and your father died a few days later from heart failure."

"I see," she said, still unsure how she felt.

"We understand that this is difficult to hear; we would have notified you sooner had we any contact information for you."

"My family and I are not close," she said, sounding somewhat brisker than she had intended.

"That is none of my business," the lawyer mumbled. "There is, however, the matter of their respective wills. They wished their possessions to be divided up equally between their three children."

Nathan, her brother. She wondered where he was. *He must be almost fifty now.* Time did funny things to memories, making them mysterious. Anna, her baby sister, in her forties. She had thought about them occasionally over the years but had not been in touch. Something had held her back.

"Your sister, Mrs Dalton, has requested the Raglan beach house owned by your parents, and Mr Reed wishes to be bought out of any property at market value. There is also the family home in Hamilton. Do you have a preference, or would you like more time?"

Dalton? Marcia was confused until she realised it must be her sister's married name. *Anna Dalton.* She rolled the words silently around her mouth, so strange. And so like her brother to want the money instead; *some things never change.* A memory drifted back of the house she had grown up in with its high Victorian ceilings and stained-glass front door. "I want the house," she said flatly.

"Will you purchase the house shares from your siblings?"

"Yes." It seemed simple and obvious.

"And do you consent to the purchase of the Raglan beach house by Mrs Dalton?"

This was the first time Marcia had heard of such a place. "Yes."

"Thank you for your time. I will send the paperwork for you to look over with your lawyer."

Marcia hung up the phone, widowed and orphaned and a little confused at her own decision, but still elated from her experience at the funeral. She reasoned that the timing of this call could be nothing other than an act of destiny.

Arriving back at the house after her walk, Marcia admired her handiwork. The garden had undergone a significant transformation, but it wasn't all visible on the surface.

The reason she had needed to move across the world was to do the inner work – the processing… it was to face her past and the things she had been running from her entire adult life.

Just like the house and the garden, there was still so much more to do. She had only tackled the tip of the iceberg, but the thing that scared her most was still too hard to contemplate.

5 2

LEA

L ea had been trying to write and getting nowhere.

Suffocating… School tedious, boring, hypnotised into vague, repetitive zombiedom. Intentionally choking the life out of those who search for meaning… suffocating.

There wasn't much more she could write about it, really. It was that dull. She wished the curriculum could provide her with more inspiration. As usual, she was glad to get home to the computer. It was one of her few sources of comfort.

Most of her online friends were overseas; Mysti, who was about her age, lived in Australia, but she was homesick for California, where she'd lived for two years with her dad. She got a bit whiney, so Lea blocked her sometimes and pretended she wasn't online.

Estella was the moderator of a chatroom that Lea had once encountered where everyone seemed to genuinely believe they were some kind of fantasy being. There were all sorts: werewolves, fairies, and demons. No roleplaying was allowed, and Lea thought it was quite strange and fascinating in a way. A few weeks before, Estella had confessed to her that she was actually Tatiana, the fairy princess and that she had to get the sword, Excalibur, surgically removed from her spine.

All the while, Alex sat on her list, always online but never accessible. She had told all her internet friends the story of Alex so many times, it had turned into a parable. It seemed to have helped; she could go over the details now without crying. She could still feel the pain, but it was muffled somehow, not so uncontrollable. She supposed it was better that way. The only problem was that it made space for her to feel the terrible loneliness that she hadn't even realised was there before Alex. When they were together, she had felt more complete, and now she knew the difference.

Grey was online today, and she was happy to see him. He kept her company on her lonely nights at the computer screen, sitting in his flat in London, a million time zones away. She had first met him in a chatroom with a witchcraft theme, and he'd seemed interesting, even if he was thirty, which was really old.

Grey: Hello
Lea: Hi
Grey: How are you holding up?
Lea: The same as usual, I guess
Grey: Hold on tight, it gets better
Lea: So you say
Grey: Well, speaking as someone with a little more life experience…
Life has this way of moving on whether you're ready or not.
Lea: I'm not. I just want things to go back to the way they were
Grey: You don't want things to get better?
Lea: I do
Grey: My favourite uncle died last year, he was like my role model.
He was a really good person, and he left behind his wife of twenty years.
Lea: I'm sorry
Grey: Thanks. The point is, it was really hard at first, for everyone.
The whole family struggled with the loss, but gradually, things got better. Even his widow is moving on now.

It was a wake-up call for Lea, giving her some perspective.

Other people had suffered more, lost far more than she had, and somehow found the strength to pull through.

Lea: I'm sorry for feeling sorry for myself. You must think I'm pathetic
Grey: No, I think you're stronger than you give yourself credit for.
Lea: Thanks Grey
Grey: NP :)

MARCIA

"The thing I've always struggled with is..." Dora said to the group assembled as usual in a circle on the carpet. "If there is a rhyme and reason for everything, if there is a God or some kind of divinity, how could he, or she, or it possibly make people suffer so much. I look at those commercials of starving children and my heart breaks. There is so much evil and pain and sadness in this world. It just doesn't seem fair."

Marcia nodded along with the rest of the group, her eyes full of empathy. "You're not alone with that question; I don't think there's a sane person in the world who hasn't wondered that very same thing at one time or another." Acknowledgement wasn't enough, and fortunately, other members of the group had become comfortable enough to contribute.

"I know this might sound bad," Aroha piped up. "Don't think I'm a terrible person, but at Uni the other day, my lecturer was talking about those ads for children's charities, and she said that most of those organisations do more harm than good. You know..." she hesitated, "like colonisation. They go in with their religion and Western views and destroy a culture. She also said that giving food aid to an over-populated country would lead to a boost in population, and then, when there was another war or drought or flood or something, it would be a much bigger disaster." She blushed.

"I see your point," Lizzy said. "But I was always raised to help people who are less fortunate."

Marcia smiled as her workshop was hijacked by Political Ethics 101.

It was Sam's turn. "I read somewhere that the traditional lifestyles of people throughout Africa before they were colonised by imperialists and religious charities were much healthier. They had higher standards of living and less disease than they do now."

Iris nodded. "I think that's still the case with the people living in cities compared to in a traditional tribal situation. I don't think it's our place to judge what is best for another country, another culture. It's ethnocentric. We can't possibly know from the outside what *should* be done on the inside," she added.

"Does that mean that meddling in other people's fortune makes thing's worse for them?" Helen asked Marcia.

"It is a complicated issue," Marcia began. "Perhaps difficult situations are part of our lesson here; perhaps we need to learn through pain, suffering and despair. I know it seems awful, but we can't judge someone else's life to be unfair. We only have our own experiences to work from. We need to understand our own boundaries."

Iris nodded. "It might sound selfish, but I actually believe it is impossible to help other people without helping yourself first, and everyone needs to take that self-responsibility before the world can become a better place. Focusing so much on outward problems may actually be a way that we run from our own… it is only drawing out the process, making it into a chronic condition."

The discussion seemed to have aired a lot of closely-held opinions, leaving the room feeling lighter and more open. Marcia sensed the change in atmosphere and decided it was a good opportunity to begin the throat centre meditation.

Focus on your throat;
Imagine a brilliant blue light emanating right through from one side to the other,
Opening this area up.

This is your true voice.
Allow the masks to fall away,
Feel its power.

This is the point where your internal self and your external self meet,
Where your private being can be translated into the public space of the world
outside.

Many people find they are afraid to voice their true feelings,
Afraid to be themselves,
Afraid of what the world will think of them,
Afraid of judgement, of persecution.

This was your way of defending yourself against an unfair world,
Now it is holding you back.

Let us take a few moments to traverse this over-grown emotional path
Into the depths of our subconscious.

It was pain that caused you to hide your true self;
Allow yourself to feel this pain now,
From the safety of your current environment.
The genuine, most intensely agonising feelings experienced now will save you
from having to bring them into more concrete, physical manifestations.

This is your chance to set yourself free.

Now you may make the choice to connect with your personal pain,
Just to witness it,
Experience,
Understand,
Acknowledge it,
And let it go;
Allow it to dissolve;
Feel it fade away.

Now you are free to be yourself,
As you feel the energy in your throat centre returning.

This is the gateway for true wisdom,

Experience what it means to be your true self,
To be comfortable in your being.

5 4

IRIS

Iris was sitting on the deck with her laptop as usual. Alex was still asleep upstairs. He seemed to stay up all night and sleep all day, a nocturnal creature.

For the moment, Iris was waiting for inspiration. All she usually had to do was look out over the wondrous evergreen forest, but this time it wasn't working. After a few attempts, frustration began to build, then the soft voice kicked in the back of her mind to guide her out. *What can I learn from this situation?* She immediately relaxed enough to realise this was exactly what she needed to write about.

Every difficult experience holds the potential for deep learning to occur. Once you have truly learned a lesson, there is no reason for it to repeat again in your life. If you feel stuck or that you are going around in circles over something, no matter how big or small, it can be extremely helpful to ask yourself, "What is the universe trying to teach me?" or "What is the ultimate lesson in this situation?" Sometimes, the answer can be as simple as learning patience or staying calm; other times, the message may be more complex. I have learnt from my experience of this exercise that there is often an element of acceptance involved. You will probably find that as soon as you have figured out the lesson you need to learn, the problem will miraculously resolve itself.

Iris could think of a dozen lost car key situations where this little process had worked wonders. Looking back, she wondered how it was possible for a human being with so much potential to get so frustrated over such a little thing. She was interrupted from her train of thought by a familiar knock at the door. It took her a moment to place it, and by that time she was halfway to the door, Ariki was already letting herself in.

"This is a surprise!" Iris was beaming. It had been too long since she'd seen her good friend.

"Well, you didn't expect me to leave you alone all the way out here on your birthday, did you?"

Iris had completely forgotten. Her parents were away on their yearly cruise, and Alex was too busy being a teenager to realise. She had turned thirty-nine without even noticing.

"Plus…" Ariki continued. "I just had to come and check this place out. You made it sound just delightful." She looked around, and her eyes fixed on the view through the sliding doors. "And it is!"

"It's wonderful to see you," Iris said, looking at her friend's warm face, chiselled in smile lines. "Would you like a cup of tea?"

"Just one, and then you're taking me to this precious beach of yours."

The day was overcast, but that didn't make the scenery any less beautiful. They walked right around the small bay and then settled on a large log of driftwood, facing the rugged open surf, which raged in absolute contrast to the calm inlet.

"Your book sounds marvellous, Darling. I'm sure it will be a big hit." Ariki, as usual, was smiling emphatically as the warm wind chaotically whipped her hair around.

"I'm enjoying the process. I'm just not sure how honest I can be. I'm not sure people will buy something that's not sugar-coated," Iris admitted, voicing a problem that had been on the edge of her mind for a few days.

"You know, everything about me is controversial, even my name," Ariki said into the waves.

Iris was surprised.

"It means Lord, as in The Lord, our God. At least, that is one common translation. It is a term of great honour, of esteem, of royalty. My Kuia, my mother's mother, she gave it to me. She said I was born for greatness, and if other people didn't like it, that was their business to deal with. She told me to carry myself with pride and never apologise for it. Now I'm going to give you the same advice. *Kia kaha*, stay strong. You have all the potential in the world, Darling; you just have to set your mind to it."

55

MARCIA

M arcia was in her garden when she noticed them. The procession of women walked back and forth from the house next door, carrying boxes. She wasn't sure whether to talk to them or not, but her curiosity got the best of her. She wiped her damp hands on her jeans, made her way down her garden path and into the property next door.

She felt shy when she introduced herself to the round-faced woman on the stoop who turned out to be called Mary, one of Mrs Everglade's nieces. She smiled at Marcia and asked her in for tea.

"We don't have a lot of time," she said over the porcelain cup that Marcia recognised from her only other tea time in the cottage.

"Sarah and I flew up from Christchurch to help sort all this out." She gestured around the room at the clutter Mrs Everglade had managed to amass in her eighty or so years. Some of it had already been packed into boxes and the other two women, Sarah and Ellie, were busy carrying them outside.

"This is a lovely little house," Marcia said, admiring the dark wooden panelling that ran halfway up the walls before it met the ancient faded, peeling wallpaper. "And the garden is so wonderful..." She took a sip of her tea, unsure how to proceed.

"It is unique, isn't it?" Mary said. "We want people who will look after it."

"You're selling then?" she asked. She had been curious about it for a while. She had actually been praying for any possibility other than developers who would obviously tear down the house, demolish the garden, and build abominable townhouses. Marcia shuddered at the thought.

"We are going to rent it out for the time being. We haven't sorted things out with the lawyers or anything. We all feel that the house should be protected. As you can see, we have great admiration for history in this family." Marcia looked at the floor around them, covered in newspaper clippings and keepsakes.

"I'm so relieved to hear that," Marcia said. "Property developers would destroy all this in an instant. It would be a tragedy."

Marcia was indeed relieved as she walked back to her own garden. At least for now, the little house, and her view of the garden, would be safe. The house might be rented out for a few years, and anything could happen in that time. It was even possible that Marcia herself would be able to purchase the property if it came on the market.

She had a brief, childlike fantasy of pulling down the fence that joined the two gardens, creating a sprawling paradise between the old farmhouse and the little cottage.

56

IRIS

I ris felt as if her energy had been renewed by Ariki's visit. Her words streamed out effortlessly into the document on the screen in front of her, joining the rest of her book.

The desire for power is natural. It is natural to want power over yourself and your surroundings, and power, in balance, is healthy. The desire to abuse power for control comes from a feeling of insecurity. This results in a separation of self. The heart, feeling vulnerable, is trying to protect itself – it creates a hard shell. The heart becomes two separate parts: the vulnerable inside and the protective outer shell. This internal dichotomy can cause many problems. To overcome it, we must embrace our vulnerability and accept it.

She sometimes wondered whether her words were difficult to understand, too technical. She needed a way to make the experience more real. She strummed her fingers against the side of the keyboard. There had to be a way. She could feel the tension build in her body as she became frustrated, unable to release her energy in a productive way. Stop! she ordered herself. Redirect.

It helped that she was sitting in front of one of the most beautiful views in the world. All it took was a moment of looking at the horizon, and the path was revealed. She turned to her own personal diva for ideas. What would Marcia do? Her mind flashed to the workshops, and she had it. Drawing on the meditations Iris had encountered, she constructed one for her own purposes.

Meditation to accept emotions:

Close your eyes.
Take a moment to relax.
You are in a dark, warm, safe place.
Relax into the darkness.
You feel completely at ease.
In front of you is a door.
On the other side of the door are your fears.
Open the door and invite them inside.
One by one.
Talk to them.

Take a moment to reflect on your emotional state right now.
Think of two or three words to describe it.
These may come easily; if not, ask yourself what colour your current feelings could be. What scent, texture, sound, or flavour could they have?

Do you know what is behind your feelings, or is it a mystery?
Are you comfortable with your feelings?
Do you feel responsible for your feelings? If so, is it a feeling of guilt or blame, or is it an empowering responsibility?
Do you blame other people or occurrences outside your control for the way you feel?

Take time to get acquainted with your emotions at this moment. Now that you know how you feel, you can begin to direct your thoughts and feelings towards how you would like to feel. If you begin by choosing the thoughts that inspire you and make you happy, the feelings will follow. If you begin by filling yourself with positive feelings, the thoughts will follow.

5 7

L E A

When Lea logged in, Alex was online. It gave her the same shot of unrealistic hope as usual. She hesitated for a moment, willing herself to resist, but of course, she was too weak. She promised herself she wasn't going to push him this time. No begging, demanding, or insulting. She was better than that.

Lea: hey
Alex: hi
Lea: how are you?
Alex: the same as usual. yourself?

There was that same dullness to his virtual tone. It made her spirits sink into the inevitable.

Lea: I'm OK, just checking emails
Alex: heh

She wished she was busy. She wished there was something more important than him. The same question burned through her mind, charring it with injustice. *Why?* Still the same damn question, still the same lurking shadows.

Lea: I have something I need to ask you, and it's really important to me.
I need to know why you changed, why you became a different person so suddenly.

As soon as she asked, she wished she hadn't. Of course, he would brush it off the way he always did. She had shown weakness and revealed that she couldn't let go. He did not respond immediately, and the suspense made her rigid. She sat glued to the screen, not even pretending to flick to her browser, to be otherwise occupied. She was about to surrender and ask him about something else, music, movies, anything, when the program showed. *Alex is typing a message.* She breathed deeply.

Alex: to be honest, I'd quite like to know the same thing.

It was a strange feeling. Like someone had let out the plug and all the pressure began to drain away. He was admitting that it had happened. This wasn't all in her head, and she could let go of the burden of carrying on the relationship all by herself. There wasn't a relationship any more, but at least, he was acknowledging there had been something, and he had made it die despite himself. *I'm still the one with the problem...* The thought brought back misery. *Because he can't feel.* All she was left with was wistfulness because emotion wasn't a currency he counted.

58

ZANE

The Sydney summer weather was exactly the wrong kind of hot. Zane had been surprised by the monsoon that managed to drench right through his clothes in the brief exposed space between the airport and the limo when they had arrived two days before. He was even more confused by the stifling muggy heat that had followed, rendering the air so thick that moisture seemed to be seeping into his pores rather than out of them. Just being outside made his head spin, and the bright sunlight did nothing to help his failing sense of clarity.

Zane was relieved that the television interviewer had been briefed by Wrench's agent not to mention anything relating to their current media crisis. They'd had enough bad press already. Just the fact that they were a hot topic right now would boost the show's ratings. People would tune in on the off-chance that there would be some drama. Some viewers were probably expecting devil worship.

Even though it had increased their album sales, it wasn't something they were proud of. They were artists, expressing themselves creatively, not evil death mongers on a mission to corrupt the youth of today.

Gavin Grono had neatly cropped, dark hair, oiled back from his forehead and a rough Australian accent. The show seemed to be leaning towards the comedic in contrast to the serious journalistic interviews the band had encountered in Tokyo.

He began with a brief bio introducing Wrench as a controversial progressive rock band "...who enjoy getting parents' knickers in a twist." He winked at the camera.

Zane flinched.

"Here we have Zane Strachan, lead singer and frontman, who all the girls scream over." He tipped his imaginary hat. "We've rounded up some screaming girls for you out the back." The studio audience evidently found this hilarious. Zane remained impassive.

"Baz, the world-renowned bassist and proud supporter of Australian tattoo parlours." Baz gave a wide grin.

"Mitch, the pommy bloke." Mitch gave his signature nod.

"And Jimmy, the band's prodigy drummer and spiritual advisor." Jimmy was as relaxed as usual.

Zane cruised through the probing questions, trying not to take himself too seriously. He answered casually so as to give nothing away and went along with Gavin's absurd accusations: that the band was starting their own religion, that they were part of an international plot to overthrow the Queen of England, that Americans never wore underwear and ate peanut butter and banana burritos for breakfast.

He laughed while Mitch took part in the newly invented Australian tradition of "spanking the kangaroo" by whacking a giant stuffed kangaroo with a cricket bat. He was actually enjoying himself when Gavin decided to push his luck.

"Now we've been told we're not allowed to ask you about the youth you've corrupted lately. Can you tell the people of Australia why this is?"

It was a serious question, thinly disguised as a joke. For once, instead of looking to Zane for the answers, they all turned to Jimmy, who seemed to be radiating serenity.

"We don't see the benefit of discussing something unless it has an element of truth in it." Zane could tell he was enjoying himself. He had spent years mastering the all-knowing yet humble tone of a lama. "We wouldn't want to waste your time." His expression was gentle and earnest.

"How perfectly sweet of you all," Gavin said through his plastered smile. "It just makes me want to give you all a great big bear hug." The audience roared in fits of laughter, and Zane, Baz and Mitch breathed a sigh of relief. Unfortunately for Zane, the worst was still to come.

"So, Zane. You're the master vocalist?"

"If you like." He was more relaxed now.

"You're from New Zealand originally, is that right?"

Zane was stunned silent. He had lost his accent years before, voluntarily adopting a Californian twang so that LA locals didn't struggle to understand him. Of course, Australia was populated by hundreds of thousands of New Zealand's ex-patriots, almost an eighth of his former homeland's total population. It was a small world; someone was bound to make the connection. His secret identity was forfeit, and for once, he had absolutely nothing to say. His mind felt like a puddle of half-formed thoughts. It had stopped communicating in words.

Then something chaotic inside him was unleashed.

"Actually," he said, smiling deviously into the camera, "I was adopted. I don't know where I originally come from." One of his secrets of origin was out; he might as well tell the world about the other one. It was more than most of his past girlfriends had ever known about him. He always kept his cards close to his chest, especially this one. It was the reason he had always felt out of place, detached but free – like he could drift around the world with nothing to hold him down, with no identity and no heritage. Like a new country: no history, no baggage.

Whenever he signed his name, he felt like a fraud. Who was this 'Zane Strachan'? Who was he really? He didn't belong to his parents or any country in particular. He only belonged to himself, and if he wasn't sure who he was, then he was completely lost.

He sat there in the studio with the audience watching him, exposed and feeling curiously relieved.

Mitch saved the day by interrupting the silence that had followed with a somewhat sexist comment about Australian women and their endowments which got Gavin's attention. The two male chauvinists got on a roll assessing the body shapes of girls of various nationalities. They seemed to be on the same page. Zane was used to Mitch's blatant objectification. The rest of the band viewed it as an eccentricity that was becoming outdated, if not yet quaint, but Gavin was a refreshing reminder of how blunt Australians could be, a walking stereotype.

When Zane finished high school, he had only one ambition: to get the hell out of there, go overseas and start his real life. He got a job working at the local video store, and before he knew it, he had fallen in love. Every time she came into the store, he pretended to be busy cataloguing, returning videos to their shelves. All the while, he listened to her witty one-liners and caught glimpses of her radiant smile, her blonde hair that she was always tucking behind her ears, her blue eyes that reminded him of something deep and serene.

So, he went to university. He convinced himself that taking a few papers would give him a head start when he left the country and finally got to somewhere worth being. Of course, this was nothing to do with her being a student. He liked bumping into her around campus, at the student magazine where she wrote cutting columns about society, which he always read. He loved the snippets of conversation he overheard and occasionally joined in on, in his casual, nonchalant way. He was almost a quarter of the way through his music degree when he finally got the courage to ask her out. Towards the end of his degree, when he was increasingly jaded, she was the only thing that kept him from leaving.

Then, a few days after graduation, she stopped returning his calls. She had moved out of her flat, and her mother wouldn't tell him anything. He was left marooned and utterly depressed. She had abandoned him, just like his birth mother had. He had to face the fact that all the women in his life would inevitably do this to him. There was probably something deeply wrong with him. He was unlovable, doomed to be alone. Once he accepted this, it was far easier than the thought of having his heart broken again. So, he borrowed a bit of the sociological discourse she used to spout and took an observer's role.

He left the country and went to the States. He started Wrench with a handful of friends he met while he was living in his first apartment in a rundown block in Echo Park, and they gradually built up an underground following at just the right time – when underground was the next big thing. Soon, they had a worldwide fanbase, which increased exponentially every time they put out an album (around every five years). And here he was, sixteen years later, with more money than he could spend and more fame than he could stomach, arriving back in the country he had wanted so badly to get away from. *Funny how things come full circle.*

LEA

Something different had come over her. Lea felt strengthened somehow. She wanted to write, but her emotions weren't as turbulent as usual. She didn't know how to express this feeling. She wished she could talk to Alex about it, but she knew better. She had finally managed to control herself in a conversation with him. Getting emotional would just take her two steps backwards. She recalled someone, maybe a television character, giving the advice to write a letter that was never meant to be sent. She turned the idea over in her mind. She wanted to get through to Alex, but she knew it wasn't working. At least this way, she could express herself.

I know you are finding this difficult, as am I, but I also know you don't want to lose this connection. You seem to be having difficulty with something internal; you want to be in control. My difficulties are usually the opposite; I want to control the external world. I want to stop it from hurting me.

You probably need time to process and adapt to all this, and I can give you space. I know it would be good for me too. It does worry me that you're so introverted that you don't seem to have room for empathy. I care about how you feel, and I would appreciate more consideration for how I feel. Our connection is such that not to consider the other is unbalanced, and it upsets me.

I would also appreciate it if you would communicate your feelings to me more openly and trust me. I would hate for miscommunication to get in the way of our beautiful connection.

As Lea finished the letter, she recalled what Alex's mum had said about external situations always being a reflection of the internal. She considered her feelings more deeply and where they might be coming from. She re-read the letter and finally, she signed off.

Love,

My self

60

IRIS

All through her youth, Iris had craved emotional intimacy. Someone to share her spirituality with, the philosophies and beliefs she had developed by herself through her own experiences.

The more she learned about the nature of reality, the more she realised how little she knew. The extent of the realisation was staggering and made her feel devastatingly lonely at times. She felt she was here, on this planet, to learn, to coordinate her spiritual being with her physicality as best as she could and to develop her soul. She had done well in high school, achieving A-grades and making lots of friends, but she had always felt she was waiting to start her real life. By the time she had moved away to go to University, she was ready for it to begin.

She was shy in her first year, preferring her own company, but she gradually grew confident and then outspoken and critical of the things she felt were wrong. She loved the freedom of living away from home. She made friends with the feminists in her Women's Studies class and the Marxists from Labour Studies. She developed her own brand of social deconstructionism that always carried with it an air of optimism.

Iris developed remarkably in those years. She tried on various relationships to see if they fit, learning a little bit more about herself every time. She became infatuated with infatuation and its roller-coaster ride, and then she gave it up in favour of a more stable existence by abstaining from relationships altogether. Not long after that, she fell in love.

Iris could wonder a million things and come to a thousand conclusions and still essentially find herself in the same place. Her mind became rather circular if she spent too much time in it, but still, she held some hope that her thoughts might help others in some way.

She thought of her school friend Amy, who would cry whenever she didn't get her way, who always needed to be the centre of attention, and who got away with the most terrible things because she could smile and sparkle and make people feel like they were important. Iris reasoned that Amy's cravings for attention often manifested in dramatic tantrums. Her eating disorders were always on display. Her numerous illnesses appeared when she was most starved of attention. She was a person who was either unable or unwilling to meet her own needs. Iris had loved her dearly but grew weary of the exploitation and the insecure feeling belonging to those who pretend to trust when in reality they cannot.

Eventually, she distanced herself completely from Amy. The last she had heard, through a friend of a friend, she had been abusing any drug she could get and had been diagnosed with depression, anxiety, borderline personality disorder, attention deficit disorder and more. Attention could be a kind of addiction.

Iris didn't know where she was going with this. She thought of all the issues people learned to live with, oblivious to their own unhealthy patterns. The invisible addictions that could cause so much misery.

Addictions are not just in the realm of substance abuse. People can become addicted to anything, for example, exercise, power, food, sex, socialising, shopping, relationships, infatuation, the attention of a particular person. Some of these are easier to recognise, such as the gym junkie or binge eater. But from that person's perspective, they may not know anything is wrong. Self-deception is very powerful when it comes to addictions.

She recalled all the dim years where she had been a slave to her own passions, out of control, unaware. She had sought to overcome them, and the first step had been recognising her own repetitive thought patterns and behavioural flaws, the cycles she had tied herself into. From her years of experience, she could spot the signs a mile away.

Addictions are always linked to excuses, 'I know I should quit BUT..." Be it a stressful job, relationship problems, or life just being so hard, the addict will always find a good excuse, a rationalisation. Even if he or she has to bend reality to do it. The excuse excuses the addiction, and the addiction excuses the excuse in a circular manner, leaving the person un-responsible (and irresponsible), free from blame – although often still feeling guilty, and ultimately a victim to themselves. Excuses are made out of guilt. They are compensation for a feeling that is not useful in itself, and they leave the cause of the feeling unresolved. There is ultimately no reason for excuses. There is a difference between excuses and explanations, and it is this: excuses are explanations with an agenda. Explanations alone have no emotional motivation like guilt or shame. They merely state what is without needing to bend it or twist it. There is no feeling of attachment to how the other person perceives the situation.

MARCIA

"The third eye energy centre is, naturally, all about perception," Marcia gestured to the centre of her forehead. "People often get caught up in a situation, and it makes them blind. They can't see the forest for the trees. Some people say that a blocked third eye is caused by ignorance, by a person not being open to greater meaning in life. A guru I once met told me that when this centre is fully opened, it reveals this world to be an illusion."

Dora looked as if she was bursting with a question; Marcia nodded at her.

"Is that why manifesting works? Like when you're putting your mind to it, you're changing the illusion."

"It could be," Marcia replied. "It's all a matter of perspective. People who view the world and their lives as something they have no control over often feel disempowered. If anything bad happens, they are hard done by; if anything good happens, it's just the luck of the draw."

"That's my father all over," Iris smiled sadly. "He won't tolerate any perspective that's any different. In his view, there are two forces: chance and hard work. It always seemed so limiting to me that in this apparently vast universe, there could be nothing more!" She laughed, although it seemed out of frustration.

"So, you all believe in this stuff?" Sam asked to a series of nods and non-committal shrugs. "I'm not saying it's not real. I'm just not convinced. Like, if I make one of those boards with the magazine cut-outs…"

"Vision board," Helen offered.

"Right – vision board," Sam continued, "I'll suddenly become a millionaire." He looked at Dora, who blushed. "But what you said before about the universe being something – an illusion – your mind can interact with – that reminded me of a book I read years ago: The Holographic Universe. It used some kind of physics to argue that the universe is a hologram and our brains are also holograms that interact with it." He looked down at his hands, unused to dominating the workshop conversation. "It was a good book. You should read it."

"I've been writing about the the power of our thoughts," Iris said. "It seems like a practical thing to pay attention to consciously in your life, like being grateful for what you do have. I always find that when I worry about money, I inevitably spend it on junk I don't need, almost as if that worry subconsciously reinforces itself. It's that scarcity mentality. When I feel content – like I have everything I need – I find I always do."

Sam nodded. Iris continued. "If I can keep myself in that good feeling, life is much easier, and I find things always fall into place – like finding the ad for this workshop and meeting you all. Or the sequence of events that led to me quitting my job and moving up here. It couldn't have been more perfect if I'd planned every detail. I only wish this stuff worked on teenagers!"

The mothers among them sighed in sympathy.

"You know, that's so true – about the money," Aroha said. "My mother earns a hundred and fifty thousand a year from her consultancy, and she's always broke. I can't believe it! I've never even earned a quarter of that, and I always have enough money for everything I need."

"And things often do fall into place," Dora added. "I was worried about not being able to afford a new couch after our old one broke. Then I decided to trust that problem to the universe, and the next day, I got a call from my friend Marie, saying she was moving to Australia and would I like any of her nice new furniture?"

"It could just be a coincidence," Sam argued. "I wouldn't put too much on faith."

"That's true. It could be," Marcia admitted. "And I would never advise anyone to put themselves at risk and assume that the universe will sort everything out. This stuff is only useful in as much as it serves you. If you sleep easier at night, trusting your energy is going into making your life better, if positive thoughts make getting through the day easier, then why not? And if it seems like magic starts to happen, then enjoy it!"

"Well, I'm going home to make my vision board tonight," Sam said, in good humour. "Let's see if I can manifest a girlfriend who looks like..." Helen kicked him, abruptly ending his sentence.

"But, aside from your views on all this hocus-pocus, Sam, are you finding these workshops helpful?"

"I am, actually." He smiled warmly. "I think the meditations have helped me work through some heavy stuff."

"That's good to hear." Marcia felt a weight lift. She had been unaware until that point how much she had been resisting Sam's criticism. *No one likes to be judged,* she reminded herself. *No one likes to be wrong.*

"There's no denying. That the way we think shapes our realities," Sam conceded.

"Right. The way we think shapes our reality," Marcia repeated. "It is very powerful. The energy centre associated with the third eye is a gateway to higher perception, to truth, insight, and awareness."

She relaxed her shoulders and watched the group shuffle into comfortable positions. They were used to this. "When you are ready, close your eyes." She went through the usual relaxation.

Imagine a bright purple light shining through the centre of your forehead,
So vibrant that it dissolves any blockages.

Allow this light to expand;
Feel your third eye centre opening.

Let it clear away illusion,
Revealing reality for what it truly is.

ZANE

Being back was eerie. Zane saw familiarity everywhere, but everything was different, as if tainted by his cynicism. It was home, but it wasn't. He didn't have a home country, not anymore. Jimmy, Baz, and Mitch were his family. Wherever they were, was home. They had tagged along for the ride. They'd always wanted to see "Nu Zeelund."

Auckland was just another city, bustling with black-clad people in a hurry to get somewhere. The suits racing to be the richest person in the graveyard. They found the first bar that didn't have a dress code and ordered the most interesting looking local beer.

"So, you're finally going home," Mitch said solemnly, then with a gleam in his eye, he added. "Finally grown some balls, eh?"

"Hey," Zane said casually. He had learned a long time ago to never take Mitch seriously. "I'm as surprised as you are."

"It's a great spiritual journey, facing your past." Jimmy seemed to be pleased.

"The timing feels right." It did. Zane couldn't explain why.

"Our little boy's all grown up." Baz put his arm around Mitch's shoulder. Mitch shrugged it off.

"It's all too poetic for me. Just get some drugs, some women and get over it."

Baz's eyes were sparkling from the few beers he'd had. "Mitch, we all know you're just a bastard because you're spiritually and emotionally unfulfilled."

"Yeah," Mitch agreed. "And we all know you've had enough therapy for the lot of us."

"What did women ever do to you?" Baz probed, half-serious.

"You fecking know already. Me mum left when I was little. Freudian issues. Et cetera."

"Don't you think it's time you faced your past and got over it?" It was Zane's turn to put Mitch on the spot.

"You should know, mate. How the feck do you get over something like that? Being abandoned." His slurring clearly indicated he'd had enough. "It's just s…somefink…" He sobbed, and his eyes became teary.

"He finally has a breakthrough, and he's probably too drunk to remember," Jimmy said, enjoying the irony of alcohol.

"Shuddup," Mitch spat.

63

LEA

Lea sat staring at her inbox, refreshing her browser every minute, waiting for a response. It felt like an old wound, and in a way, it was, pulling her chest. A deep yearning. She thought it was over, that she was over it, but she had been wrong. All it took was one little email to send her right back into the middle of her suffering again. He shouldn't have contacted her. She shouldn't have responded, spilling her heart out all over again. He had asked how she was, and she had been honest. She regretted it once she had clicked 'send' and transmitted her feelings through fibre optics to him, but it was too late, and she was desperately awaiting a response, hoping for redemption. Again, writing was the only outlet for the intensity of her emotion.

Again and again, it comes, repeats in my mind, over and over until I can't tell if it is me thinking for myself or if it's controlling me. It attaches itself to me, covers my eyes, blocks out the light, and sucks out all life. It devours me... but sometimes I wonder if I need it more than it needs me.

She pulled her attention away from the screen and let her eyelids close. All she could hear was her breathing and the hum of the computer fan. The feeling tightened, and then it dissipated. It surprised her that it could be so strong one minute and then go so quickly.

She let her thoughts run wild through her mind: worries about uncompleted homework, the pang of hunger followed by possible solutions of spaghetti toasted sandwiches or cheese and crackers. These mundane things occupied her for moments at a time until she turned her attention to a higher purpose. The Goddess.

In her mind's eye, she saw the mystical feminine figure enshrined in silver moonlight. The image was pushed from her as Alex came back into her head, and emotion rose like nausea in her chest. She needed him. She needed him to understand. She was desperate. And then the feeling faded again. This made her question if it was even real. It was a sort of craving, the way addicts in the movies went crazy over cocaine or heroin, but it disappeared and then returned of its own accord. After what seemed like an eternity, she began to recognise the pattern and it lost some of its power over her.

Peace Within

What I want is peace
From the whirling chaos of my mind
From the dark, entrapped, burdened abysses of my soul
Chained to this mundane reality
Torture
Pure torture.
To this mundane world
I need to escape
I need to find peace here
Inside.

64

MARCIA

Marcia pulled at a stem, and the plant came loose. Dry earth crumpled from its shallow roots. She was freeing her garden from the stranglehold of a plant she used to recognise as Deadly Nightshade, but after living in England for years, she knew better. The real Nightshade, Belladonna, was a very different plant from this. The starry white flowers were nothing like the menacing and seductive purple green of *Atropa belladonna*.

The plants she savagely ripped from the garden were commonly known as blackberry nightshade. The jewelled black berries were edible when cooked. Early colonial settlers in New Zealand had made jam from them. Marcia had read about it years before, in a library in Edinburgh, in an effort to prove her father wrong, or at least, his voice that still echoed in her mind.

Once you've buried one child, you've buried them all.

Her father had given up on her a long time before she left home.

All the hope and joy of expectation culminating in loss, a void too deep and terrifying to ponder.

She tossed the weed aside and reached for another.

That's how it was when Thomas died. She remembered her lost baby sibling. Life had gone on, but it was not really life; no promise of heaven, no funeral.

We were too sensible for florid ritual.

The child Marcia had imagined him lying there in a box, cold and lonely, a lost cause like her.

The problem with weeds like this was that they seeded everywhere; it seemed like she was making progress, but it wouldn't be long before more would shoot up to fill the place of the one before.

She sometimes thought it fortunate that she was the only other child at the time, the oldest taking responsibility; she got the worst of it.

Dad couldn't escape his guilt, but he couldn't face it either, so it seethed beneath the surface; the corpse of his lost dreams, odious decaying pet, his tortured ego. He couldn't bear to be wrong but was blind to the reality that it was no one's fault, no place to be right. Cot death leaves no villain except the one we already possess: our own internalised culpable conscience.

And so, she became his villain. She could see the anger in his eyes, still hear the words echo in her head: "*It should have been you.*"

65

IRIS

As Iris pulled up, she noticed Marcia and Helen standing on the footpath outside Marcia's house, looking up. Iris turned to see the sky on fire. She got out of her car to stand beside Marcia and watch the sky glow, enflamed in brilliant gold. *It's funny*, Iris thought, *how these beautiful spontaneous things make acceptance so natural, so easy*. As they stood in the street watching in awe, Iris sat down on the grass and let herself relax into the moment. The people in the cars that passed seemed to think that these women starring at the sky were more interesting than the sunset, only noticing their social deviation and not the heavenly display stretched out right in front of their eyes.

Moments saw it ended. The gold evolved to vermillion before fading. The clouds, feathery and light, textured like a colonial oil painting, were ablaze against the turquoise sky. Then dusk was upon them, and the group, which had grown to include Sam, Lizzie, and Dora, collected their dinner contributions and retreated to the warm, welcoming light of the old villa.

It had been Marcia's idea to hold the final workshop at her house, and the others had suggested that if change was in the air, they might as well go with the flow and have it in the evening over a pot luck meal. For all except Iris, it was their first time there, and they admired the Victorian architecture and gushed over Marcia's interior renovations and great taste, making her blush girlishly. After a colourful dinner, they continued to gorge themselves on the last feijoas and the first tamarillos from Marcia's trees. Then they all settled in around the potbelly stove. The autumn night had suddenly become chilly.

66

MARCIA

M arcia sat, looking into the flames that peeped through the holes in the potbelly's door, mesmerised.

"Can I ask you something?" It was Dora.

"Yes." Marcia turned to her. The group were lounging around the fire.

"I've been wondering this since the first workshop, and I just never found the right moment to ask... I really want to know what you believe. I mean... Do you believe in God?

Marcia felt unusually awkward. Questions about religion always put her on edge because she didn't want to offend anyone who had different ideas from her own.

"God?" she said, a half question. Dora nodded

"I used to wonder a lot about God. So many people have different ideas about divinity and supreme beings and such... I don't question whether there is a God or not, not anymore. I have seen and experienced enough in my own life to know that there is much more than just the physical world, and we've covered that before..."

"Maybe..." Iris interrupted. "A more appropriate question would be: How do you perceive God to be?" Dora nodded at her, grateful to be let off the hook.

Marcia paused for a moment, although she already knew what her answer would be.

"I think we are all God. God is part of everything, and everything is part of God. So, in this way, I think God is the creative source of life itself. That is why we are conscious creators. That is why we can influence things in this world… Why we are aware. Every atom is God… So here we all are." She gestured around the room. "We are God interacting with itself."

There was a moment of understanding, of insight, a shiver that passed through everyone in the room. Marcia found her opportunity to begin the meditation.

We can never stay in a moment for long no matter how nice it is;
It soon becomes the past, and holding on only brings pain, regret, sorrow, guilt, longing, misery.
We cannot become too attached to any time, experience, person or object unless we are willing to experience the feelings of its loss.
If we are to let go, we must be centred in the present moment…
To surrender to life as it unfolds, right now.
Imagine a brilliant white light shining through the crown of your head.
Allow this light to open your crown energy centre.
A direct channel to the divine,
Letting universal light energy in.
You are a complete being,
Perfect in every way.
Feel this connection to the universe as all blockages dissolve;
Feel yourself becoming lighter, freer.
Surrender your will to your higher self;
Allow yourself to be guided deeper into yourself.
Feel this iridescent light spreading
Down through your other energy centres.
Connecting with the purple of your third eye,
The illuminated perspective you find there.
Let it spread further, to your throat centre
To the blue of your inner wisdom
Allow it to flow into the green of your heart centre,
Connecting with unconditional love and compassion.

Now it descends into the yellow of your solar plexus;
Allow it to cleanse your mind, your mental body.
Let it flow down to your sacral centre and connect with the orange light,
Purifying and healing your instinctual self.
And now it meets your root centre;
Let it combine with the red energy of your physical body.
Allow this healing to take place...
Throughout every layer of your self.
Now feel this energy as it flows down your spine like a waterfall,
Cascading over all your energy centres,
Healing your life.
Feel this energy descend from your root centre
Down, down, down,
Deep into the Earth,
Spreading out like the roots of a tree.
Feel this connection to the Earth mother,
To the physical world,
To life itself.
Allow the incredible strength of the Earth, this golden light, to flow up into your
body, right into your heart.
Now from above you, silver light, divine light, descends into your crown centre,
connecting you to the universe.
Allow this energy to flow down until it meets the gold energy in your heart.
Feel yourself opening up to your full potential.
Now, allow any excess energy from your body to drain away into the Earth,
To be recycled into new life,
To fertilise the planet.
Allow the universal energy to lift any burdens from your soul.

IRIS

It had been a perfect evening. As Iris walked out to her car, she was sure the stars were shining brighter than usual. The air was crisp, but she dawdled anyway, admiring the garden by night, grateful for all that she had learned from the workshops. She heard a noise behind her and turned to find Marcia, wrapped in a dressing gown as if it were a jacket over her clothes.

"It's been so wonderful," Iris said, her voice musical.

Marcia smiled sadly. "I wish this wasn't the end. I've learnt so much from all of you."

"The feeling's mutual." Iris smiled at the woman she admired more than any other in the world. "Thank you."

"I'm not who you think I am," Marcia said, still smiling in a way. "I'm not all wise and perfect."

"We're all perfect," Iris reminded her.

Her drive home was peaceful. The land that spread out beneath the car seemed to carry her along. The magnificent sky opened up, revealing its true beauty to her. She felt her energy expanding. She felt aware.

She drove past a familiar beach, and before she knew it, she had pulled over into the viewing bay. A memory sprang from the back of her mind.

She was young, in her early twenties, stumbling over the rocks as he held her hand, offering support. It was a mild autumn day, but night had fallen quickly, turning the sky an inky blue-black. They found large, curvy, volcanic boulders and lounged on them. They had smoked a joint and looked up at the stars and spoken their minds, full of garbled thoughts.

"Do you think you'll ever have kids?" she had asked casually, although the question came from a serious place, an ache that twisted inside her. His laughter chastised her.

"I don't want to spread humanity. We're like a virus on the face of the Earth. All we do is pollute and destroy. Sooner or later, this planet is going to invent the cure."

That was it. Ground zero. The breaking point.

Iris watched the waves throw themselves against the rocks. The sound always calmed her. It had been so long ago, but the memory was still fresh in her mind. She let it drift away. Her mind went blank, and she had an epiphany.

At university, she had taken a paper in Moral Philosophy. It had inspired her to study virtues. Her spirit soared as she connected the pieces. Virtues were the ultimate positive goals and, therefore, the ultimate affirmations. Each one could be summed up in a word, an ideal, and each word could fit perfectly with an energy centre.

The heart centre could be *Compassion*. That was obvious. The solar plexus she had learned to heal through *Acceptance*. That made perfect sense as a virtue for that potentially controlling mental energy. She pondered the others as she drove home. The sacral centre was all about survival. She thought on this for a moment.

Marcia's meditation had taken Iris on a journey into herself through her fears. She had felt her own fragile mortality and grasped for salvation. It was such a struggle, at times, that she had almost given up. She had been ready to get up and walk right out of the room, never to return, when a little voice whispered from the back of her mind, *just trust...* That was all it said, and that was all she needed. She had let go of the fears and hovered in her mind. *Trust* wasn't a typical virtue. 'Faith' was probably the traditional word, but Iris had never particularly liked its sanctimonious connotations. Trust was all she needed.

As soon as she was through the door, she flung herself at her laptop and began to type. The physical body was a tricky one, 'Health' perhaps, although that could pertain to any level. An image flashed through her mind of blood coursing through her veins. She vaguely remembered she had once heard Louise Hay describe blood as pure joy, transporting essential nutrients around the body in celebration. She liked *Joy*. It had a good feeling about it. She typed next to the word: *The sublime experience of being.*

So far, so good. The throat centre was about wisdom, but that wasn't exactly a virtue. She racked her brain. It was also about communication and the internal and external selves. She wrote down the keywords and moved on to the next one.

The third eye was the centre for insight and higher awareness. These were wonderful things, but she wanted a word that inspired bliss. *What's the goal?* She wondered. *What is it we ultimately want to see?* The truth. *Perfection* in everything.

Her thoughts drifted to the crown centre. There was no word great enough to describe the divine light she had experienced as it flowed down her spine, connecting with the other centres on its way. It was too wonderful. The only experience that even came close was one she had reached in her own meditation at home after the first workshop.

She created a digital table and filled in the blanks with a concise version of everything she had learnt about energy centres, knowing she could elaborate in the text of her book.

That was it, everything except the throat centre. She looked back at what she had written. Communication. What was the ultimate communication, the virtue that true wisdom wanted to share? As soon as she thought it, the word gave her a warm bubbly feeling, and she knew it was right. *Gratitude.*

Centre	Colour	Description	Blocks/Imbalance	Relationship	Virtue
Crown	White	This centre represents your alignment with life force energy and your connection with your higher self	Feelings of being disconnected, off balance, misguided, lacking purpose	Universal	**Love** the true nature of the universe, the source which filters through our different facets
Third eye	Purple	This represents your perspective and when in balance can bring insights and understanding, this can also be the gateway to the collective unconscious	Closed mindedness, lack of perspective, fogginess, resistance to different views	Extrasensory	**Perfection** the goal, ever expanding wonder, Alignment naturally brings everything into divine balance
Throat	Blue	This centre is related to communication and wisdom, it is also the gateway for change and the connection between your internal and external selves	Communication difficulties, self-esteem problems, resistance to change	Wisdom	**Gratitude** expressing the natural response to the magnificent nature of existence
Heart	Green	This is where compassion, generosity and unconditional love come from, your ability to empathise with others.	Emotional coldness, emotional pain, lack of empathy	Unconditional	**Compassion** connecting with everyone, only through pain can we understand its opposite
Solar Plexus	Yellow	This centre is your rational mind, the control centre. Your logical thought processed and internal dialogue come from here	Control issues, anxiety, fear	Control	**Acceptance** being in the flow of the universe, releasing the need to control
Sacral	Orange	This is where your survival drives come from, hunger, desire. This level of your being is geared towards meeting physical needs	Dependency, compulsive behaviour	Survival	**Trust** everything will work out in the best possible way, this counters destructive fear based survival drives.
Root	Red	This centre represents the purely physical level of your being, your physical body	Health problems, difficulty with physical reality	Physical	**Joy** the sublime experience or being, becoming aware and choosing happiness and celebrating life

ZANE

Zane had not realised how much he missed his mother until he saw how she had aged. Her smile lines were deeper, her hair had lost all its colour to grey, and there was a heaviness in her shoulders he did not recognise.

"I'm so sorry, Zane," she said, tears welling up in the corners of her eyes. "There's something I should have told you years ago. Something you need to see." She made her way over to the hall bureau and withdrew two envelopes with shaky hands.

"This…" she said, thrusting the first at him. Its paper was aged to the colour of weak tea.

"This came just after you left us."

Zane was perplexed. His mother seemed to be overreacting to a few delayed letters. He noted the rim, carefully torn with the family heirloom letter opener. Zane cast his mind to its gilt handle rather than confront the sight of his mother breaking down. "And this," she said, her hand shaking with the second envelope, "arrived a few months ago."

The kind of surprise that hits you in the stomach like a brick, that throws your plans, the life you thought you had, everything, out of the window... Zane was still reeling. He finally felt he understood the way a devoted spouse would feel when divorce was announced. *The kind of shock that wrings tears from what feels like a dry sponge. The way parents must feel when they hear of their angelic child being suspended from school for reckless behaviour.* Pandora's box was opened, and there was no going back. *The choice is yours,* his internal monologue stated. *Let go or bring yourself more pain, take a step back or be pulled into a void of unhappiness.*

IRIS

I ris had just put the final touches on the draft of her book. Everything had clicked into place, and she was amazingly, astoundingly, perfectly happy. Then the phone rang.

"Hello?" Her voice was full of joy.

"Iris," the voice on the other end was sharp like a pin to her temple, but her consciousness reeled in confusion. "It's Zane."

Her mind caught up quickly, like a slap to the face as her ordered mental world crumbled.

"Why are you calling? Why now?" There was panic in her voice.

"I just got your letter," he sighed. "I just found out."

7 0

MARCIA

L*osing a child is something you never get over.* Marcia had watched her parents live with the daily grief of the little boy they had lost. She wondered why adopting Nathan hadn't stopped them from looking so sad. She also wondered why they never spoke about her brother. She missed him too, but they never asked. They only ever asked about school and homework.

Marcia felt she understood now, reviewing this snippet of child-hood as she pulled ivy away from the fence line. They didn't talk because it hurt too much. It hurt to remember. They focussed on the daily chores that kept them occupied, devoted themselves to work and being busy because it kept the pain at bay. It was too huge to deal with and too deep to comprehend. She felt herself forgiving her parents a little bit more with every weed she stripped away; each, a tiny step towards clearing her family legacy of anguish.

The garden was looking good now. She had made a satisfying difference in just a few months, and it now barely stood out in the tidy neighbourhood, but Marcia knew that on closer inspection, there was still a lot to do. *If you dig a little deeper, you find there's always so much more to overcome.* It was in this sentiment that she walked to the letterbox one morning in late February in her pale silk dressing gown and found exactly what she had been looking for. It was the most terrifying feeling in the world.

LEA

Lea felt empty inside. She was back on the anti-depressants, despite the fact that they didn't work, and she was sure they were shorting the synapses in her brain when she forgot to take them, and they did that electric shock thing. They made her feel dull. They made everything grey. Her mother insisted that she do something. She had been doing everything – everything in her power anyway. She had even gotten to the point where she felt she was in control before it all spiralled out again.

Everything's blurred. I don't know how to handle this insatiable vortex, never-ending hunger for some fixation. Perhaps I need someone to love. I feel so empty after having known this love. Now I cannot live contentedly without it. Not that I have ever lived contentedly, but after tasting it, I'm hooked.

Prescription medicine and cigarettes and alcohol were nothing compared to Alex. He was something like heroin, she imagined. So intense.

The strongest thing I have ever known. Alex was my lifeline, but he's escaped from my grasp. I need to be strong, independent, but I have this need to love… I should meditate.

It was easier said than done. She closed her eyes and immediately needed to scratch her arm then readjust her legs. She became frustrated with herself, which didn't help her relax. She gave up and dived face-first into her duvet, burying her face. Her warm breath threatened to choke her, but she didn't care if it did. She felt worse than she had without taking those stupid pills. It was simple. They didn't help. She didn't need them. She got up and threw the packet into the cane rubbish bin beside her dresser.

I can do this on my own.

Just when things had started to look up, Lea found herself plunged back into her old pain. The darkness was familiar as always.

I bleed between these pages what I cannot speak aloud: my agonising torment, myself despise, my inner child clutching at my conscious mind, my apathy and contradicting empathy, at times, my un-revoked cynicism, and sometimes I let other thoughts seep through just enough to crush them with malevolent paradox… in order to amuse my pessimism most probably. I can never tell.

She looked down at the words she had just written and saw, as if for the first time, how melodramatic she could be. It made her laugh at herself. It felt good, freeing. But there was still so much work to do.

Forgive myself, splitting myself apart in bright purifying light, releasing guilt. Breathing through, right through me. Letting go, forgiving everything, even the choice to be here. All the pain, all that I may have caused others, even the potential for experiencing and inflicting pain. Release.

Will you forgive God?

For God, or gods or goddesses, was surely the reason for all the suffering human beings faced. It was a cruel thought, but not as threateningly barren as the perspective that there was no God at all, nothing. There had to be another way.

I am my own God, my own fragment of the universe. I chose to be here. I need no repentance. I can choose to set myself free. I need no externalised deity of my divinity. We are all part of God.

She felt light, as if she were floating. She could feel that the corners of her mouth were reaching up towards her eyes, smiling. So, this was what happiness felt like. It seemed unfamiliar after such a long absence.

Realisation: everything is as it is meant to be… looking at my current situation, I am exactly where I need to be right now. All worries dissolve.

Of course, not all her worries had, but she was definitely heading in the right direction, and this she could tell by the way she was feeling.

IRIS

Alexi. That was what she had named him, after the last Russian prince. She called him Lexi as a baby, but as soon as he started school, he was Alex. That was that. This was what Iris was thinking about as she struggled to find the right words to tell him his life was not as he'd thought it to be all along.

The bath was getting uncomfortably cold, but there was no more hot water. She watched her hands, their wrinkled fingers clasped under the water like a lotus, distorted by the ripples her breath caused on the surface. She wanted to melt like chocolate, smooth, sweet, and delectable, into the water. She had run the bath to escape, to get perspective and take stock of her life. There was a chill in her mind. The icy past had cut with precision into her world, and she was at a complete loss.

She needed to tell her son that the father he thought had abandoned him hadn't actually left; he'd never even known he existed. Alex had left a few minutes before. He was outside for once, kicking his soccer ball around the uneven driveway. Iris could hear him in the distance, an irregular thudding that mocked her heartbeat.

The book that had seemed so near completion only minutes ago was now clearly unfinished. Iris had a lot of work to do. She needed to find a way to communicate the important truths she had just learnt into her book. She needed to tell people that sometimes the things they wanted most in the world were buried so deeply in their subconscious, the resistance to them so strong that they couldn't even be aware of them. She wanted people to know that when things finally make sense and come together in the most wonderful way, the contentment, like the calm before the storm, causes a paramount shift, allowing something huge and altogether surprising to occur. *There is no end*, she thought. *Like the seasons, we just keep cycling.*

ZANE

Z ane had told the guys about Iris. They knew almost everything about each other after ten years of living in each other's pockets – literally at first because they didn't have much money. He had told them he had been in love once, that everything had been wonderful until she left suddenly without saying goodbye.

"She probably had her reasons," Baz had said, but Zane could not, for the life of him, work out what those could have been. He waited outside her flat until her flatmates had felt sorry for him and taken him in, and when she did not return home, he had called her parents, who brushed him off. If they knew anything, they didn't tell him. Finally, he had given up. He left for the States with no hope. He knew his pain had enriched his music, given it depth.

"Life happens," was Jimmy's response. He seemed to escape his life with religion, visiting Buddhist monasteries in every country they toured. It gave him a lightness unexpected of a large, hairy man. Zane sometimes admired his diligence, and at the same time, he scorned his refusal to swim in the cesspool of reality with the rest of them. Ultimately, he was jealous of anyone who glided through life, aware or not.

Mitch had just shrugged when he heard about Zane's tragedy. Zane doubted he had ever really been in love with any of the stick-figure girls he bought home and said as much. Mitch had agreed easily enough.

"It's the image I'm in love with, mate," he'd said, lolling back in his recliner. "Perfection." The word was crisp yet intangible.

Zane didn't have patience for ideals when the world was falling apart around him. Ideals were dangerous.

Just hearing her voice had cost him a lot. He could feel his self-assured personality crumbling away. He had lived for years with the idea that she had left him because of some kind of mysterious thing. He couldn't tell whether it was him or her. He had, of course, wondered if she had met someone else. That was the obvious explanation, wasn't it?

It had never crossed his mind that she could have been pregnant, *with his child*. The thought was so strange and intense it made his insides twist around. He didn't even know she'd wanted kids. They were still pretty young, and it was true; he hadn't been ready.

He picked up the other letter, knowing fully well that if he had received it at any other time in his life, there would have been a good chance he would have thrown it away and not thought about it until he was drunk.

His birth mother had always been an enigma. He had hated her and yearned for her alternately. He had told himself over and over that he didn't care. He had loving parents. He had everything he wanted. He didn't need another mother. He didn't need anyone. It was hard not to resent someone for rejecting you so totally when they had every obligation not to; when, by birth, she was the one person in the world who was supposed to love him, and she hadn't even given him a chance.

Iris had made him do it, just after he turned twenty. She had told him it would give him closure. He'd sent a letter to the department of something and gotten nothing back. They hadn't been able to contact her. Since then, he had blocked her out of his mind as best he could. If she wanted nothing to do with him, he would be the same way.

If he hadn't simultaneously found out that he had, in ignorance, done exactly the same thing to his child, he might never have picked up the phone and dialled her number.

74

IRIS

Iris had been lying to herself for a long time. She had avoided the truth, avoided telling Alex about his father. There was a lot she felt she had to make up for, but first of all, she had some internal work to do: uncovering a pattern of self-deceit. There were always excuses, ways of justifying her position. She had become adept at this form of lying. It started innocently enough.

She thought it might have arisen out of her childhood intolerance for injustice. Any time she encountered unfairness, she always fought against it, whether it was for herself, for her siblings or even strangers. She had taught herself how to argue, how to bend reality around her little finger in order to balance out the power. The positive effect of this was that she became good at explaining things and relating points together in a meaningful way, good at convincing others. The negative pole was that she resisted change, uncomfortable situations, excusing herself, being sick, weak – anything to evade – being tired, lost, sad: these were the socially acceptable ways out of responsibility.

In much the same way, she convinced herself that Alex didn't need to know things that might hurt him... that might hurt her.

I can change this pattern. I am changing it. I am always safe. I have no need to protect myself, no need for stress, no need for excuses. I release the need behind this pattern, behind my stress and guilt. I release my burdens. I release emotional pain. I am strong, able, happy, warm, inspired. I choose my situation. I choose my reality.

75

MARCIA

Marcia had spent her entire adult life in denial of something so colossal she could not confront it until, through running, she came full circle and ran right into it. The baby she had held in her arms for moments after the hardest 16 hours of her life, whose eyes she had looked into and prayed for mercy, for forgiveness, had called her. She did not recognise his voice, but the man on the other end of the phone line had answered her prayers, almost four decades after she had lost him.

She could not respond to him. She could not speak for the tears that clawed their way through every inch of her skin, trying to escape. Her heart, the one she felt she had lost all those years ago, now throbbed erratically in her chest, absurdly loud. She did not feel real.

"Hello?" The voice demanded her attention, and she wanted to bottle its essence, to imbibe it in order to redeem herself.

She uttered the only words she could say.

"I'm sorry. I'm so sorry."

He had called her, after all these years of not knowing, and all she could do was apologise. There were no words that could make up for what she'd done, no words to express the intense emotion that overwhelmed her. It was over too soon. He had let her feeble words fall into silence, and then he had hung up, leaving her to listen to the beeping that represented her failure as a mother, as a human being.

On the table in front of her sat a letter from the Registrar-General of Births, Deaths and Marriage. She had received it two months before, and it had filled her with hope. It was an official letter, acknowledging her inquiry. It said that her son was willing to be contacted, and it mentioned a previous inquiry lodged eighteen years before. He had tried to find her, but no one had known where she was.

She wondered if her parents had known. Had they read her mail? The thought filled her with the terrible pain of injustice. It was their fault, and yet, they were the ones to whom his letter was sent. She hoped they felt guilty. She read and re-read the page in front of her, hoping it would give her some clue, but of course, it didn't. It protected him from her.

She didn't have a way to contact him, to call him back. She didn't know what to say to him anyway. How could she undo her biggest mistake? How could she let him know that he was all she could think about for so long, no matter where she was or what she did? Her baby. How could she explain that she had been utterly powerless at the time when she couldn't even believe that herself? Hadn't she spent thirty-five years, reliving those days in her mind, going over every possibility to see where she could have done something differently?

She could have run away from home before he was born. She could have found somewhere safe to have him and then brought him up on her own, but at sixteen, she feared for her safety and for his. She didn't know how she could provide for herself, let alone someone else who depended on her so completely.

In the hours that followed his birth, she had been drugged without consent. It was something she regretted despite having no choice in the matter. She could never get those precious moments back, where she could have held him and let him know he was loved, even if she couldn't keep him. In the days that followed, she had felt hollow, empty; every thought made her cry. She couldn't do anything at all, just lie there in bed with the curtains drawn, speaking to no one, not even eating. She thought she would die that way, waste away until there was nothing left of her. She wanted to.

Something that had always surprised her since that time was the utterly enduring nature of life. It carried on indefinitely so that as the weeks dragged on, Marcia had felt something returning to her. Not happiness, but some form of strength, and it built up until it was enough to get her out of there. She swore she'd never return.

She looked around the room, at the house she had reclaimed in more than one way. It gave her hope. She couldn't change the past, but she could make a difference in the present. She would have called him back then if she could. She would have told him that she wanted to know him, that she wanted to be as much a part of his life as he would allow, that she loved him more than anything in the world and always had. There was so much to say, so she picked the phone up and called the only person she could bear to share it with.

IRIS

I ris was already in the twilight zone, so it came as no surprise when Marcia called her in a state. From what she could gather from her friend's garbled sobs, the baby she had adopted out a long time ago had just called her as a fully grown man. It would have astonished Iris to find out that her close friend, who always seemed so 'together', had such a tortured past, but she was beyond surprise.

"I had no idea," she said. "That must have been a shock for you."

"I contacted the agency a few months ago; I didn't know if he would care, I didn't think I deserved him to. Now I don't know if I feel better or worse. It's amazing, I'm happy that he's alive, that he's doing well. It didn't even sound like he hates me, but it brings it all back, the worst time in my life." She sobbed again.

"That's so strange," Iris said, not wanting to detract from the valid drama Marcia was obviously in the thrall of, but she couldn't help herself. "I just got a call from Alex's dad."

Marcia was silent on the other end of the line, probably pulling herself together.

"I didn't think I'd ever hear from him again. It's been sixteen years with no contact at all."

"Oh." Marcia seemed stunned out of her state. "That's shocking."

"Do you know what the worst part is?" Iris was whispering despite the fact there was no one else in the house. "He didn't even *know*. He's been out of the country, and his adopted mother – I can't believe her! She kept the letter from Zane this whole time!" Iris passed through the shock and rage again too quickly. It made her nauseous.

"Zane?" There was something in Marcia's voice that Iris didn't recognise.

"Yes, that's his name."

"That's *his* name."

It took Iris a moment to comprehend what Marcia was getting at.

"No!" It was genuine denial.

"Zane Strachan."

"No. No. No." Iris's head was spinning. It was impossible.

Marcia was silent, putting the pieces together while Iris uttered any word that made sense.

"No way! This can't be happening. My life is a soap opera. You're his mother? You were the one who... I can't believe this." It wasn't meant as an accusation, but it sounded like one.

"I didn't... I had no choice." Marcia was trying to justify herself.

"It doesn't matter." Iris didn't mean it to sound so blunt. "I mean it does. I believe you. It must have been awful." She couldn't imagine the agony she would have gone through if her parents had made her give Alex up, which her mother had been in a mind to do when she first heard of her impending grandchild. No one could have torn him away from her, but it was a different time and she was older than Marcia had been. Iris tried to understand it, but it was too awful.

"If Zane is your biological son, that means... Alex is..." She didn't need to finish the sentence; Marcia had already worked it out.

When Iris put down the phone, her head was spinning, trying to accommodate this new reality where things were not as they seemed to be. Something else surprised her: a feeling in her solar plexus that could only be betrayal. It didn't seem reasonable. She could see Marcia's side of the story, but something had shifted between them. Even though they were friends, Marcia was something of a role model to Iris, someone worthy of her admiration. She had put her on a pedestal in her mind, and now the reality that her idol was only human had cracked the ceramic.

MARCIA

Marcia felt like a terrible fraud as she walked up to the hotel. Iris had given her the details that *he* hadn't. She couldn't wait by the phone just in case he called her back. It would drive her insane. She knew it was too soon, but she needed a chance to explain. It was the only thing on her mind. She was compelled to see him, despite her better judgement.

She could tell it was a new building, with that modern architecture that looked like and had all the aesthetic appeal of misshapen shoe boxes, as one of her English friends had once commented. It was made up of concrete squares which had been angled strangely, with sloping roofs and lots of glass. The man at the desk wore a silk scarf around his collar. He was prim and polite but eyed her suspiciously when she asked for the room number.

"I'll just call, shall I, and let him know you're coming." It wasn't a question; he was already reaching for the receiver.

Marcia raised her arm. "I'd rather you didn't. I'm his mother. I wanted to surprise him."

He frowned slightly and then righted his expression into a fake smile.

"Up you go then, ma'am." His voice was cheerful but strained – a little too high-pitched.

Her heart thumped so loudly it seemed to echo through the glass elevator. As it rose, it revealed a view of the river which would have calmed her on any other day. The back doors opened into a long, narrow hallway with dim, upward-facing light fittings torched against the wall. As she approached, panic screamed through her chest. She struggled against it. Her clenched hand felt weak as she knocked on the door.

Light poured out as it opened, revealing a man who looked like Jesus. She scanned his face, looking for some similarity, something of her.

He seemed calm, even as puzzlement crossed his face. It was replaced by some kind of distant recognition. "Zane, it's for you."

She heard the sound of a chair falling over. "What?"

It was obviously a surprise. Her chest felt as if it might cave in as she heard him approach. She took in his beautiful dark hair, his penetrating eyes that seemed disappointed somehow. *He was hoping to see Iris.* As soon as the thought crossed her mind, she saw his expression change into one of fear, and then he seemed to be examining her, taking in the features that were so familiar. Similar and yet different from his own, in the same way that she was looking at him.

Marcia was struck by an overwhelming wave of complex emotion. She wanted to reach out and touch him, to cradle him in her arms as she hadn't been able to after his birth. It was a longing so strong she was taken aback.

The other man had disappeared, giving them privacy. She was still feeling edgy, not sure if she was welcome or an impostor in his life.

"Would you like a drink?" he asked. His expression seemed so familiar, and her mind wanted to place it but could not.

She nodded readily. She would have accepted anything, hot or cold or alcoholic. It made no difference; it was something, an olive branch. She stepped further into the room, allowing the door to close behind her. It was an open, airy space, probably expensive. Clothing and baggage were strewn carelessly around the room, which made it feel more comfortable somehow. She sat down at the glass-topped coffee table, admiring the river view she had barely noticed moments before. Now it lulled her.

She gratefully accepted the tumbler of whiskey he handed her, allowing it to scorch her throat.

"You know," he said, sitting down opposite her. "I always did wonder about you."

78

ZANE

He knew he was overdoing it as he reclined in his seat with his boots resting against the table. The posture was too relaxed for the occasion, and a small, young part of his mind somersaulted in protest as if he were arriving at a cocktail party in pyjamas, something he had gained a reputation for doing in Los Angeles. He ignored it and remained ludicrously laid back. He knew meeting one's birth mother was supposed to be emotional and awkward, but he wasn't into tradition or social norms, so he sat and casually asked her about her day.

At first, she seemed taken aback by this, but she recovered quickly. She told him she had been gardening.

"Vegetables?" he had asked.

"Some. The harvest season is over, but there are always carrots and potatoes..." She trailed off. He couldn't help but appraise her as she spoke, her lips moving eloquently, her English accent, her face, so symmetrical, finer than his, but there was a resemblance. If he saw her walking down the street, wrapped in that emerald shawl, her dark peasant skirt billowing out behind her, he would have been intrigued by the mystery she seemed to possess. Her dark eyes were almost the colour of his, her skin so much paler. She was classically beautiful, and there was something about her that made her ageless.

Not young but impossible to place. He would never have guessed she could have been old enough to be his mother, with that dark ruby-streaked hair.

"So, what did you wonder?" she asked when silence indicated he planned no more than the trivial questions already posed.

"I'm only beginning to figure that out," he said, looking her in the eye for the first time. "I think it was more of a general wondering." He leant back again, hiding behind his nonchalant guise.

It was in much the same way that the conversation came to an end, never reaching an obvious conclusion. She left her phone number and address, never asking him for more than he offered, giving him miles of emotional space. Part of him appreciated her for going along with his game; the other part was furious. *Doesn't she care who I am? Where I've been since she abandoned me?* The voices began to shout as she exited, but the last look she gave him silenced them. It was intense but unreadable. Her eyes bored into him with so much unsatisfied energy that he held his breath for moments after the door had closed. He knew it wasn't really over.

79

IRIS

Alex had not spoken since she told him. He'd been in the kitchen when she finally plucked up the courage. She tried to explain that she'd recently discovered something important.

"Is it about my father?"

How did he know?

"So, what is he? A window cleaner? A druggie?"

"Actually, he's a musician."

"Great, a bum musician."

"I think he does quite well."

"So, what does he want? To feel less guilty about abandoning us?"

The anger in his voice was so powerful it knocked Iris in the chest.

"Alex. He didn't know." Her eyes pleaded forgiveness, but his were cold.

"You said…" Through the accusation, his voice was breaking with emotion. "You said you told him. You said he never replied."

"I did," she said, breaking down herself. She didn't want Alex to hate either Zane or her, but she could see something had to give. There were sixteen years of unasked and unanswered questions to be spoken for. "I wrote him a letter; he never responded. I thought…"

"You just assumed he'd got it. You thought he'd want nothing to do with me, so you made that choice for me."

"I didn't know," she beseeched. "He hasn't been in New Zealand your entire life. I didn't want to force him to be involved if he didn't…" Her words broke off, brittle.

"Yeah," he said with a blackness in his eyes she had never seen before. "Who would want to be *my* dad? Who would want that kind of burden?"

"That's not what I meant," she said, in a voice she usually used in an argument. "There are so many things I should have told you, Alex." Her voice became tender. "Your father never planned you, but I did. I wanted to have a baby, but he wasn't ready. It's not his fault or yours." *Or mine*, she thought, but she didn't believe it herself.

Alex had gone quiet then as if processing. She didn't dare tell him about his grandmother as well; she reasoned he had enough to deal with. He hadn't met Marcia. It probably wouldn't mean much to him.

He became a zombie to her, eating, sleeping, not bothering to go to school. He sat at the computer a lot, but with blank eyes, not even moving the mouse. At times, he did not bother to turn it on. Sometimes he sat in front of the TV and stared at his knuckles.

Iris tried to speak to him casually, to ask if he was hungry, if he wanted anything, but he never replied. It seemed to her to go on forever; more likely, it was a couple of days. Then one evening, he walked right up to her and asked her a question. It was so uncharacteristic of him that she shuddered.

"What's his name?"

Iris knew this was something he should have known all his life. It was absurd that she hadn't told him, and now it was difficult. She had seen his name credited on the back of the CDs she had inspected when Alex left them lying around. *What's worse*, she wondered, *having a father who is a complete stranger or finding out that the same absent parent happens to be one of your heroes?*

"Zane Strachan." When she said it, she watched his face carefully. She waited for the surprise that didn't come. She watched closely for a colour change. She waited for a response. Nothing. He just turned around and walked out of the room. His stoic footfalls echoed in her mind through her entire sleepless night.

The next day, when she went to rouse him mid-morning, he was gone.

All the usual thoughts occupied her mind. She should call the police, who she knew would have little interest in a teenager missing for such a short time. She should contact the school, his friends, the neighbours, but if she knew her son at all, he wouldn't turn up on anyone's radar. She should go out and look for him, but what if he returned? In the end, she resigned herself to the optimistic duty of sitting by the telephone and praying.

ZANE

Z ane had to see her again. It was all he could think about, an urge he could not shake, even through the brief encounter with his birth mother. He had things to do, publicity crap. He opted out of the TV interviews, leaving his band to deal with the bright lights and plastic smiles. The guys had joked that he had finally grown some balls after all these years.

He called the directory and found her address, somewhere in the middle of nowhere past Raglan. It surprised him that she could be so close, an hour or so away. It was surreal. He felt his skin prickle when he thought of it: coming face-to-face after all this time. So many years had elapsed. They were worlds away and still so connected somehow. He felt it in his chest, like invisible chords oblivious to time and space, that anchored him to her.

The country was prettier than he remembered. So green compared to the yellows and greys of Los Angeles, so much grass adorning the rolling hills dotted with livestock and clumps of trees. He wanted to watch it all as it went by, to take it all in, but he had to pay attention to his driving.

The road wound on, becoming steeper, the corners sharp, never giving him a chance to relax. Then it gave way to straighter stretches. It was a beautiful autumn day, his second autumn in the last few months, and the leaves were beginning to turn gold and vermilion; nature always accepted the change that people struggled against.

After driving for what seemed like forever, the hills began to reveal peeps of ocean between them. He passed through the little town, remembering the turnoff from the map he'd found online. He crossed a one-way bridge and watched the houses thinning out and the native trees becoming more prolific, all the while, tension was building in his chest.

It took him a while to find the driveway, hidden away in the bush, and once he had pulled up outside what could possibly be a house but was too obscured by trees to be certain, he realised he could not go on. It was too much. He looked around, engulfed by ferns and other familiar plants, the names of which he could not remember.

They had come out here, to this coast. They were just kids, really, but thought they were so grown up. Iris had held his hand as they clambered over rocks, using each other for balance. He had looked out to the horizon and lost himself in infinity until Iris kissed him unexpectedly. That was the first time she had told him she loved him, as if she'd planned it all along. She was crazy like that; she had the whole world tucked away in her head, just waiting for the right moment to surprise him.

He took a deep breath and fidgeted with the windscreen wipers. He had a child. A child who had been living for the past sixteen years without his knowledge. It was too big to grasp, but it was starting to sink in, giving his body the most unusual sensations, alternating hot and cold.

One minute, he was furious with her. *How could she?* But then logic broke through. *She tried to tell me.* His mind swung back and forth like a pendulum, giving him motion sickness.

Everything had changed for him in the course of one day, two letters, three betrayals. The three most important women in his life had turned all the certainty he once possessed into jelly. His adoptive mother, his first love, and his birth mother. There was a poetic beauty to it, which he felt he couldn't appreciate fully because he was caught in the middle of it all.

The thought of going on was paralysing but going back was absurd. He got out of the car and waded through the most intense emotions on his way to the brick steps etched into the side of the bank. Native grasses and seedlings were growing all over them. *Jesus, what the hell is Iris doing out here?* But he knew before he even asked himself the question. *She needs this place just as much as I need to see her.* There was a sense of destiny about it as if his future self was guiding him.

He got to the porch and tapped on the glass of the door. Nothing. Relieved, he turned to go but was stopped in his tracks by a clambering sound in the house. He turned to find he was staring into those forget-me-not eyes, and it was too late to go back.

IRIS

Zane was at the door. Iris did a double-take. Zane. At the door. Something did not compute. She stood there, looking stupidly at him through the streaked glass, which she realised was covered in fingerprints. *I should clean the glass.* She felt embarrassed by it, although she knew he was looking straight through it, straight through her to the other side of the world, back into the past when everything was different and perfect and they'd been happy. Together. But between them and the present, there was so much baggage. She realised he was still standing outside, and not to be rude, she reached for the handle, only to find it slipped from her hand. She felt like a ghost in a movie, unable to touch, made of something different than reality. She tried again and clasped the cold metal. How odd that there was still cold in the world when she was burning up. She opened it reluctantly, unsure if it was the wisest thing to do, to remove the protective layer between them. His eyes were on hers the whole time.

"Zane," she said. It was a statement; it sounded disembodied somehow.

"Iris." He nodded at her, and she heard him swallow hard.

"Come in." It was awkward, but she meant it. She continued to stand there, staring at him, allowing her eyes to remember the latte shade of his skin, his dark eyes, the curve of his shoulder where she used to bury her head. It took her a while to realise she was blocking his entrance. She moved to the side, embarrassed again. She led him to the sofa where they sat, looking out over the horizon, in intimate conversation though no words passed between them.

ZANE

It was as if they were speaking telepathically, remembering the same events at the same time. Each breath she took, Zane could relate to. Each subtle movement of her body was another story, filling in the years they'd been apart.

He knew he needed to speak. There were so many things he needed to know. Actually, there was only one.

"I have a child." It was half question, half statement. He believed her letter, but it was all still sinking in. "I'm a father." The title didn't sit well. It was unfamiliar, older than him. It represented responsibility and authority and rules, things that weren't really *him*.

At the same time, it was a miracle, something impossible yet infinitely good. Iris was still there. She had never really left him. The mystery that had torn his world apart was solved and in such an unexpected way.

"He's gone." Her voice was thin and cold.

"A son?" Zane was confronted with mental images of a younger version of himself; it took him a while to grasp what Iris had said.

"Alex," she said, nodding her head and keeping it downcast.

"Alex," Zane repeated as if it had been on the tip of his tongue all these years. "Where is he?" It was baffling; could it be possible to gain something so significant and lose it all in the same instant?

"I told him who you are."

Zane looked into her eyes, and they were full of apology.

"I think he has all of your albums... He didn't know... He never asked your name."

Zane's anger flared up again. "You run your household on a don't-ask-don't-tell policy?"

"I know." Her words were full of sharp guilt, causing him to deflate.

"He'll be back." Zane wasn't sure why he was reassuring her; he just knew.

"I'm so sorry, Zane," Iris broke down. "I shouldn't have run away like that. I should have made sure you knew." It was old emotion, but it came out in an engulfing wave that made him feel like he was drowning.

"You said..." she continued, her voice rising between sobs, "... you didn't want kids, you didn't want to make the world even worse than it was by spreading the human virus."

"But I didn't know that you *did*." He knew it would have made all the difference. She could have changed any of his strong opinions in moments. It made him feel weak, but he didn't care.

"I should have been there for you. I can't believe you had to do this on your own." He looked around the room for evidence that she was, indeed, on her own. Everything from the carefully arranged fruit bowl to the pink fluffy slippers screamed Iris.

"I think it was just something I needed to do." Her voice was stronger, and then it broke as another wave rolled in. "I just wish I didn't screw it up so badly."

Zane couldn't imagine Iris screwing anything up. She was a complete being, perfect in and of herself. That was what drew him to her in the first place. That was why he loved her.

"What's done is done," he said. There was no point lamenting. "He's what, sixteen by now? He has to work some things out for himself." Zane felt odd talking about this person who he didn't know, had never met but was intimately connected with. It felt wrong to make assumptions about him, but there was a part of him that intuitively knew his son. He was only just realising it.

LEA

Lea sat in the darkness, praying silently to any god that would hear, hoping desperately to be rescued from her own sadness. She instinctively found her way to her desk, opening the bottom drawer. She let her hands run through the textures until she found something smooth. Retreating to her bed, she set the candle on her bedside table and lit it. As the flame illuminated the room, she remembered a line from a poem she'd once written. *When a candle is lit, a shadow is cast.*

She had not been raised with any faith, and right now, she felt desperately alone. She prayed to the Christian God, the Muslim God, the many Hindu gods of which she knew little, the ancient Greek gods she had learnt about in Classics class: *Athena, Zeus, Artemis.* She prayed to the native gods she knew about only through children's storybooks: *Ranginui, the sky father, Papatūānuku, the Earth mother.* She prayed to the goddess in all of her many facets.

She let herself drop into her bed, exhausted from this desperate attempt at faith. She felt dizzy. She remembered she hadn't taken her anti-depressants for days. She was supposed to wean herself off them, not just stop taking them.

She had the strange sensation that she was falling, through the bed, out of her body, rising up. She saw herself lying there, looking small and sad. She felt herself rising further up, up, up, through the roof, towards the stars. She felt as if she was expanding like a balloon the higher she rose. She felt so light, so wonderful as she reached the outer limits of the Earth's atmosphere and found herself in another world entirely.

Other beings like her were milling around; they looked like little lights moving in formation. A bright light moved towards her, greeting her. Was she in heaven? Was this Jesus coming to her? It was someone familiar. The bright light embraced her, filling her with understanding and joy. All the wisdom in the universe was accessible to her at that moment. Everything was perfect and good and right.

Then she knew she had to go back. She saw her body, so far below, so small. She wondered how she could possibly fit, as vast and expansive as she had become. She felt herself being pulled back down, sucked into her body like a genie into a bottle and into a peaceful sleep.

Waking refreshed the next morning, she felt lighter somehow, like a huge burden had melted away overnight. The reality that was torturous yesterday was a faint memory, and the world around her seemed more abstract. Something had changed. She just couldn't put her finger on what it was.

It was obvious to Lea. A transformation had occurred. She knew it was something to do with the dream she'd had. Something told her that it was more than a dream, but her internal sceptic doubted whether it was possible that she had actually left her body. She didn't struggle with this cynical voice. She no longer needed to believe because she knew. She understood.

She liked to think of it as divine equilibrium, a term she had read about on one of her favourite websites on paganism. The autumn equinox had restored her balance. It had made her mind clear. Overnight, her worries about what other people thought of her had vanished as she realised that judgement was actually an internal process. Whatever other people thought about, it wasn't for her to know or care. *I am the only one who can judge myself,* she thought.

It's all up to me. The realisation had brought a light, harmonious feeling with it that complimented her stoic determination to overcome.

84

IRIS

I ris loved her son like nothing else in the world, but she sometimes felt her attachment to him was unnecessary, that it only caused her to pull and push him, to want to control him in order to be in control of her own feelings. The more she tried to control him, the more distant he became, punishing her for her transgression, making her feel guilty.

She had no idea where he could be, and although she desperately needed to find out, she needed to be in a fit emotional state to do it. She needed to detach, to accept him and his actions, to love him purely, simply, for himself.

I expect you to be yourself,
To do what you feel you need to do,
To do what you think is best,
To do what you think will cause you the least amount of pain;
That is all I expect of you;
Because that is what I know I can expect from myself, from anyone;
That is human nature.
I feel unconditional love and compassion for you,
I appreciate you;
You are magnificence in human form;

You are indescribably beautiful;
You are ever-changing perfection;
You are God.

She looked down at the message she had written neatly, the black ink seeping into her thick white letter paper. It was perfect. It was her message to Alex. To everyone. It was God's message to creation. And as Iris believed God was the creative force of the universe, it was God's message to itself.

Marcia had expressed a similar sentiment in the last workshop, and Iris had felt incredibly pleased. Universal truths had this way of repeating themselves over and over, and people on similar wave-lengths seemed to somehow congregate together.

Everything in its place. This was the way relationships could be if they were fully realised; love and appreciation, unmarred by the need for control, free of the expectations that cause stress, giving each person the freedom and acceptance to be themselves. *Now I'm ready to find Alex.*

She found him nestled in the windswept grass that struggled to grow between ancient volcanic boulders on the hill above the beach. It was not her usual walk, but Iris had strayed in the hopes that he would be somewhere close.

He was curled up, his back to the wind and Iris noticed little shards around him, which she thought at first to be glass, but then their reflection was too much a mirror, and she realised they were the broken fragments of CDs.

Alex was awake but not fully conscious. He stared blankly at the lichen growing on the stone in front of him, and she knew he felt her presence only when he spoke. His words were disordered at first as if there were too many conflicting thoughts trying to escape at once.

"Is... What... bler... doing." He gave up and breathed deeply.

Iris got down on her knees and wrapped him in her arms. She didn't care if he was nearly grown up and hated this kind of attention; he was her baby. He didn't move, and so she stayed that way, just breathing in the sea air and feeling utterly grateful he was still hers. She had always believed that children were not the property of their parents; rather, they were entrusted with each other. Now, although she knew it was her role to be his guardian and his guide, she realised she would always be his mother.

85

MARCIA

M arcia smiled like an ecstatic child as she saw the silver rental car pull up outside the lichen-covered stone fence in front of her house. She recognised her son's profile instantly. She watched from a shady corner of the afternoon-sun drenched garden, where she had been weeding. He got out of the car and seemed to size the place up, taking in the masses of trees and the Victorian villa, which, to her credit, looked much less derelict than it had a year before. He negotiated her gravelled driveway, stepping over puddles left by the autumn rain. He moved in a way that was graceful for a man, as if the world was carrying him and the ground came up to meet his every step. He looked unbelievably happy, happy and curious like a child.

She waited until he was almost at the house to make him aware of her presence.

"Over here," she called, waving out to him.

He seemed stunned but made his way over quickly enough.

"I owe you an explanation," she said. Her head was lowered slightly, but she kept her eyes on his.

He just nodded.

"This is where I grew up… mostly. We moved here when I was

about six." She continued to weed as she spoke, allowing her thoughts and words to flow with the motion.

"My father was a proud, angry, controlling man. We didn't get on. We always seemed to clash. To me, this house was like a war zone." Her expression was sad as she recalled the past.

"I was fifteen when I met him." It was obvious who she was talking about. "He was a labourer. My father hired him to do some renovations. He was removing some walls to make the living room bigger." The memory was still clear in her mind: white sheets covered the furniture, which was pushed into the far corner of the room, white plaster dust that stuck in her throat.

"He was sixteen. His name was Tama. We had this magnetic connection. He became my obsession, and it didn't take long before he returned the attention.

My father caught us in my bed, and he went wild. He yelled louder than I'd ever heard him. He picked up the chair from my nightstand, and he was about to hit Tama, but Tama bolted." Marcia began to laugh. "No pants on or anything." She continued to chuckle through her tears. "It would have been hilarious at the time, but I was so scared." Zane reached out and put his hand on her shoulder. She could feel his warmth spreading through her body, healing her.

"He locked me in my room for days. I never saw Tama after that." She sighed.

"A month later, I woke up with nausea before dawn and had to rush to the bathroom to throw up. I knew then. It was the late 70s, and I was pretty clued up. Of course, I didn't tell my father, but after a few months, I had to tell someone. So I told mum." Marcia remembered the comforting feeling of finally confiding in someone. She was stung with betrayal.

"She went running to him the first chance she got. She could never keep a secret. I should have known. He was angry then, but I didn't care. All I cared about was you." Her eyes implored him.

"He didn't let me leave the house. He locked the door and boarded up the window. I felt so trapped, so powerless. Sometimes he came into my room and yelled at me. Sometimes he was quiet, and he said he was disappointed. He never said it, but I knew he was a racist bastard. He was always racist about my mother's Indian heritage too. He didn't like that Tama was Māori. After you were born, they let me hold you, just for a minute, and then they took you away. I screamed for you, and they injected me with something. When I woke up again, it was all over. They just took you away."

Marcia looked at Zane through her tears and saw his own glistening down his cheeks.

"I sat in the room nine days later and made the biggest mistake of my life. I had nothing but you, and I had to choose whether to keep you or give you up to people who could give you everything I couldn't. It seemed selfish to consider my own future, any plans for the rest of my life that I might have had. By that time, everything I had been through had obliterated any positive thoughts about the future from my mind. I could see no way that I could look after you. I had no money, and my father had told me he would throw us out on the streets. I sat in that office, and I watched myself sign you away as if from a distance. I was giving up the only thing that mattered to me. Sometimes when I look back at that situation, I see things the way I did then, that I had no choice, but most of the time, I just see the way things could have been. I have picked at every loose end, every possibility, so many times, but nothing can change the past."

Marcia's eyes had become unfocussed, catatonic. She still held a strand of stray ivy. It dangled loosely from her hand as the tears continued to flow down her face.

ZANE

Zane had been standing silently, more focused than he had ever been in his life. As he looked down at this woman, his birth mother, he felt he could see back into the past she spoke of. He could comprehend the connections, the coincidences, and the sacrifices that had been made so that he could have his life. He grasped her hand, sending the ivy fluttering to the ground, and pulled her into a long, quiet embrace.

IRIS

I ris sobbed into her cafe napkin as Marcia shared the story.

"It's so unfair, Iris said. She didn't care if half of Hamilton saw her smudged mascara.

"I feel that pull. I think every mother does: that possibility of losing your child. It's the worst thing in the world – just the thought of it."

"I never understood how they could do it. My parents. They had already lost a child. My little brother died of cot death. They knew how awful it was. How could they make me lose my baby as well?"

Iris couldn't answer that question. "I don't know how you managed to cope with all that unfairness." The word was heavy and painful all by itself.

Marcia looked up at the apartments across the street, at the people on the veranda above the shops who were watching pedestrians walk by but never suspecting they were being watched themselves. Iris followed her gaze and watched her demeanour change as her tone became lighter.

"You know, in some ways, I think it made me appreciate my life more. I think it taught me to be grateful for what I did have. I had nothing at the time, but that set me free. I lost everything, and I had nothing to lose. I could travel the world without fear because the worst had already happened; there was nothing to worry about. I learned so much through my journey, and that wisdom is priceless."

"It's amazing that you could even come to such a positive revelation," Iris exclaimed. "But hearing that story does make me grateful I have Alex. As pesky as he can be sometimes, he is the single most wonderful thing in my life." Iris breathed in the cool morning air, feeling lighter somehow. The unfairness of loss could teach gratitude. That made sense.

Differentiation and polarity

It's important not to condemn things too quickly. Everything has its place. We need to know what darkness is, or we wouldn't understand that light existed; we would be too immersed in it to notice. In this way, contrast helps us to differentiate between one thing and another. We wouldn't truly appreciate happiness if we never felt sad at all. We wouldn't appreciate what we have if there was no possibility of losing it.

The unfairness you feel when you lose something can teach you to be grateful for what you do have. If you view life in this way, there is nothing that is completely without benefit. The polarities of black and white, good and bad, day and night, right and wrong are helpful tools by which we can compare other things. It is also important to recognise the many shades in between one extreme and another to understand the complexity of every human experience.

What is it you hate?
Do you hate to protect something you love?

88

ZANE

Zane listened to the whirr of plane engines as he stood at the airport to say goodbye to Jimmy, Baz, and Mitch, promising them that he would be back soon enough so that they could work on some new material.

"Hey, man," Mitch said, grasping Zane's hand in a static handshake. "Say hi to Iris for us." He winked. "Oh, and tell your mum she's hot." Zane pushed him in the direction of the flight gate.

"Thanks for the adventure," Baz grinned. Plastic wrap was still covering his newest shoulder tattoo, which he had explained to Zane was a Māori style and probably culturally insensitive.

"I bet you've got a lot of new inspiration," Jimmy said while his eyes sparkled in a smile.

Zane sighed, letting the burden of the last few days roll off his shoulders.

"Yeah," he said, breathing deeply. "My life is blessed."

It was an odd phrase because it was entirely true and yet equally as ironic. He had been through emotional hell and back. He had had to face betrayal and to forgive, to question the core of his identity and take on an entirely new title.

MARCIA

Anyone who was watching from a distance would have seen them assemble there on the beach, an unremarkable group. The man was alone at first. His hands were in his pockets as he kicked at the sand while his long, dark hair blew in the wind. A cloud passed over the sun, leaving him still, calm. He looked out to the horizon, shielding his eyes from the light reflecting off the sea. He was in this state when they joined him. The woman and the boy, almost a man. Their arms were linked as they walked down to the shore. She seemed to lean on him slightly, as if she were lost, over-whelmed. He stood tall, proud, a little awkward as if it was unusual for him.

Marcia watched all this, hidden behind the changing sheds. The woman she knew well and the two men she didn't, but wanted to more than anything else in the world. Her son and her grandson. When the three of them met, she knew it was her turn to join them. She watched herself as if she were a stranger. Her dark wavy hair blowing uncontrollably, her bright-red coat like a beacon as she bridged the gap that had haunted her for most of her life.

It was an unusual feeling. If they had met one-on-one, she knew it would have been uncomfortable, but in this way, in this beautiful place, there was a lot to look at. When she felt she was falling, she could look at Iris, who now seemed radiant as if she was completely together.

Her son stood in front of her, her beautiful baby. Just looking at him made the tears stream. He was not angry, the way she had expected him to be. He had a right to be. He hadn't even been angry during their first two encounters. He seemed to be integrating it all behind those dark eyes.

Her grandson let go of Iris' hand and looked from her to Zane as if putting the pieces of the puzzle together, looking for his own features and finding them. His skin wasn't quite as olive as Zane's; his build was heavier, and his eyes were Iris' blue, but the resemblance was striking.

It had been Alex's idea to meet like this. Iris had called Marcia and requested her attendance at this perfect event: this coming together of lost family.

After a moment that seemed to stretch for eternity, the edge vanished from the air and was replaced with a sense of acceptance. Marcia felt as if she was breathing for the first time, filling her lungs with air and her spirit with joy. Then Alex spoke.

"Can we get some food?" Their collective laughter was lost in the wind, and the atmosphere lifted into one of celebration.

IRIS

The cafe was bustling, full of locals. Iris was surprised she didn't feel nervous or awkward, the odd one out at this family union. She wanted to stay close to Alex, to protect him, but he seemed to be managing well on his own. He had an awed expression as he looked at Zane as if he were not real. Iris wondered whether it was one of those moments for him where he was sure he must be dreaming. That was the way she felt.

Iris sipped her latte and watched her friend bond with her ex-boyfriend and her son in a quiet but deliberate way. It made more sense now why she had been so drawn to Marcia. It wasn't just her charisma or her wisdom. It was the familiarity. She had Zane's dark penetrating eyes, and although her skin was much lighter than his, his face bore some resemblance to hers. Alex's did, too, although she'd never noticed it before. She had always thought he looked a lot like Zane. She was reminded of it every day. He had never let her forget.

Zane glanced at her, his expression uncertain as if he was wondering whether she might disappear into thin air. *That kind of history can't be undone.* She wondered whether she would ever regain his trust. She wanted to.

Alex went to order some more curly fries, and Marcia excused herself and headed to the bathroom.

"Why did you only try to contact me once in sixteen years?" His voice was probing, and there was a hint of pain but no anger. She could hear the unasked question: *Did you think so little of me... that I would have nothing to do with you?*

Iris searched his eyes for an answer.

"I honestly thought you would have received the first letter, and if you wanted to contact me, you would have. I thought you didn't want anything to do with me after what I'd done."

She was faced with the side of herself that thought she was a terrible person. It thrashed in her mind, but she let it go.

"Why didn't you ever try to reach me?" Iris asked. "After the first time, I mean? Mum told me you called, but only once... I wasn't ready to tell you then. It took me weeks to write that letter."

She looked down at her hands and was surprised to see his light brown skin covering her own. His palm felt smooth and warm against the back of her hand.

"Probably for the same reason. Except..." He looked off into the distance. "I couldn't for the life of me work out what I'd done wrong." Iris felt sorry for him then, not in pity but sympathy. It must have been awful not knowing.

There wasn't much else to say, and a calm silence fell between them until Alex returned with change. Iris didn't notice Zane's hand mysteriously disappear until she had reached for her handbag. How astute of him to know that public displays of parental affection did not go down with the teen folk.

Alex offered to show Zane around town, leaving the two women to finish their second round of espresso. Iris watched Marcia closely, noticing the lightness of her presence as if the past trauma had been erased from her being.

"Thank you," Marcia said, her dark eyes filled with joy. "You've made all of this possible, you and your wonderful son." She was almost in tears. She wiped her eyes with the back of her hand. "I've done enough crying this year already, probably more than I've ever cried in my life."

"I've learnt so much from you. I should be the one who's grateful," Iris admitted.

"Well, who says we can't both be?" Marcia smiled.

They both looked out of the window at the exact same moment that the sun broke free from the clouds, its warm golden rays shining over the town.

ZANE

"Thanks for showing me around," Zane said as they walked up the main street. He knew it wasn't a necessary thing, more of an excuse. He wondered what Alex's motivation had been. To leave the café, to get away from his mum, or just to spend some quality time with his dad. *Dad. Such a strange word.*

"I can't believe you're my dad." Alex kept his face calm. He was talented at it, but Zane could detect a slight smile in his voice.

"Hey, you can call me whatever you like."

"Cool." He was silent for a while, then he added. "You make awesome music."

"I can't take all the credit." Although at that moment, he wanted to. He was positively beaming. "The rest of the band does a little bit of work too."

"Can I meet them?" His voice sounded eager. Zane could tell he deliberately toned it down. "I mean, would that be sweet with you?"

"Sure," Zane said casually, and then because he thought he might like to play the role of the father who tried to be cool but always came off looking like a dweeb, he added, "Sweet as."

By this time, they were at the top of the hill that led into the little town.

"That's pretty much it," Alex said.

"It's changed a lot since I was young." Zane did his best impression of an old man voice, making Alex laugh a little. They both turned and looked out over the township towards the sea; just as they did, the overcast day was suddenly perfectly sunny. The golden light gleamed off the flat waters of the harbour. It was a postcard moment that made Zane feel free to appreciate the present moment and enjoy the delights of being.

Zane made himself comfortable on the couch in Iris' house. It was something he thought he could get used to.

"Shove over," she said, nudging his feet from the other side so she could sit down.

"Even when you're being rude, you're graceful."

"And you're as much of a master of flattery as you always were." Her smile was warm and familiar. Everything about the setting made him comfortable.

"I heard you were in trouble with the media a while ago."

"You've been keeping tabs on me?" he smirked. "It was just another fear frenzy, which is, ironically, the kind of thing we make music about."

"Have you been stalked by paparazzi lately?" she asked lazily.

"No, come to think of it, Guru Jimmy must have been right. It has all blown over already."

"Guru Jimmy?"

"Our drummer. You should meet him. I think you'd get along quite well. He's very… Buddhist."

"He sounds charming," Iris said, leaning her head a little closer to Zane. The intimacy thickened the air, and he could feel it, like velvet as he breathed it in. He casually inched himself closer to her while they both stared out through the glass sliding doors that opened on to the deck at the darkening sky.

"So, I hear you're writing a book." Zane made his offering to the conversation.

"Oh," Iris said, her eyes darkening. "You'd taken my mind off it.

Yes, I am. As a matter of fact, I'm in an internal struggle with it at the moment."

Zane couldn't help but laugh at that, and she elbowed him for it and gave him a look of mock hatred.

"Don't laugh. It's because I'm such a hypocrite. I've been keeping things from Alex all his life and lying to myself about it. I have a feeling that it's only the tip of the iceberg. I'm really in no place to give other people advice."

"No one's perfect, Iris." He made his voice as simultaneously gentle and serious as he could. "You're probably one of the most 'together' people I know. One of the wisest, too." He couldn't help himself. "Even if you did bear and raise my child without telling me." His voice cracked into laughter.

"I'm glad you can laugh about it," she said, folding her arms and pouting slightly.

"My point is, you have a lot to offer the world. Don't let a personal crisis stop you."

Iris turned to look at him, and in her eyes, he could see that he was right, and he internally congratulated himself. He turned back to look at the beautiful view of the falling night and smiled to himself as Iris rested her head against his shoulder.

"You know," she mused. "There are probably thousands of fangirls out there who would kill to be in my position now."

"Millions," he corrected in his quiet, self-assured way. "And not just girls, either."

They both burst into laughter.

"You always were good at keeping a straight face," Iris said amidst fits of giggles.

92

IRIS

Was it possible that just days ago, she had wanted more to do? Iris bustled about the kitchen making coffee. She had woken up with a running monologue of a to-do list in her head. Her book was almost finished, in theory. That meant she needed to find a willing publisher. She would have to summarise every chapter in order to submit her work.

Her lease was running out fast, and that meant finding a new place to live, paying rent on her meagre benefit or finding some sort of job. The idea was perplexing and frightening. There was no way she could go back to working ten hours a day in an office with artificial lighting and air conditioning. She had no idea what else she could possibly do. The only jobs available in Raglan were probably in the hospitality industry, which didn't pay well, and she didn't think she would be much good at them anyway. She was reluctant to move and uproot Alex again with all the changes he had already been through.

"*Stop making plans,*" Zane's whispered song in her ear. "*It will all work out in the end.*"

She let herself relax in his arms.

"*Time to reflect, see whatever life sends...*"

It was all too easy. "This is one addiction I need to lose," she said, pushing his arms away so she could continue with her business.

"Wow, you came up with the chorus all by yourself!"

"Seriously, Zane. It's so confusing. I feel like we're back where we started almost two decades ago. We're not the same people. It's like we're going round in circles." She hated that he was always cheerful in the morning.

"You are more talented than I ever gave you credit for." His smile still made her melt. *"This is one addiction I need to lose – going round in circles, get so confused,"* he sang in his chocolaty voice. "It almost rhymes! You know if this book-writing gig doesn't pan out, you could be one hell of a lyricist."

93

ZANE

Just like that, the anger had gone. He didn't see it go, and it didn't trouble him with goodbyes. He only noticed it in the silence in his mind. Whether it had faded slowly or disappeared into thin air, Zane couldn't tell, but it had affected everything.

The guitaring was just as powerful, and the bass flowed as dark and seductive as it ever had. The drumming wasn't any less complex, and yet, there was a definitive change. It was not just the lyrics; it was the way the music massaged Zane's mind and ran through his body. It lifted him higher than he had ever been, to a place of greater perspective, to a place where he could see all the shadows for what they were, and the conflicts that had seemed to dominate his life before were now minuscule like the little trees and houses set amid endless square dry grass plots that he watched from the plane window on his flight back to LA.

He pulled off his headphones and stopped their album playing on his headphones. The roar of the engines offered their own kind of music. There was a rhythm amid the chaos. Part of him wanted to stay, but there were too many things drawing him back. He had loose ends to tie and new projects to begin, whatever they may be.

Something told him that it wouldn't be long until he returned to New Zealand.

MARCIA

M arcia looked through the window, watching the last of the autumn leaves drift down to join the sediment forming on the small brick courtyard outside. It was picturesque in a nostalgic way. She was already missing everything she would have to leave behind.

She had been avoiding returning her London friends' phone calls for too long. James had asked her if she was planning on selling the apartment where she and William had lived or whether she would be renting it out. She was surprised to have to think about it again. People only let her get away with being a grieving widow for so long before they made her accountable. She had so many decisions to make, and she couldn't make them all from her secret garden. She needed to face the world again.

Maybe she would return to being a counsellor. Maybe she would do something different altogether. Maybe she would live in London, maybe in Hamilton. She had a yearning for freedom that she hadn't felt since her youth, to travel the world as a free spirit once more, but this time, she would have a family to come back to.

She finally felt she could shut the painful volume of her life, the youth that she had been avoiding for so long, and move on into something fresh and delicious. She smiled to herself as she sipped her spiced cocoa. *William would like to be here now, at this moment with me*, she thought, and the thought was more happy than sad as she felt his presence wrapped around her on the sofa. *I'm always with you,* he seemed to say.

IRIS

I ris lay in bed, visualising completion. A perfect synthesis of mind, body, and spirit. It was a wonderful feeling, as if she was attaining perfection of being by realising that everything was perfect to begin with.

It had been an incredible year. She had learnt through journeys into herself and out of herself, through triumph and catastrophe, through action and inaction, through change. She now *understood* the things that she already knew, that each external experience mirrored her internal reality. She knew how to let go of everything, and in the process, find the world.

She opened her eyes and found herself just as human and fallible as before and ready to be fooled all over again by reality, the most astute teacher.

There were bags and boxes to pack and a house to clean. The lease was almost up. She had to figure out how she would manage to transport all her belongings, and she had to decide whether to take Marcia up on her offer and housesit for her in the big old house in Hamilton while she was gone. Iris could picture it in her mind; she would tend the gardens and live a life just as reclusive as her current one, even if she wasn't blessed with the sound of the ocean.

She had sent out the first four chapters of her book and an overview to every publishing company she could find online. Now she was playing the waiting game. Living rent-free for a while sounded like a good idea, just while she figured out her next step.

There was just a hint of longing, and it surprised her. It had been a long time since she had missed anyone other than Alex when he was away, and Zane had only been gone two days. He had said goodbye in his non-committal way that she knew was a thin veil for caring too much. He would have liked her to ask him to stay, but it was really his choice. Instead, she gave him an open invitation to return. She knew he would take it, sooner or later. He was already so familiar. It was strangely comforting.

ALEX

Alex figured things had turned out ok, probably better than expected; after all, how many people could say their hero became their father, far from the other way around. Zane wasn't really a 'dad', but he was pretty cool for someone biologically related to him. He had the LA plane tickets in his drawer. Zane had sent them as a kind of "if you want to" thing for his birthday. *I might even go*. He tossed the thought back through his mind; it seemed pleasant enough just to have the possibility.

MARCIA

I t was with a strange sense of déjà vu that Marcia wandered through the rooms of the old villa that had become her home over the past year, for it had been almost exactly a year since she had done the same thing in her flat in London, taking stock of the things she loved and would leave behind. Everything in the house seemed to fit so well; the items she had acquired in this short time complimented the colours she had chosen. She would miss the light-cream walls and spring-green furniture, peppered with pink and red. She couldn't take it with her, and part of her felt comfort in leaving it behind, waiting for her return. There wasn't much she needed. Her humble suitcase was largely dominated by clothing.

As a last sentimental gesture, she retrieved her tarot deck from the bedroom cabinet. She unwrapped the cards from their silk scarf and held them close to her face, inhaling the subtle scent of incense and the rose oil they had been anointed with. As she lowered the deck back into their wrapping, a solitary card darted out and fell to the floor, face down. It felt as if destiny had leant on Marcia at that moment. She felt its weight enter the room, and already she knew which card had made itself known. She leant down and gently picked it up, admiring the depiction of a torch-bearing woman, smiling in the centre of a circle of rejoicing people. She had always felt it was a strange illustration for the World card, but now it seemed to fit. She had found her place in the world, centred in a circle of people she loved.

LEA

L ea had nothing better to do. Her mother had insisted on her going to the Raglan beach house for the weekend. She wandered down to the beach alone, enjoying the mid-morning winter sunlight and the salty sea air. She sat down on a large piece of driftwood, part of an old tree, somehow washed up by the tide. She had brought her notebook with her, and she flipped through its pages, browsing over her darker moments. It was hard to believe her life had ever been that bad. She could see the progression she had made over the year. Her earlier writing had been concerned with anti-depressants. It had complained about her family and about school.

Her poetry had been obscenely, theatrically dramatic. She would surely die of embarrassment if anyone else ever read this stuff. A third of the way through the story of her year, she had become unbelievably, ridiculously, stupidly in love. Some of her entries had been jubilant; others ached with an addict's hunger.

Looking back, she wondered whether it had actually been love or just some kind of chemical reaction in her brain. Maybe that was all that love was. It seemed like it from what she had gleaned from Hollywood movies. Surely there was more to life than that. She knew there was. She had experienced it: the understanding that she was connected to all things and that all things were made out of the same basic positive matter. That was a kind of love that eclipsed the mundane romantic variety.

There was an obvious break where some of the pages had been torn out and others were wavy with dried tears. She could still feel the agony as if it were yesterday as her old words stung her. Armed with her new sense of perspective, she could easily unburden herself of these feelings. They had no power over her anymore.

She turned to the most recent contribution, so unlike all the others.

Paint my heart tangerine and watch the stars drip down.
Paint my soul opaque-grey and watch the heavens drown.

It was a celebration of sorts. She liked the feeling the words gave her, some new kind of indulgent joy. She leant back against the tree root that reached unnaturally towards the sky. As she looked out at the horizon, she felt her mind spreading out along it, becoming calm and flat. It was a peculiar feeling but quite relaxing. She enjoyed the nothingness inside her head before being interrupted by inspiration.

One glimpse of purity,
The essence of something positive,
Eclipses all cynicism and negativity,
Epiphany,
Bliss.

TWO YEARS LATER

Never give out your password or credit card number in an instant message conversation.

Alex: you ever go to Atheist Forum anymore?
Lea: nah
Lea: it sucks now
Alex: I haven't been basically since they stopped allowing us to be mean and kick the fundies with amusing boot things
Lea: lol
Lea: fair enough
Alex: yeah, because they were trying to expand and become an actual influence somewhere. Where, I don't know, but they were trying to become an influence there
Lea: yeah i guess
Lea: the rift that ruins every revolution.
Oh, hey, congratulate your mum for me. I saw her book in whitcouls
Alex: Yeah I think all the fame's gone to her head. She never stops smiling
Lea: do you realise how long it's been since we've talked this much?
Alex: Nope, I can't say I do to tell the truth
Lea: i cant remember

Alex: I have trouble remembering anything when I think about you actually

Lea: why is that?

trying to block it out lol

Alex: no, I wouldn't want to have blocked it out, maybe I just have a shit memory

Lea: i have awful memory too, for anything that isn't pointless and random

Alex: I remember little things, like that tree we first kissed under

Lea: lol

Alex: but other things I can't remember at all

Lea: i don't think about it too much

Alex: I think about it from time to time

Lea: why?

Alex: I dunno, because we had good times together?

Lea: hmm

i guess we did

Alex: I kinda regret screwing it up I guess

Lea: i never thought id ever hear you say that lol

Alex: heh

Lea: odd

Alex: why?

Lea: just is, coming from you

Alex: I think I've changed over the past however long its been

Lea: so it seems

Alex: yeah

or I can blame it on this dip, which I'm certain is bad

Lea: lmao

Alex: anyways

Lea: yeah

Alex: well I'm sorry

Lea: why?

Alex: because i messed up and you deserve an apology

Lea: omg

no way

Alex: way

Lea: thank you

Alex: you're welcome
Lea: thats the last thing i ever expected from you
seriously
Alex: it's probably the least I could do
Lea: it really does mean a lot to me for some reason
Alex: well you do deserve it
Lea: :)
Alex: :)
Alex: so yeah
Lea: yeah

ACKNOWLEDGMENTS

This book would not have been possible without the feedback, support and encouragement of a number of special people. Big thanks to Nadine Isler and Jane Ritchie for reading early drafts all those years ago and providing such comprehensive feedback. Thanks to Jana Mittelstädt for the brilliant editorial support. Thank you Stella Peg Carruthers for your insightful perspectives. My eternal gratitude to my dear friends Laura Jansen and Chantal Cropp who have always believed in, and loved, this book.

Fishing for Māui

Selected in the Listener 100 Best Books of 2018

A novel about food, whānau, and mental illness.

Valerie reads George Eliot to get to sleep – just to take her mind off worries over her patients, her children, their father and the next family dinner. Elena is so obsessed with health, traditional food, her pregnancy and her blog she doesn't notice that her partner, Malcolm the ethicist, is getting himself into a moral dilemma of his own making. Evie wants to save the world one chicken at a time. Meanwhile her boyfriend, Michael is on a quest to reconnect with his Māori heritage and discover his own identity. Rosa is eight years old and lost in her own fantasy world, but she's the only one who can tell something's not right. Crisis has the power to bring this family together, but will it be too late?

"An accomplished story of a family in crisis - Ritchie's great skill is her ability to conjure the inner lives if her characters. Fishing For Maui is a compassionate meditation on what it means to be well". - Sarah Jane Barnett

ABOUT THE AUTHOR

Isa Pearl Ritchie is a New Zealand writer with a PhD in social science. She writes novels for adults and for young people. Her novel *Fishing for Māui* was named one of the best books of 2018 in *The Listener* Magazine and was a finalist in the NZ Booklovers awards 2019. She has also written articles for *The Spinoff, Pantograph Punch* and *Organic NZ*. Isa lives in Wellington.